ART
GIRLS
ARE
EASY

ART GIRLS ARE EASY

A novel by
Julie Klausner

poppy

LITTLE, BROWN AND COMPANY
New York   Boston

Copyright © 2013 by Julie Klausner

Poppy
Hachette Book Group
237 Park Avenue, New York, NY 10017

For more of your favorite series and novels, visit our website at www.pickapoppy.com

Poppy is an imprint of Little, Brown and Company.
The Poppy name and logo are trademarks of Hachette Book Group, Inc.

The publisher is not responsible for websites (or their content) that are not owned by the publisher.

First Print Edition: June 2013
First published as an e-book in May 2013 by Poppy

ISBN: 978-0-316-24362-9

For Phil

1

Indigo Hamlisch stared out the window of her father's gray Mercedes Coupe and thought about sex.

It was 5:30 AM, and even though the early summer sun had already risen over the suburban vanishing point where golf course met sky, it was still way too early for anybody in her right mind to be thinking about anything besides caffeine. But Indigo was thirty minutes out of a vivid, if pedestrian, erotic daydream about her art teacher, Nick Estep. She squirmed around in the tight backseat trying to find a comfortable position for her long legs. Up front, Leo Hamlisch merged onto the northbound Taconic Parkway while her stepmom, Yoshiko, futzed with the stereo. Yoshiko had managed to tune the radio to an odd number between the classical station, 888 AM, and the "traffic and weather together" news standby, 1015 AM. Soft, creaking violins whinnied into static, broken up only by the faint announcements of the time and temperature. The effect was far from soothing.

Yoshiko was probably trying to make some sort of statement by lingering between the two stations, though Indigo had no idea what it could be this time. Maybe she was trying to say something about limbo—being stuck between two places, or something equally as convoluted. Yoshiko, an experimental performance artist, was a little eccentric. Not that Indigo could really judge her. In fact, the whole reason for this very car trip might have seemed strange to any outsider.

It was the last time Indigo would be making this trip to the bus that took her where she'd spent every summer since she was seven years old: Silver Springs Academy for Fine and Performing Arts for Girls. She was fifteen, the oldest you can be at Silver Springs, and she'd been looking forward to this day throughout the entire school year. When she took that trip to camp it always felt like she was going home, instead of the other way around.

The crackling stereo grew louder, and Indigo's dad turned down the volume without saying a word. "How does it feel back there?"

Indigo shrugged. "It's all right, I guess. More cramped than the last car. I'm pretty sure I lost feeling in my left foot an hour ago." She wiggled her toes until pins and needles darted though them.

"Well, not much longer now, peanut." Leo smiled and resisted the pull of sentimentality, choosing not to remark on how little Indy used to be when they'd drop her at camp on their way to Nantucket. The Hamlisches were from New York City but always summered with power-WASPs in between Leo's meetings with the rest of the board of directors of the American Civil Liberties Union and Yoshiko's experimental art performances. Which were…interesting.

Yoshiko Hamlisch's most recent work involved her sitting in a freestanding bathtub filled with lukewarm borscht, while she folded paper cranes and placed them on top of the magenta soup like rubber ducks. It was supposed to be a commentary about mixed marriages and assimilation. It was extremely well received.

When Indy's dad married Yoshiko, Indy was pleased to have a kindred artistic spirit in the family, even if she was sort of bizarre. Yoshiko was kind, and she always encouraged Leo to fund his daughter's requests for new paints or annual memberships to the Museum of Modern Art. But it didn't change the fact that Indy had always needed nurturing from mentors whose talents were more closely aligned with her own. When Indy was in first grade, Leo had searched online and discovered Silver Springs: it seemed like the perfect place for his daughter's star to rise.

Yoshiko twisted the radio dial again, and Leo cleared his throat. Indy shut out the parental distractions and thought about her imaginary make-out session with Nick, the painting teacher at Silver Springs who taught her, in a feat of spectacular irony, how to draw things in perspective. She felt the tingle of what it would be like to see him once she arrived. Even though she'd had a secret crush on him for years, this summer seemed different somehow. Or maybe it was just Indy who was different. Older. Probably better looking. Definitely more mature.

"So is Lucy excited about her position? Will you two girls still be joined at the hip even though she has those new responsibilities?" Leo asked, making eye contact with Indy in the rearview mirror. It had been a full year since she and Lucy Serrano saw each other in person, and although they were BFFs in the most meaningful way you can be best friends with somebody you see only once a year, Lucy, who spent her last summer at Silver Springs as a camper, was now returning to the Springs as a C.I.T. And while Indy and Lucy's one-year age gap had never amounted to much, this year would be the first time it made a difference—at least superficially. But Indy didn't really think much would change. How could it?

When Lucy and Indigo first met, they clung to each other with a tenacity known only to the very strong and the very afraid. They were seven and eight, respectively, and their first summers away from home met sporadic jags of crying between rounds of being picked on by kids used to spending their holidays away from the safe hearth of their parents' condos, McMansions, and Park Slope brownstones. What started out as a bond sprung from commiseration soon blossomed into the kind of friendship that came with all the trappings of a love affair. Indy and Lucy were newly head over heels each July, inseparable each August. Each summer they'd eat meals, gaze at stars, gossip about crushes, sneak first cigarettes, and create and cackle at their own inside jokes—together.

They were a mutual admiration society of two, muses and creators at the same turn. And they weren't even competitive with each other—even though everyone expected that to change. But it never did.

While most best friends became entrenched with the thorny trimmings of adolescence—who's thinner, who's better at stuff, who's going to get which guy sooner—Indigo and Lucy seemed to defy stereotypes by just growing closer as the years wore on. Maybe it was because they had the distance of the school year, but maybe it was just because they were both known for being the best at what they did. They were secure in their respective talents, and Indy felt grateful to have Lucy in her life. She knew that she was unlike other artists who felt they weren't completely alone only when they were absorbed in the act of creating their work. Indigo didn't feel lonely when she was painting, but she also didn't feel lonely whenever she spoke to Lucy.

Lucy, having grown up in a show business family, never doubted her future as an actor (she won't say "actress" without drawing the comparison to the outdated term for "flight attendant"). And Indy, an art major at Silver Springs, had been developing her voice in all forms of visual media since she was old enough to make a sound.

When Indigo was only six years old, she lost her mom. At the time, Indy hadn't completely understood breast cancer, but she'd known that it was something big. Something horrible. As she struggled to make sense of everything, she retreated into herself and ended up finding solace in the watercolor paint set she'd gotten for her birthday that year. Making art didn't bring back her mom, but once her pain had been transformed into something beautiful, she remembered being amazed at the power of art.

Since then, Indy had expressed herself best in her paintings, drawings, sculptures, and prints. All the right people had begun to take notice of her work—she'd even been called a prodigy by an art scout who'd visited the Springs one summer. Indy wasn't sure how legit that praise was, but she knew she was good. It was the one thing she had unwavering confidence about.

As trees flew by in a green blur outside her window, Indigo wondered about what Nick would think, or even do, when he saw her newly voluptuous body. Instead of being a flat-chested pudge, now she was curvy, with freckles spattered everywhere there was skin, and long, straight legs like Big Bird's that jutted out from generous hips. Her boobs, which she hated, made her look pornographic in a tank top, even with a minimizer bra, and her long, dark hair looked less like the winning side of a compromise with her dad to keep it "princess length" and more like the deliberate decision of a young woman with her own style. Maybe people, namely Nick, would take notice of more than just her paintings this year. The notion was intoxicating. She glanced at her reflection in the rearview again for affirmation that she looked presentable. Her big brown eyes stared back.

By the time Leo Hamlisch had pulled up to the bus stop in White Plains, New York, Indy's daydreams had dissolved into pointillist, colorful debris, like pretty dots that make up the shapes of numbers from color-blindness tests. All that was left in her stomach was the flutter of anticipation that came along with the start of something new. This summer was filled with possibility, and like a blank canvas, it was daunting but exciting. She took a deep breath and flipped her long, straight hair.

"Well, this is your stop, kiddo," Leo announced. Indigo took a beat to stare at the exodus of kids leaving their parents' foreign sports cars to board the hybrid double-decker parked in front of them. Then she hoisted herself out of the back of her dad's Coupe, stretching out her stiff limbs like a newborn colt.

"You write to us if you need anything, Indy. You still want that bag of rubber gloves I saved for you? For a collage or something? Just say the word, and I'll have them sent right over." When Yoshiko was done with her offer, she started crying and snapping photos on her vintage Polaroid camera, documenting the event and experiencing it in tandem. Indigo gave her blubbering stepmom a set of double air-kisses, European-style.

"Right! Thanks, Yosh. I'll let you know if I want them," she said, knowing full well that she would have no use for seventy-five sets of rubber surgical gloves. Not now, at least. But it was still kind of sweet. She felt an unexpected pang of affection for her weird parents.

Leo awkwardly placed his hand on Indy's shoulder. His crisp blue button-down was already slightly wrinkled, and sweat stains had begun forming under his arms. Indy fought the urge to recoil, and instead pulled her dad close to her for a real hug, even though she was self-conscious about her breasts smooshing against him.

"Make us proud," he said as he shielded his eyes, sizing up the other parents in the lot.

"She always does, Leo." Yoshiko sniffled and added, "Go! Create things!" while she shooed Indy away with her toothpick arms.

Indigo couldn't help but smile. "Bye, Dad. I love you. Bye, Yoshiko. I'll write."

And with that, she was off, wheeling her TUMI suitcases atop the gravel to the gaping maw of the waiting bus across the lot. The crunch of the pebbles under her wheels and feet felt satisfying, like the first thrust of a shovel into warm, soft soil. It was finally time to dig into what Indy was sure would be the best summer of her life.

2

As she made her way down the bus aisle, Indy waved breezily to Puja Nair, the aspiring playwright, and Yvonne Bremis, the frizzy-haired stand-up comedian. Beside them was teacher and adviser Jen Rant, a onetime Silver Springs camper who was now a twentysomething performance artist. Jen won an Obie award that winter for her one-woman show at P.S. 122 in New York City, themed on slaughterhouses and her experience of growing up adopted. And finally, like a blinding turn into a sunny street or a record scratch in the middle of a movie preview, there was Lucy.

Lucy Serrano, who stood five-foot-two in kitten heels, was a petite slip of a girl, with a heart-shaped face and big, straight teeth. Lucy couldn't tan—she only burned—and her white-blond hair was the kind you'd see only on dolls and in shampoo commercials. So it was no surprise when Lucy landed the gig as the spokesmodel for Pantene's new line of tween hair care when she went out for the role last fall. Indigo walked to her private school in Manhattan during the year and often passed bus-shelter ads starring Lucy and her golden mop. At first, Indy would swell with pride when she saw them—she felt the need to snap cell-phone pictures of each billboard and text them to Lucy constantly. But the novelty had worn off after a while, and it got to the point where Indy's brain no longer associated the posters with her best friend. Plus, it didn't really replace the experience of seeing Lucy in person. It kind of just highlighted the fact that they couldn't hang out as much as Indy wanted, which was sort of a bummer.

But now her famous friend was there in the flesh, standing tall for such a tiny girl, with the confidence of a tabloid mainstay who *knew* she wore it better. As Lucy floated down the aisle toward her, Indy shoved the army-navy bag she used as a purse under her seat to make room for Lucy.

"*Indy!*" Lucy bleated.

"Luce!" she squealed back.

Lucy flung her black Dolce & Gabbana leather duffel into the overhead compartment, exposing her navel as she did. Indigo noticed the flatness of her friend's stomach, and instinctively compared it to the bellies of the statues she'd seen just yesterday at the Metropolitan Museum of Art, where she went to sketch every Saturday morning. Indy had become especially interested in drawing the human form lately, maybe because her own body had just undergone such an epic transformation.

But Lucy was another story. Hers wasn't a tummy, or belly, or anything else with a *y* at the end of it. Lucy had abs, a core, a midriff—it was the anatomical shorthand of the term "hard work." Like a swimmer who shaves his legs to move faster in the water, Lucy had shed the weight she thought was getting in her way on camera. Her ambition was great enough that the vague promise of stardom was enough to make her forget, most of the time, that she hated her life a little more now that ravioli and cake

were no longer a part of it. But sometimes art was worth sacrific-
ing things for. Indy knew that all too well, but was relieved hers
didn't involve giving up grilled cheese or anything.

Lucy scooted over next to Indigo and hugged her like it was
the last time she'd ever see her. "Girl, I *missed* you," Lucy said.
Indy squeezed her back, then playfully shoved her aside. "All
right, all right. You're suffocating me with Pantween fumes. Do
you get a free case of that shit with every paycheck or something?" Indy joked as Lucy took off her cropped jean jacket and
settled in. Her best friend laughed. "Not with *every* one."

Indigo noticed the bright yellow "Staff" T-shirt Lucy was
wearing, which fit her like a worn, broken-in pair of jeans. The
sleeves rested at the exact right spot of her slender upper arms,
and the fabric was perfectly faded. She looked effortless, casual,
and gorgeous. Suddenly, next to Lucy, Indy felt childish and over-
dressed in her sunflower-print baby-doll minidress. Why hadn't
she just worn her favorite Ramones shirt instead? She hoisted up
the front of her dress to minimize cleavage exposure.

"So," Lucy gushed, popping the cap off a tube of Carmex and
applying the lip balm. "The first thing I have to update you about:
remember that guy I told you about on G-chat? Tyler? From
Cedarquist?" Lucy's school seemed to host an endless supply of
attractive boys who wanted to date her.

"Tyler or Taylor?" Indigo asked. She vaguely remembered IM-
ing with Lucy in the last month or two and fielding some
heartbreak-related exposition about a guy in her class who'd been
jerking her around over an invitation to his junior prom. It was one
of those chats where Indy could go to the kitchen and fix herself a
snack—even toast—and upon her return, Lucy would still be going on and on about so and so's text and what does it mean, and
here's what *she* thinks it means, and why. Lucy's brand of drama

did not, on many occasions, need an audience. But usually Indigo didn't mind typing the appropriate responses, which ranged anywhere from "Aww, how sweet!" to "Ugh. Eff that psycho."

"Tyler. Not Taylor. Tyler. With the skateboard."

"The one with all the head injuries?"

"Right, him. He's semipro now." Lucy beamed before she launched into the complicated saga of their courtship.

Indy only half listened, relieved to be back in the company of a girl who made her feel like she was the relatively sane one. She was baffled by Lucy's interest in guys their age. And they were always *guys*, teenagers that Lucy herself would call "boys" or "kids"—never men. Indy, meanwhile, lusted after authority figures: actors in their forties, friends of her dad's. She liked the unavailability of older men, and their libido-charged appreciation of her precocity. Indigo couldn't really take a compliment seriously unless it came from a man who remembered a time before the dial-up modem. Maybe it came from hanging out with her dad's friends at their cocktail parties growing up, maybe she'd read *Lolita* before she was old enough to know it was a comedy. Either way, Lucy's appreciation of boys their age was another of their differences.

In actuality, Indigo was pretty inexperienced with guys. She'd never gone further than an ill-advised make-out or two, but all of the dirty thoughts and scenarios she'd played out in her mind made her feel ten times more experienced than her bubbly friend. And while Lucy cast a wide net with her romantic pursuits, Indy crushed on only a select few. But when a man she liked finally did come around, Indy fell *hard*. As she did for Nick. She wanted him like crazy.

Lucy grabbed Indy's arm, practically bursting with girlish excitement. "And, oh my God, Indy. You should see his body. It was just *sick*. I mean, he wasn't *Jersey Shore* buff, but he was fit. We only made out, but I swear, I remember thinking I would go all the way with him." Now she had Indigo's full attention. Lucy leaned in close and added in a dramatic stage whisper, "I'd never felt that with anybody else before."

"So are you going to do it, then?" Indy asked, wide-eyed. "Lose your virginity to Tyler the hot skateboarder?" This was big news. The kind of dirt she was hoping for.

Lucy exhaled loudly, and her mouth twisted into a pout. "Probably not. I mean, we're going to be at camp for so long and everything.... Also, he started writing me some really weird poems."

"What kind?" Indy giggled. "Dirty sonnets? Haikus?"

"Not even. Just some really poorly written stuff comparing my body to a smooth half-pipe ramp that he'd like to ride for all eternity."

Indy guffawed. "Ew! A half-pipe? He sounds like a creep. And maybe a stalker!"

Lucy shrugged her shoulders. "At least he was hot."

"Speaking of stalking," Indigo remembered, "I read an article in the *Post* about this guy that would root around in his ex-girlfriend's garbage for old Q-tips."

"Ew! For reals?"

"Yup. Apparently, he was collecting her earwax so he could make a candle out of it. He was obsessed with her."

"Oh my God!"

"I know. Isn't that insane?"

Indigo began to smile just as the sound in the distance of fifth graders singing show tunes hit Lucy's ears like a scent reaching a cartoon skunk.

"Ooh!" Lucy squealed. "That's my cue! See you in a bit?"

Lucy bolted to the front of the bus, where the theater majors held court, and sat next to an annoying actress-y girl whose name Indigo didn't know. Tiffany? Melissa? Something. Soon, the vehicle ached with a three-part-harmony version of an emo anthem from *Spring Awakening*. The Silver Springs musical theater geeks had clearly warmed up before boarding the bus.

Before going any further, a distinction should be made between Silver Springs and other camps—the ones with counselors and bunks and color war and relay races and campfires and mosquitos and those kinds of things. Because Silver Springs was by no means a typical summer camp experience.

Set in the dominantly Unitarian section of the Massachusetts Berkshires, Silver Springs was founded in 1972 by the since-deceased "it" couple of Nic and Sunny Heavenfeather-Strauss, a beat poet and ballerina who, before embarking on a dual suicide pact, retired to the least humid section of the Northeast to focus on their mission of teaching watercolors and the Alexander technique to disabled children.

Since then, Silver Springs, named after Sunny's hometown near Bethesda, Maryland—as well as the haunting Stevie Nicks song—evolved into the premier fine and performing arts summer institution for 175 lucky young women.

There were no counselors at Silver Springs, despite the *C* in Lucy's C.I.T. title. There were only instructors and professors that specialized in the camp's four fields of study: drama, music, dance, and visual art. The Silver Springs campers slept in air-conditioned chalets, not cabins, named after famous composers and choreographers—not woodland creatures. The young women of S.S. looked toward Broadway. SoHo galleries. Juilliard. Mark Morris Dance Group. Lincoln Center. And the ones self-aware enough to know that theirs was a mediocre talent were already figuring out how to marry well.

But Indigo and Lucy were never mediocre talents.

Indigo plugged her headphones into her iPod and blasted a playlist made up of Shins and Vampire Weekend songs as she watched the scenery wipe her window from left to right with new trees and sky. They were driving into the Greenwich area of Connecticut for another pickup, and this stop boasted even bigger SUVs, glitzier luggage, and more natural-looking face-lifts and fillers on campers' mothers than the stop before. Indy scrambled for her bag or for something else she could put on Lucy's vacated seat next to her so that Eleanor Dash wouldn't take it. But it was too late.

Eleanor Dash, alpha bitch and professional anorexic, took small, deliberate steps toward her target. Her tiny dancer's feet made no noise as she approached with intention, and her small eyes narrowed back into her gel-slicked, dirty-blond widow's peak. She had eyebrows that were plucked into apostrophes. Eleanor looked like a snake circling a mouse, or a Disney villainess.

"Hello, Indigo." Eleanor slid her bony silhouette into the aisle seat next to Indy.

"Eleanor," she replied curtly. "How are you?"

"I'm *extremely* well," she sneered, crossing her knock-kneed legs, which were already tucked into saggy ballerina tights. Indy shrank toward the window so she didn't have to be so close—what if her horrible personality was contagious? Eleanor wore a knitted shrug and a short black dress. It seemed basic but probably cost a fortune.

Eleanor's spiky elbow jabbed Indy in the side as she slid her purse below the seat in front of her. She didn't apologize. Indy was aghast that Eleanor managed to somehow lose weight since last summer; she was so flat-chested she was practically concave, hav-

14

ing halted her body's baby steps toward puberty with unhealthy weight-loss methods. Indy and Lucy used to joke that for a girl named Dash, it was funny that Eleanor didn't come with a period.

"So. Did you hear the latest?" asked Eleanor, with the matter-of-factness of a seasoned gossiper. Indigo didn't respond, and even put one of her earbuds back in. But her seatmate persisted.

"...About Nick Estep."

Indigo dropped her iPod onto the floor, where it narrowly missed the remains of Yvonne's Caramel Frapp, which seeped aggressively toward the back of the bus. Indy's chest heaved as she fumbled with the cords, blushing and hiding her face from Eleanor as best she could.

"No," Indy stammered. "What happened with Nick?"

"He's not coming back this year."

Indigo felt her heart begin to thump, and a feeling of dread crept up into her throat like acid reflux.

"Oh, yeah?" she asked. "Why not?" Indy tried to sound casual.

What did Eleanor know about Nick, anyway? She was a dance major; her interactions with the art department were few to none. It went without saying that Nick was the best-looking instructor on site, and you'd have to be blind or from outer space not to know it. But the way Eleanor spoke, it was like she knew him socially. And that made Indy feel sick.

"Why isn't Nick coming back?"

"I don't know," Eleanor continued, inspecting her perfectly manicured pink claws. "Maybe somebody got him fired. And maybe he should have been more careful when it came to pissing off campers with influential parents."

Indigo's panic level rose. Eleanor was a creative genius when it came to making up the right lie in order to get people fired—specifically, teachers who'd "wronged" her in some way.

Two years ago, an Alvin Ailey dancer who taught a master class at Silver Springs made the mistake of expressing concern to Eleanor that her pelvis was possibly misaligned. He was fired shortly after Eleanor found a blurry clip of an episode of *My Strange Addiction* about a man who ate rocks and happened to bear a slight physical resemblance to that very teacher. Apparently, gravel-munching staff members—who were dumb enough to go on TV—did not reflect well on the camp's reputation.

"So," Eleanor continued, "what's new with you and Lucy? Does she still return your calls now that she's a shampoo star?"

At the mention of her name, Lucy peeked her head into the aisle and glanced her blue mosaic-tile eyes toward Eleanor and Indy. The theater majors around her were still singing, but Lucy's attention shifted back toward the closely seated duo. She looked concerned and mouthed, "I'm sorry!" It *was* kind of her fault Indigo was now stuck sitting next to Eleanor.

Indy and Lucy both knew about Eleanor's rich history of trying to undermine their friendship and generally being the worst person alive. But even so, there was a chance that what Eleanor said was true. Indy's belly churned with anxiety and melancholy. Hers was a belly, not a 'riff or a stomach or anything else that could be described by words with sharp guttural consonants.

She thought about the e-mail Nick had sent her back in May. Indy didn't tell anyone about it—not even Lucy, who knew about her crush on Nick since it began, at age eleven, when Nick took Indy's pudgy hand to guide her as she mixed red powdered pigment and linseed oil with her palette knife. Nick, who was as good on e-mail as he was dispensing quippy advice to the room of art students he taught, had written to Indy to see whether she was coming back to camp this summer. He said he hoped she definitely would, and that she was a "talented girl." He also mentioned that there was a Gilbert and George exhibition at the New Museum she might want to check out, and ended his e-mail with "Later," and then "xo, Nick." Just seeing his name in her inbox made Indy sweat. What's more, she couldn't believe that Nick had remembered a detail so specific as that she liked the bold, odd art of Gilbert and George.

Indy wasn't sure if he was suggesting they go to the show together, but it still took her two weeks to formulate the perfect, casual-seeming response. She signed it with the same "xo" and hoped to God it meant that they were flirting. Much to her disappointment, he'd never written back, but Indy still held on to the original e-mail like a secret treasure. Telling anyone about it—even Lucy—would have caused her to overanalyze Nick's intentions. It was better to think he'd wanted to meet up with her but just couldn't.

Indy pictured his face for the millionth time that morning. Nick Estep could be described only as handsome. Not "cute," as Lucy often called her crushes. *Handsome.* With his scruffy, dark hair and eyes that seemed to alternate between brooding and amused, Nick looked mature in a way that Indigo found irresistible. He looked strong and real—capable of heavy physical exertion, like he could pick her up in an excited embrace and swing her around after a long time apart.

But the most attractive thing about Nick was his passion. For the process of creating art, the beauty of free speech, his opinion about how the Rolling Stones were better than the Beatles. He was never serious but always serious, in that if he wasn't committed to his artwork, he would have long ago taken his father up on his offer to work for him back in Newton, Massachusetts. It was lucky he didn't. Nick was so incredible and amazing at what he did. His art mainly consisted of elaborate photorealistic paintings and metal sculptures that were dark and twisty. His work made him even more deep and fascinating—especially since, in person, he was usually warm and friendly. At least he was whenever he saw Indy.

Indigo hoped Eleanor was just trying to mess with her, saying Nick wouldn't be there this year. The thought was so unappealing, Indigo closed her eyes and willed it to go away.

She didn't even realize she'd drifted off until she received another bony jab to the ribs. "Wake up!" Eleanor hissed. Sure enough, the bus was pulling up to campus, and the sign welcoming motorists to Silver Springs elicited cheers and general rabble from the peanut gallery of young campers at the front.

Indigo felt disoriented and groggy. She rubbed her eyes carefully so as not to smudge her mascara and looked out the window. They were just pulling up to the front of the camp. Indy could make out the lush lawn and blue buildings with sloping gray roofs in the near distance. Massive shady trees were spaced evenly throughout the campus, and the Silver Springs camp flag, which bore a feminized coat of arms that represented each discipline taught at camp above the Latin phrase *Ars Gratia Artis* ("Art is the reward of art"), danced lightly in the breeze. The overall effect was quite ethereal. Indigo began to imagine which colors she would mix to achieve the specific shades of the scene if she were to paint a landscape right now. Chartreuse and goldenrod. Maybe some cerulean.

"You were snoring." Eleanor smirked, her thin lips a line graph of contempt under her Lancôme burgundy matte stick. "It was pretty annoying."

That was rich, coming from her. Indy gathered her things: she couldn't wait to get off this bus and avoid Eleanor for the rest of the summer.

As the girls lined up like elegant, talented cattle down the bus aisle, the camp director, Lillian Meehan, greeted each camper as she exited with a lei made from organic peonies tied together with red kabbalah string. Lillian was tall and amiable, and thin enough to look great in clothes, though not necessarily pretty. Basically, she was Glenn Close with dark hair and a whistle around her neck.

Lucy looked back at a still-sleepy, rumpled Indigo before getting off the bus. As the two girls made eye contact for the first time since their light dish session about Tyler or Taylor or whoever, Lucy smiled and winked at her friend, and Indy felt the warm rush of camaraderie wash over her. She smiled back and soon enough emerged from the bus into the warm kiss of sunlight on the grassy patch, where Lillian greeted her with a lei. And when she lifted her face to take in the familiar postcard of the sprawling green campus before her, Indigo found something small and sublime in its composition.

There, on the lawn of the main sprawl of Silver Springs, right near the office, stood Nick Estep, holding a blowtorch to a life-size rectangular metal sculpture. Goggles rested over his longish hair, which trickled onto the collar of his Nirvana T-shirt in the Berkshires sunlight. Indigo's heart rocketed to every point on the surface of her skin. He was here after all.

"What. The *fuck*." Eleanor said, to no one in particular, putting her spindly hand on her hip in protest. Indy crossed her hands over her chest as though she was trying to keep her heart from leaping out into the fire at the end of Nick's torch, and made her way toward the main house, where the staff were handing out bunk assignments. Indigo smiled. She was in a beautiful setting with an endless supply of paints; her best friend was there, and so was Nick. All of the elements of a brilliant summer were perfectly in place. Now it was just up to her to create it.

3

Nick Estep, a twenty-one-year-old sculptor and oil painter with a penchant for cow skulls and futurescapes, stood six-foot-four in his bare, filthy feet. He smelled like wood and sweat, and he always had stubble. His nose was an isosceles triangle, his thick black hair spilled around his ears and neck, and his intense green eyes were the star of the show. He was handsome, distinguished. Super-fucking-hot.

Indy fought the urge to run right up to him and start chatting about the art shows she'd visited during the school year. She could tell him about the Jenny Holzer show she'd seen at MoMA, and casually drop into the conversation that she'd taken his advice and seen the Gilbert and George exhibit after all. She really wanted to bring up his e-mail. But there would be time for that later. Maybe in the art studio, when they were more...alone.

Indigo strode toward the registration table outside the main house with autopilot confidence. She waited with the huddled masses from every age group until Lucy, in authority-figure mode, came over to the back of the line.

"There you are!" Lucy sang, touching Indigo's arm. "You don't have to wait with the others." She pulled her out of the line. "Come with!"

"Seriously?" Indy looked around. "I mean—thanks...."

Lucy smiled. "Dude. Of *course*. One of the many perks of being my best friend." Indy was pleasantly surprised that Lucy was already abusing her C.I.T. power a bit.

Lucy walked Indy to the front of the registration line, where the cafeteria and swimming staff waited behind the giant table. Indy glanced back in Nick's direction, just to make sure he was still there—he looked up from his work and nodded in recognition. *Oh my God.* Was that meant for her? She didn't want to smile back and risk looking lame if it wasn't, so she began to look around as slyly as possible to see if there was anyone else in her general vicinity who he might have acknowledged instead. But no one else was looking in Nick's direction. Indy turned back to the table, her cheeks burning.

"*Bonjour*, Indigo!" said Michel, an award-winning pâtissier who specialized in making low-lactose desserts for Silver Springs campers during his summers. He scanned the list of names in front of him. "Hamlisch, right?"

Indy nodded. "I'm a tenth-year. I assume I'm in the Beat cabin."

"Ah, yes." Michel crossed her name off a list. "Ferlinghetti."

While all Silver Springs camper housing was reasonably lush, Ferlinghetti was one of the largest, most appointed bunks on the campus. It was named for the famous poet and painter, Lawrence Ferlinghetti, who cofounded City Lights Books in San Francisco and hung out with many influential Beat Generation writers during the fifties and sixties. The girls in Ferlinghetti lived two to a room instead of four or five, and the A/C was the coldest at camp. Indy was psyched that she'd made it to the

21

summer of her cushiest accommodations yet.

"Here you go, Indigo." Michel handed her a recyclable key card from a rubber-banded stack he held like a Vegas dealer. "Your luggage is already in your room. You're in suite three."

"Thanks." She nodded.

As Indy scootched out of the way to let the next girl take her place at the front of the line, she rubbed her thumb over the embossed design on her key. One side of the card was the Silver Springs coat of arms. The other said simply "Ferlinghetti" in a serif font. She began to head toward the path that led east, away from the main house and toward the upper-hill campus, where the older girls stayed in the O'Keeffe, Streep, and Beat Poet cabins.

On her way, she passed Lucy again, who was chatting with Lena Ho, a violin major with an unfortunate last name.

"Hey." Indy smiled at her friend. "Catch you later?"

"Of course!" Lucy grinned back. "After dinner hangout?"

"Sounds good. Because I have something I'm *dying* to tell you…." Indigo replied, raising her eyebrows suggestively.

Lucy's eyes widened. "Whoa. I can't wait."

She'd decided to tell Lucy about Nick's e-mail—it was really the only juicy thing to have happened to her all year. Maybe part of her wanted to confide in Lucy just so she could feel closer to her best friend. Indy had a passing suspicion that now that Lucy might be preoccupied with C.I.T. stuff, they might grow apart unless both of them were completely honest with each other. Indy decided there'd be no secrets this summer.

She strode leisurely to the Beat cabin, taking the scenic route along the shady pebble path that looped around massive oak trees and past the cabins named after Marxist thinkers and Pre-Raphaelite painters she'd stayed in during past summers. There was the swing set, and the entrance to the steps that led up to the Esther Williams Pool. And wherever there were clearings, massive outdoor sculptures rested atop pristine grass.

She noticed a new addition on the lawn glinting in the sunlight, and immediately recognized it as one of Jeff Koons's famous pieces from his "Celebration" series. The sculpture was a massive diamond, the kind you'd find on a ring, made of chromium steel and coated in a vibrant royal-blue patina. It had to be part of the Silver Springs Professional Art Lending program, in which select professionals and collectors would lend their famous works to camp each summer, to educate and inspire future artists. Indy had seen a similar Koons piece—a giant yellow balloon animal—on the Met rooftop garden back in New York. So this was awesome.

Indy finally arrived at Ferlinghetti—a Dutch colonial cottage with decoupaged rocking chairs and flowerpots scattered on the front porch. As she stood there, trying to adjust to the serene atmosphere of the perfect Massachusettsness of the campus on a beautiful summer day, her mind crept back to Eleanor's rumor. It was clearly bullshit. Nick was here: she'd seen him with her own eyes, and Indy was pretty sure Nick had seen her, too. Reliving the moment caused a bolt of excitement to shiver down Indy's spine like a Slinky down a flight of stairs. She couldn't wait to get into the studio and start channeling some of this nervous energy into her work. It felt like every cell in her body was buzzing with activity.

Indigo slid her key card into the front-door slot and made her way down the hallway, which was adorned with black-and-white photos of the suite's namesake in his heyday. There was one of Lawrence Ferlinghetti outside his bookshop in San Francisco, another of him reading a poem onstage, and a shot of him drinking coffee with Allen Ginsberg. She passed suites one and two and wound up in the corner double, where she found her luggage next to three Chanel trunks and two Louis Vuitton rolling suitcases.

The room itself was like a boutique hotel's. The beds were already made with Silver Springs–issued five-hundred-thread-count Egyptian sheets, and the walls and bedding were draped in fresh shades of ochre and chartreuse. Two dressers, two night-stands, overhead lighting, and generous closet space filled out suite three. It was actually quite cozy and chic. Indigo took advantage of being the first girl in the room by claiming the bed she wanted. She began to unpack her bags.

A shrill voice broke the silence.

"Hey, Slut." It could be only one person. *Of course*, Indy thought. She turned around to greet her new bunkmate: Eleanor Dash. It was a cruel joke that they would be forced to spend so much time together in the next month.

"Welcome, Roomie," Indigo said, with sarcastic overenthusi-asm.

Eleanor slammed the bedroom door behind her, leaving the two of them alone in their suite.

"I can't *believe* Nick is here," Eleanor hissed, tossing her fuchsia Coach purse on top of the dresser. She bounded over to her bed and spread out on the floral-print cotton comforter. "Who does Lillian think she works for? Our parents pay her effing salary!"

Indigo began to refold her clothes and put them into her dresser, pretending to listen. She was good at tuning out super-fluous noises, a skill that came in handy in New York and around yentas like Eleanor.

"I mean, it's not like there aren't other art teachers that could use the salary he makes," Eleanor continued, unzipping one of her Chanel trunks full of expensive dance clothes. "What does Lillian pay him? Five figures for eight weeks? There are homeless people who sell homemade rubber stamps in McCarren Park who would smother their grandparents for one-sixteenth of that!"

"Are you thinking of hipsters or homeless people, Eleanor?" Indy asked, rolling her eyes. "And since when have you even been to McCarren Park? Isn't that in Brooklyn?"

"I was seeing a guy who lived there last year. His dad is in a band, his mother makes artisanal cheese in their loft space. I got over him once I found out he didn't smoke or drink. *Don't change the subject, Indy*," Eleanor snapped. "This Nick stuff is bullshit, and you know as well as I do that he doesn't belong back at Silver Springs, considering what he did. I mean, you in particular!"

"What are you talking about?" Indy asked, as nonchalantly as she could. Did Eleanor know she had a crush on Nick?

Her new roommate took a deep breath and sat up on her bed, like she had the weight of the world on her bony shoulders.

"Well," she continued deliberately, "there's something you may not know about your art instructor." Eleanor reached over for her purse and removed a photo of an emaciated model from her wallet, then tacked it up over her bedside mirror with her gum.

"I heard he was fired because there were *indiscretions*," Eleanor said. "With campers. Specifically, your pal Lucy." Done with her Thinspo interior design project, Eleanor tucked a phantom strand of blond hair behind her ear and sat down on the bed again while Indy puttered on her side of the room. "I heard Nick took her virginity in his cabin, by the pool, last summer."

There was a pause then, as Indy put down a pile of her sketchbooks and slowly absorbed what she had just heard. She finally turned her head and looked Eleanor right in the eyes.

"What?" Indy said, with as little emotion as she could.

Eleanor smirked. "I mean, I assumed you knew when Lucy lost her virginity because you guys are so close. She didn't tell you? Or isn't that what best friends are for?" Eleanor stood up, slunk over to the full-length mirror, and began to examine her posture in ballet positions one through five. She looked like a stick bug trying to do yoga. It was nauseating.

Indigo stood by her bed with her arms at her sides, deciding when and how exactly she was going to tell Eleanor to shut the hell up. But Eleanor took her reaction as a cue to keep talking. She was enjoying this.

"What's more," Eleanor said, sneering, "Lucy was dumb enough to leave herself logged in to her Gmail on one of the iPads in the computer lab." She began to stretch her body into another unflattering shape. "And Nick e-mailed her a very raunchy message."

Indigo's heart felt like it had dropped into her stomach. Nick had e-mailed Lucy, too? This was the first thing that Eleanor had said that seemed plausible. "Really?" she heard herself ask. "What did it say?"

"Oh, the usual," Eleanor continued casually. "'Thanks for last night, I'll never forget it. I'm so glad I was your first, hope I didn't get you preggers.' That kind of thing. I can't remember it by heart, but I have a copy of it somewhere."

"Why do you have a copy of it?" Indy was suddenly invigorated by the challenge Eleanor seemed to present. She felt baited, but nobody could argue with black-and-white evidence. That is, if the e-mail even existed. Indy tried desperately to maintain a calm exterior.

"I printed it out," Eleanor replied. "It was right there, out in the open. It's almost like Lucy *wanted* to get caught."

"That's ridiculous," Indy shot back.

"I swear!"

Indy extended her palm. "Let me see it, then."

"Well, I don't have it here."

Indigo began to relax. There was no way this story could be true. She and Lucy may have not seen each other in the last year, but they were best friends—Indy still would have been the first one to know if she'd lost her virginity. Plus, there was no way that Lucy would have ever hooked up with Nick, knowing Indy's feelings for him. Not a chance. But despite all of this, a tiny seed of doubt had been planted in Indy's mind. Just because Eleanor didn't have the actual e-mail in her possession didn't mean that Nick hadn't sent Lucy a flirty message, too. Or that he hadn't e-mailed anyone else at camp, for that matter. Indy felt a bit sick.

She had to get out of there. *Now.*

"I'm going to take my stuff to the bathroom," Indigo announced, reaching into her suitcase to get a transparent cosmetics case stuffed to its creases with organic skin products and battery-powered tooth care.

"I'm sure this is hard for you…." Eleanor began, but Indy made her swift exit.

Not as hard as it's going to be for you if you don't keep your mouth shut this summer, thought Indy. Eleanor really knew how to set her off.

The shared Ferlinghetti bathroom boasted state-of-the-art modern Kohler sinks that were mounted in a tidy row onto gleaming, pearl-colored tiled walls. Above the sinks, a giant immaculate mirror reflected the ten shower stalls, each one housed in its own cloudy glass tower with teak bathmats in front of them, like little welcome mats in front of phone booths. Around the corner were toilets and bidets, which were appointed to the girls in the upper-hill bunks (the lower-hill campers tended to fill water balloons in them), and an assortment of cubbies and hooks for the campers' massive selection of creams, pills, cleansers, toners, makeup, hair care, and everything else it took to keep the Ferlinghetti girls looking and feeling exactly as they were accustomed.

Around the cubby area, Yvonne the aspiring stand-up comedian was unpacking a sprawling array of scrubs, creams, and devices around one of the sinks in the bathroom. She dropped a chubby armful of various cuticle nippers onto the floor in theatrical panic when Indy came in, and Indigo half smiled, knowing Yvonne was amping up her shtick for the attention.

"Hi, Yvonne. How was your school year?"

"Oh, not bad, thanks!" Yvonne stammered. "My love life is nothing to speak of, but I'm on a new seafood diet. Basically, I eat a ton of shrimp!" She chuckled at her own joke, then waited for Indy to do the same.

Indigo smiled generously, and Yvonne brightened. She had given up on fitting in long ago, and lived for any kind of positive response to her jokes—even mercy laughs. The joy she got from being well received disappeared as quickly as it came. But at least at Silver Springs, Yvonne wasn't picked on the way she was at home. It was lucky that her defense mechanism had blossomed into a skill—something she could be passionate about. She was actually pretty funny, in small doses.

"How are *you*?" Yvonne asked awkwardly. She tried hard to be normal, but when she was friendly without joking, the effect was sweaty with effort. "I remember reading online about that fellowship you won. Was that the piece you were finishing up last summer? The installation?"

"Yeah." Indy nodded, unpacking her cleansers and acne stuff.

"*Jon Benet Descending a Staircase*. I ended up building the whole thing out of sculpting clay, and those flippers? You know those teeth that beauty-pageant girls wear?"

"Totally! Oh, God. I have a whole bit about *Toddlers & Tiaras* in my act." Yvonne grinned. She had clearly missed being around other creative nerds as much as Indy had.

"So I built the stairs by stacking a bunch of those nasty fake teeth. It was supposed to be about how exploitative pageant culture is, and how it's really just a microcosm of the entire beauty and entertainment industry, even for adults."

"Whoa," Yvonne murmured. "That's impressive. My take on that whole show basically has more to do with how jealous I am of those little kids! I *wish* I'd gotten lipo for my fifth birthday instead of that stupid tricycle!" Yvonne laughed awkwardly.

Puja Nair, a petite Indian American hipster girl, came out of the shower with wet hair and wearing a towel, a pair of flip-flops, and her Woody Allen glasses, to join Yvonne and Indy at the sinks.

"Hey!" Puja could be a little intense, but she was, for the most part, a sweet girl—and an insanely talented writer.

"How was your school year?" Indy asked.

"Oh, you know! It was pretty lackluster. I tried to do a table-read of my last script with some kids from the drama club, and it was subpar. I'm just so relieved it's summer now. I can finally get some *real* work done, you know?"

"Definitely," Indy replied, realizing she was the alpha girl by default. Puja and Yvonne stared at her like she was in charge of the conversation. "Are you guys psyched for the workshops?" she asked.

"I can't wait for the Judy Tenuta intensive!" Yvonne yelped. One of her favorite comediennes was scheduled to come teach a stand-up comedy workshop in August.

"I hope I get a good adviser," Puja said, starting to floss.

"Who did you work with last year?" Indy asked.

"Jen Rant," Puja answered, mid-floss.

"Oh," Yvonne snarked. "You mean *Debbie Downer*? That girl's got less sunshine up her ass than a miner trapped underground during a Scandinavian winter." She paused for a beat. "Too soon for trapped-miner jokes? Is that still a thing?"

"She's not *that* bad." Puja giggled. "She helped me take a play I wrote and turn it into a feature script. It ended up being terrible, but that's my own fault for not realizing that a helicopter landing onstage is really not that big of a deal when you're aiming to shoot it instead of stage it."

Puja used to write a Vietnam War–themed play each week, after spending her Christmas break two years ago in San Francisco on a food tour and seeing lots of homeless Vietnam vets on the street. She implored her parents, a food critic and a Bollywood actress, to rent *Apocalypse Now* so she could figure out what "made the bums tick," and, even though Puja was only eight at the time, the Nairs relented, knowing they had a precocious auteur-to-be on their hands.

"God, I remember that!" Yvonne squawked, rubbing a foam cleanser onto her slablike cheeks. "Remember how my parents walked out of that one play you did? *What's That Sound?*"

"And all of the younger girls started screaming during the amputee scene?" Indy chimed in, recalling how hilarious it had been, despite the serious subject matter.

"What can I say?" Puja shrugged. "I love making a splash!"

"Hey, hookers." Eleanor waltzed into the bathroom with the eerie calm of somebody who shouldn't have been as angry as she was moments before.

Puja and Yvonne instinctively averted their eyes to the tiled floor in the presence of a high-status bully. Eleanor kept talking as she unpacked.

"So, P.S.?" she hissed into the mirror, though she had said nothing to justify a postscript. "It's already five-forty-five, which means we have to be at the dinner hall in fifteeeeeeeeen."

Grateful for the excuse, Puja and Yvonne darted to their room to change, muttering "Thanks" to the notorious skeleton Medusa as they left.

"Are you going to dinner?" Eleanor asked Indy as she pulled out a pair of pointy tweezers and began to pluck her already sparse brows.

"I was planning on it," Indigo replied flatly.

"Ehhh, I don't think I'm going to go," Eleanor decided, in between plucks. "I'll see you at the campfire after, yeah?"

She had an infuriating affectation of saying "Yeah?" like a question at the end of her conversations, like a poseur Emma Watson or something. And Indy wasn't really surprised Eleanor was avoiding the public consumption of food.

"Later." She left Eleanor at the sink to arrange her own palette of diet pills and department-store creams. Back in their bedroom, Indy grabbed her tinted cherry ChapStick and dabbed some onto her lips. It was a tradition at Silver Springs for all of the campers to wear white during the Welcome Dinner and campfire activities, so she slid on a brand-new pair of white jeans over her newly massive-seeming hips and butt. She traded her sunflower baby-doll dress for a white tank top, which clung to her small waist, then pulled on a big white hoodie sweatshirt.

Indy slid her feet into white flip-flops so her purple pedicure showed, and took a moment to check herself out in the full-length mirror that hung behind the chaise longue in the suite, which was still messy with their unpacked stuff.

Here we go, she thought. She used the soothing inner voice her shrink recommended when it became tempting to recede into darker thoughts.

But she wasn't even going there. Her secret crush was safe, and it was in a place nobody could see. Indy decided to believe that Lucy and Nick never had anything between them. There was no way. She renewed the goal of putting her feelings—even the dark ones—on paper and into her work this summer. If anything, it was bound to make her art more meaningful.

Indigo kissed her own fingertips, getting them waxy, then pressed them to her own mirror reflection. She hit the lights and left the Beat cabin, head held high, into the peach-and-mauve-drenched dusk that settled into the lush campgrounds just outside the door.

4

On the first night of camp, the girls ate dinner with campers of all ages for the purposes of avoiding, for one evening, the cliqueishness that went along with the social workings of Silver Springs. Last year Indy had been forced to sit next to Lily Nagel, an eight-year-old aspiring film director. Lily had insisted on asking her trivia questions from the American Film Institute's top 100 films throughout the entire meal, like whether or not *Sunset Boulevard* is in the top ten (it's not). Every time Indy got a question wrong, Lily would laugh and make a game-show buzzer noise. Having to eat with girls half your age was totally humiliating in its own right, but getting berated by one was just surreal. That said, there *were* certain perks to being the oldest at camp, and one of them was that this year, Indigo got to spend her last official Welcome Dinner with the Ferlinghetti girls.

Indy entered the dining hall, which was closer to a four-star restaurant than a school cafeteria. Each table was decorated with a tasteful centerpiece made up of peonies and snapdragons, the colors of which popped among the sea of white outfits worn by the Silver Springs campers. Indy noticed Puja sitting next to

Yvonne, who waved enthusiastically from a round table in the corner. Eleanor was, true to her word, mercifully absent.

As Indigo walked toward her table, she caught Lucy's eye. She was wearing a gauzy white sundress with a flattering scoop neckline and sat with the staffers, laughing and tossing back her glossy hair. Indy felt a little pang of jealousy but gave Lucy a friendly half-wave and continued on.

"Hey guys. How's the game hen?" Indy plopped down in her chair. "I'm starving."

"Best I've ever tasted. Seriously. I even got seconds!" Yvonne shook some salt over her polenta and poached white asparagus.

"So," Puja began, turning to Indy, "we need to talk about the social with the Kinnetonka boys. Is there anybody new there this year? Have you talked to Jay?"

"Gross, *no*." Indy pulled a face.

"Can't you e-mail him or something?" Puja whimpered. "We want to know who's coming this year." It struck Indy as funny that the prospect of interacting with boys transformed even the incredibly talented, driven, and otherwise mature young women of Silver Springs into drooling, giggling idiots. Sort of like the puddle of quivering porridge she herself turned into every time she saw Nick.

Suddenly a plate of food appeared in front of her, set down by one of the kitchen staff. "Bon appétit," said a server she didn't recognize from last year.

"Thanks," Indy said, digging in and grateful for an excuse to change the subject. "Oh my God, this is so good."

"Right?" Yvonne took a forkful of game hen and raised it in mock-salute to Indy. She spent the rest of the meal catching up with the girls, occasionally glancing over at Lucy, and scanning the room for Nick. For some reason, he was missing from the Welcome Dinner so far.

Lillian's booming voice over the dining hall P.A. system halted everyone's conversations. "Attention, campers! We'll be serving a locally sourced hypoallergenic dessert at the front of the hall. Please line up, ladies—then meet us in the Harpsichord Room for our campfire activities."

Indy trudged toward Lillian, who distributed dairy-free single serving portions of panna cotta to the campers. She smiled dutifully when she met the camp director's gaze.

"Indigo, you look fantastic." Lillian couldn't help complimenting Indy on her newly buxom figure, even though she tried her best to avoid any mention of a camper's shifting weight or body shape.

"Thanks, Lillian." Indy took a panna cotta and a wooden minispoon. She followed the queue of campers shuffling down the hallway, and soon she was in the Harpsichord Room—a former ballroom furnished with Victorian accoutrements, both real and faux, and adorned with framed articles about alumni achievements in the world of stage, screen, art, film, and beyond.

The Harpsichord Room and the dining hall were all part of what was known as the "main house"—the Victorian mansion that Lillian and her partner, Debra Fishpaw, inherited years ago and converted into a summer camp. Inside the Harpsichord Room, shelves of sheet music stood alongside music stands carved from teak, and cases for wind instruments of every size and shape lined the walls, which were papered with sumptuous wine and mustard patterns.

That night, the instruments and chairs were cast aside, and a simulated campfire made out of orange crepe paper, Christmas lights, and leaf blowers sat in the middle of the space. The fire simulacrum was a Silver Springs tradition, born of the avalanche of complaints from the campers and their parents about mosquito bites and ash-laden wind after Lillian hosted an authentic outdoor campfire. Since then, the welcome ceremony for new and returning campers was held indoors, under the blissful hum of central A/C and the pleasant glow of dimmed track lighting.

As the other girls settled in, Indigo sat cross-legged on the antique floorboards and chewed on her cuticles until Lillian walked in, wearing a head wreath of discarded lei peonies. She stood in front of the "campfire" and spoke into a wireless microphone she produced from one of her cargo pockets.

"Silver Springs women! It is a blessing to be back in the powerful presence of your creative spirit!"

After that came a smattering of applause led enthusiastically by Debra, who stood to the side with a whistle around her neck. Indigo surveyed the sea of familiar and strange faces she'd be spending her final summer as camper alongside.

"Okay, ladies!" Lillian continued into the mic. "Let's get on our feet and get ready for some bonding games!"

Indigo groaned in dread. Silver Springs had its own version of fuzzy, getting-to-know-you crapola. It happened only on the first night of camp, when Lillian decided to pretend she was a traditional camp director and that girls came here for reasons of friendship, and not because their parents wanted them to demolish the competition in their fields of choice.

"Here we go, everybody!" Lillian practically sang with delight. "It's time for…Graham and Pollock!"

Indigo winced as Debra hit play on the Bose sound system on top of the actual harpsichord in the corner, which the room was named after. Soon, Philip Glass music filled every rococo crevice around her.

"Tree in the wind!" Lillian shouted, and the girls all halfheartedly lifted their arms like branches and swayed in the imaginary wind, a lame homage to legendary modern dancer Martha Graham. It was so fruity and theatery. Indy felt ridiculous pretending to be a tree or anything else.

After making her campers pretend to be pebbles, butterflies, and fetuses for the game, Lillian led everyone to an adjoining room, where several large blank canvases lined the floor. It was time for Pollock, which was exponentially more fun because it involved making a mess with paint. The girls were split into groups, each group was given a canvas, and they were all instructed to splatter jars of paint in the style of the famous abstract expressionist artist Jackson Pollock. It was the Silver Springs version of Color War.

When everyone was finished and their white clothes totally ruined by a kaleidoscope of wayward paint splatters, the staff would judge which piece was best, and the winning painting would be displayed in the dining hall for the rest of the summer. It was a pretty high honor for an arts camp, where paint-covered canvases were a dime a dozen.

Indigo loved playing Pollock, but this year she was tired of all of it before it even began. Maybe she'd outgrown it.

Still, once Indy got started splattering violet tempera paint against the blinding white canvas, she got into it. Their canvas looked good. Her teammates, Puja and Yvonne, shrieked and squealed as they flung paint at one another. Indy eventually joined in, laughing at how inane this all really was.

She'd stop every so often to distribute polite hellos to all the instructors she remembered from summers past, from Sydney Fogel, the hard-edged Atlantic Theater Company veteran who begrudgingly taught drama to the advanced acting majors, to Renée Cornillion, the beautiful, angry, and broken ballet instructor, who lived every day like it was her last chance to punish her students for being younger than she was. And there was Jen Rant from the bus, looking dour in an off-white minidress with yellow stains on it, paired with knee-high striped socks with black flats. There were so many different shades of bitter on the faculty rainbow.

Lillian had handed over emcee duties to Harry Glibbe, the chipper musical theater director whose enthusiasm was so fierce, it seemed like he was making fun of everybody. Indy loved Harry Glibbe. He was sarcastic and warm at the same time—a balance that so many of the other staff members lacked. It really was too bad she didn't get to take any classes with him—he was always super-sweet when she saw him at meals and at Lucy's shows.

Indy ended up near the front of the room as soon as Harry took the mic from Lillian. They were obviously about to announce the winner, but she suddenly felt suffocated by the paint fumes and the crowd. Everybody was chattering and still play-fighting. She needed some fresh air.

"All right!!!" Harry said, with extra exclamation points. "It's time for the biiiig winner!" Indy pushed through the horde of rainbow-splattered girls, teachers, and C.I.T.s milling about. She was almost to the exit when she stepped into a massive puddle of slippery mauve paint. Slipping and falling, Indigo skidded through the paint. And there she went, flip-flops and all, falling backward like Alice through the rabbit hole for a scary and awful half-second.

As Indy fell, a moment stretched into eternity, as things seem to do when you lose control. She wished she could take that last step back, but all she could do at that point in time and space was to try her best to fall gracefully.

And then she felt the sturdy relief of a man's hands catch her from both sides, holding her up from under each arm, supporting the back of her head with his chest.

"Careful, there," Nick whispered to Indy, his stubble brushing up against her neck. She felt his breath get under her shirt. She smelled him on her skin. Feeling him next to her was like trying to embrace the suds in a warm bath so you have a collection of them in your arms for the time between when they exist and disappear.

Indigo exhaled in full for the first time all day.

Nick propped Indy up and let her go. "You okay, Indy?" He smiled at her.

"Yeah, thanks," she managed to squeak in response, cursing herself for being so clumsy and then so awkward. And then, just as suddenly as he came, Nick was gone.

Indigo steadied herself against the wall, inspecting the soles of her flip-flops to make sure there was no paint left for her to slip on again. But the official activities were breaking up now, and spontaneous choruses of everything from Lady Gaga to *Porgy and Bess* began to erupt among the music majors. They even started to bring out the odd uke or harp to strum, and Indigo figured that was her official cue to sneak out to her bunk, change her clothes, and start getting settled in her studio.

She slipped out the French doors leading to the Esther Williams Pool, which shimmered with the reflection of the sconces that lit up the inside of the main house. She passed the terra-cotta planters around the back of the mansion and the big elm tree that shaded the East Wing, clicking on her mini-flashlight, and made her way alone down the pebble path back to Ferlinghetti. The trees made the walk seem cooler, and the sky dazzled with stars that seemed to be pluckable from her reach. It was so quiet, Indigo could hear her own breath.

"Hey! Indy! Wait up!"

Indigo turned her head to shine her flashlight on Lucy, who squinted in its beam behind her. Lucy bounded toward her on the path.

"Oh, it's you!" Indy exclaimed. In all the madness, she'd completely forgotten about their scheduled after-dinner chat.

"Hey, stranger. Blind me much?"

"Sor-ry, Princess." Indy shoved Lucy playfully, leaving a faint violet handprint on her shoulder. Lucy had somehow managed to avoid getting splattered during Pollock. "You bitch!" Lucy squealed, erupting into giggles. Lucy had this way of flirting with everybody, or at least it seemed that way. Maybe that was just what friendly, outgoing girls did to make themselves seem prettier. Indigo smiled to herself as they walked together.

"So, what's new? Whatcha been working on?" Lucy asked, her turquoise-jewelry eyes gleaming with interest.

"I think I'm going to do something about technology for my final project this year," Indigo explained. "I saw a special on MSNBC about the influence of the Internet on the human brain, and it really fascinated me. My piece could be themed around social networks and texting and stuff, and how even though we're more connected than we've ever been before, we're also somehow more out of touch."

"You mean how you and I IMed all year and I still have no idea how you really feel about that fellowship you won? And whether you're still worried that it's too late to be a prodigy?"

Indy blushed and Lucy grinned back. She knew her so well.

"The fellowship was awesome," Indy said, nodding. "It meant a lot to my parents, too. God, they place so much stock in that stuff. Grants, scholarships, you know?"

"I know what you mean. When I got that Pantene spot, it was like I'd finally proved to my dad that I could one day, *possibly,* with the right series of lucky breaks, maybe, working a part-time day job, support myself. He's always so concerned about my acting ambitions not being commercial enough, and I'm like—hello! I'm in a *commercial.*" Indigo nodded along in agreement, but sometimes she had trouble relating whenever Lucy got "actressy."

"Yeah, I mean—I think your career is doing all right if you've got your face plastered around half of Manhattan. And not in the, like, come-to-this-Gentlemen's-Club-on-Fifty-fourth-Street sort of way."

They both laughed.

"Anyway…" Lucy continued. "What's this big, juicy secret you wanted to tell me?"

"Oh, it was…" Indy began, kicking a clump of dirt on the path. Her toe was still mauve from the paint slip. "It was nothing."

"Aw, man. It sounded so good. You sure?"

"Yeah." Indy shrugged. "Really, it was nothing."

Part of her still wanted to tell Lucy about the e-mail, but she decided to wait a bit longer. As much as she wanted to confront Lucy about her alleged interaction with Nick just in the hope of hearing Lucy contradict the rumor, Indy decided to withhold this little nugget of information for now. She wanted to observe Nick and Lucy from a safe distance before making any silly accusations that might hurt her friend's feelings.

"Hey, listen," Indigo said and sighed. "I'm going to go to bed. I'm pretty spent, you know? It was a long day. See you at breakfast tomorrow?"

"Yes!" Lucy exclaimed. Then she marveled aloud, "God, it's so weird to be at the staff table. I missed sitting next to you tonight." Indy knew Lucy had added that last part only to make her feel better—but it worked. She smiled.

"Well, *I* thought it looked pretty fun," Indy said, offering her own little permission for Lucy to have fun without her. She shone her spotlight toward the path anew. "Good night, Luce."

"Night, Ind."

By the time Indy reached the Beat cabin, the stars had reached a nearly obscene level of brightness. Indigo crept into Ferlinghetti to shower, change her outfit, and grab her art supplies, stealthily avoiding any interaction with a sleeping Eleanor, who'd evidently spent the dinner hour rearranging their room to her liking. Indigo threw her paint-splattered campfire clothes in the laundry basket and found her favorite navy hoodie, then began packing tubes of oils and brushes and pencil cases into her backpack. Just as she was about to head out of the bedroom, she overheard Puja and Yvonne across the hallway, cackling like cartoon witches.

"Did you see how he looked at her?" said Yvonne, her speech muddled by what sounded like openmouthed bites of snack crackers.

"Oh, totally. Like he was a dog and she was made out of bacon." Puja laughed.

"It's…*bacon*!!!" Yvonne imitated that commercial for dog treats, then howled.

Indigo couldn't help hearing Nick's name in their conversation, even though they hadn't mentioned anyone specifically. Had Yvonne and Puja seen Nick rescue her from her fall? Had they picked up on any sexual tension between them? Or was it all in her head?

"Well, we don't know for sure whether or not they really did it," Puja surmised. "I mean, Eleanor makes up as much shit as she spreads around."

Her paranoia was only half-founded. They were talking about Nick and *Lucy*. Weren't they? What else could it have been? And

Jesus, were they loud. How was Eleanor sleeping through this? Indy pictured her roommate turning her head slowly, like a mannequin in a horror movie, and smiling back, eyes open and blank. Her heart began to race.

Indigo strapped her backpack to her shoulders and popped her sweatshirt hood over her damp ponytail. She silently closed the door behind her suite, then made her way out the squeaky front door, leaving Puja and Yvonne to wallow in the sweet rush of schadenfreude.

As the screen door flapped behind her, Indy realized she had forgotten her flashlight. She didn't want to go back inside and risk interacting with her bunk mates, so instead she walked into the darkness around her cabin. Slowly but intently, and with the muscle memory of her many summers embedded within her sense of direction, Indigo made her way west toward the art studios, which were kept illuminated by the small, bright lamp of somebody else, working into the late night.

5

As soon as Indigo stepped into the paint-splattered floor of the art studio, the smell brought her back to summers past. The aroma of thinner and clay dust made her feel before she could think—the emotional nostalgia from just standing there raised the hairs on her arms and gave her goose bumps, along with the chill of the night air, even inside the industrial space that was Silver Springs's main art studio. It was electrifying to be back where she belonged.

"Well, hello."

Nick's shaggy head peeked around the giant easel that bisected the space. He looked intense, distracted—like he was caught working on the piece of a lifetime. And he probably was. But he didn't look annoyed at the interruption. After a moment, Nick lent the same gaze to Indy that he had to the canvas he stood in front of. All five-foot-two of her, standing in front of the glass door, strapped to a backpack, holding an armful of pads and two huge tote bags bursting with supplies.

"Hi," Indigo said shyly. Her voice echoed in the vastness of the empty room.

"Hey, take a load off! Look at all the crap you're schlepping. Lemme give you a hand."

Nick walked around the easel, wiping his paint-smeared hands on his jean shorts. Then he reached out for Indy's bags. "Jeez," Nick said. "You're going to end up a hunchback if you carry all this stuff around. Don't you know this is too heavy for a little girl like you?"

Indy's cheeks flamed up at the term "little girl," but not in offense. It was kind of hot the way Nick said it, like she was thin, or young, or fragile.

"I'm good, thanks," Indigo said, struggling to transfer her sketchpads onto the long wooden table in front of her. She looked around at the familiar space—there were the slanted drafting tables, the corner with the pencil sharpener and the cutting board, the wall of massive aluminum sinks behind the garbage cans for recycling and trash. Off the main space was the sculpture studio, with welding equipment and ceramic supplies, including a working kiln that Lillian had commissioned from a team of Amish lesbians out of Pennsylvania, who crafted the thing from naturally occurring stone and organic mud. The whole place felt cold and homey at the same time—like you could get work done here for hours on end, but you wouldn't want to take a nap in any of the chairs.

Nick rolled his eyes and slipped his hands beneath the straps of Indy's backpack, grazing her shoulders through her hoodie.

"Don't be a hero," he said, taking the bag. "And be careful; you seem a little shaky on your legs today." Nick gestured with a nod toward Indy as he put her backpack on the table next to her stuff.

"I will." She blushed at his mention of their earlier run-in, unzipping her knapsack as she looked over at the lockers, which lined the glass wall facing her bunk. Indy paused before starting to unload all of her stuff.

There was an awkwardly long silence. Not sure what to say, Indigo resisted the urge to mention the e-mail he'd sent her. She knew it wasn't the time to talk about it—but she wanted to badly.

"Aren't you exhausted from the trip? I always feel like the first day of camp is the longest." Nick broke the silence, taking his place back in front of the easel. It was the second time he'd saved her from humiliation that night.

"I just wanted to get a head start on settling in, before every-thing gets crazy."

"I like that about you. Indigo Hamlisch, Serious Artist. You might be the only one at the camp, you know."

"Really?"

"Nah. Everybody here is serious to a fault." Nick laughed. "But at least from your work, you get the sense that you're into what you do—for *you*. You're not just following your parents' orders, or drumming up whatever requisite 'A for effort' kind of com-mitment that would get you in to a good college one day for extracurriculars. You're like Supergirl or something. Plus, you're talented as fuck."

Indigo smiled, feeling flattered that Nick would swear around her liberally. It meant he regarded her as a peer, not as a camper—or a mentee, even. "Thanks." She tried to be confident for once instead of self-deprecating. "Do you mind if I take this big locker?"

"Help yourself." Nick rinsed his brushes in coffee cans full of Turpenoid while Indy stacked pads and boxes of charcoals, pen-cils, pastels, and colored pencils in the roomiest locker of the studio.

"Is that Liz Taylor?" Nick looked over at one of the many

bulging sketchbooks Indigo was transferring from the pile on the table to the locker next to the sink. Indeed, she had duct-taped a vintage black-and-white photo of Elizabeth Taylor, busting out of a halter top and looking sultry and freckled in some 1960s pinup, onto the cover of the sketchbook she used for life drawing. She had books she kept for research and inspiration, ones she kept for writing, some she kept for collage work, and some for drafting ideas for three-dimensional projects. But this one was full of drawings of people she saw on the subway, in the park, and occasionally, naked, when she went down to Prince Street in SoHo for evenings of life-drawing classes that featured live models and jazz.

Indy nodded. "I found that photo in an old *Life* magazine I bought from a street vendor in the Village."

"She was smokin' hot," Nick said as he put a brush up to his canvas and marked it with intention. "One of my all-time favorites. But it wasn't until, like, *Cleopatra* and *Butterfield 8*, when she, you know, started looking like that." He ran a hand through his shiny dark hair and it fell down, a piece at time. Indigo tried not to stare. "I always had a huge crush on her. Liz Taylor, Jane Russell, Diana Rigg. Shall we say, statuesque brunettes. That's my type."

Was that a come-on? Indy was a busty brunette and had the style of all those sixties bombshells, at least in her mind. Surely this was about her, wasn't it?

"I hate Audrey Hepburn," she heard herself say.

Nick laughed out loud.

"Really? Girls your age generally go bananas for her whole *Breakfast at Tiffany's* shtick. But I know what you mean, she was never really my thing. Too skinny, too cold. And that accent always seemed forced. I mean, I know she was English, but it always just seemed sort of overly stylized, hearing her talk.…"

"Affected," Indigo added.

"Yeah," Nick said. Then he went back to work.

Indigo decided to set up an easel perpendicular to his and work on what would soon be a painted version of one of the still lifes from her sketchbook—a bowl of rotted fruit on her kitchen table from home, surrounded by boxes of Duracell batteries, Mop & Glo, Sudafed, and Twinkies. It would be a cool statement about the effects of meth on poor white American bodies. She was excited to add the rich colors of the decaying fruit.

Indy adjusted the legs of the easel to match her height and put a prestretched canvas on the bottom clamp. As she taped her reference photos to the top of the easel, she peeked over at Nick, who had stopped working on his painting to stand back and look at it. She went around to join him and examined his piece, too.

It was a five-by-ten-foot landscape of a postapocalyptic desert scene. Miles of soot and sand were littered with cow skulls and machine-gun shells under a green, ominous sky. It was dark stuff they stood before, but Indigo could tell that once it was finished, Nick's piece was going to be really powerful. Nick shook his head as he stared at what he'd made. He was a perfectionist, too.

"That's looking pretty cool," Indy said, cringing as she heard the words escape her mouth. *"Pretty cool"*? Ugh. It would have sounded so much smarter to draw a comparison to the stark, violent paintings of Francis Bacon. Nick probably would have been thrilled at the reference to one of his idols.

"Yeah, I dunno," Nick said. He didn't look over at her. "I'm a little concerned about the composition."

"Do you think it needs one more big thing, like, off to the side?" Indy asked, thinking that's what she would have done to the painting. Not that this was anything even close to a piece Indy had ever produced.

48

"Maybe. I could also just need a break from it."

"Sure."

Indigo was thrilled at having just had an artist-to-artist conversation with the guy she'd spent half her life fantasizing about. She tried to play it cool, like she was totally used to giving grown men she idolized casual advice about their work. She started sketching on her canvas just to look busy—like she was just doing her own thing, not anxiously waiting for Nick to respond. Or for him to ask her what she thought of his other paintings. Or to come over to her and spin her around with his big hands, holding her narrow shoulders and bringing her close, then touching his lips to her ropy, pale neck before he'd finally kiss her, in exquisite relief.

She just stood there and sketched her still life as Nick stepped away from his canvas entirely and washed his hands in the sink. Finally, he made his way over to the crappy Panasonic boom box in the corner of the painting studio. Indy heard the sound of a cassette ejecting from the outdated contraption, then Nick popping in another tape. It was hilarious, this antique technology. Indigo had never even seen a cassette tape until she came to Silver Springs her first year and listened to a tinny recording of The Violent Femmes while she learned to throw pots on the wheel. And though Lillian kept trying to install iPod docks in all of the studios, the art students refused. There was just something superior about the nostalgia of cassette decks.

Nick hit a button, and Indy instantly recognized the first track of R.E.M.'s *Automatic for the People* from its opening guitar plucking notes. As Michael Stipe's deep voice filled the studio with rickety earnestness, Indy felt herself become engrossed in what she was doing.

She drew and drew, until her piece started to resemble something she was excited about. It always amazed her how things took shape. Most of the time it happened in a totally unexpected way. Or just with time.

She went over to her scuffed taupe metal locker and removed her paints, a palette knife, and a rubber-banded cluster of her favorite brushes. She started setting up for the next step of the process, taking pleasure in keeping everything neat and organized while she did.

She squeezed the new tubes of paint Yoshiko had charged to her AmEx last week, delighting in how it felt to dent the plumpness of the aluminum tubes with her thumb. Dots of color went onto her waxed-paper palette pad; the first leaf since she'd unwrapped it moments before, like a Christmas present. She dumped her brushes next to the pad on the counter surface and walked over to the sinks to fill an old coffee can with Turpenoid.

There she paused to notice Nick, who'd already painted over the sky of his landscape in bold strokes of crimson red, negating all of the progress he'd made on that part of his spacescape. At first she was sad to see what he'd done, but then she shrugged it off as an artist's choice. They were peers now, and she knew as well as Nick that when you were making art, the only important person to please was yourself.

She also couldn't help but think about herself decked out in lipstick that color, reclining on some kind of comfy, secondhand couch in the apartment in Brooklyn she'd one day share with him. She would be dressed up in vintage-looking lingerie like Liz Taylor's and waiting for her future husband to finish up his work so they could make out.

As she mixed her colors, side one of the tape ran out, causing the button to pop up on its own. She wordlessly turned the cassette over, hit play, and the sounds of side two kept Indy and Nick company. *This is it*, she thought. *This is what I am meant to do.*

6

Indy could barely keep her eyes open at breakfast the next morning.

"Remind me one more time why campers aren't allowed to have coffee?" Puja, who sat next to Indigo in the dining hall, moaned out loud to nobody in particular.

"I have no idea," Yvonne said, appearing from nowhere to sit with them. She slid her tray between theirs. "But I don't know how I'm supposed to stay regular without my morning Americano." She took a bite of croissant. "Too much information?"

Indy forced a smile at Yvonne, who meant well but was just way too loud at this hour. She sat and stared at her poached egg. It lay on the corner of her plate next to the financier she'd grabbed when the silver pastry platter was passed around her table. She basically had some version of a hangover.

Last night felt so good. She'd finally been able to get back into a flow of working that came naturally. It wasn't so easy to get that coordination right; the process of brain to eye to brain to hand to canvas sometimes felt like a horrible, complicated dance routine.

But last night in the studio with Nick, Indigo wasn't distracted or stuck or stubborn or uninspired or hard on herself. The still life she'd drawn, then painted, completely exceeded her own expectations. She just made something beautiful as easily as she breathed air.

Indigo tried not to credit her surge of productivity to Nick's presence, but she couldn't help it. He had some kind of magical influence on her creative brain. Around him, even her mood was calmer, more light.

In a way, Indigo was happy to be half asleep right now. It was like she was extending the dream state of last night—blissfully buzzing with good ideas alongside the man she wanted to lose her virginity to, and marry, and live with, and make babies with, and all of it, right now, forever and ever, amen. She knew her fantasies could get bananas, but sometimes she liked feeling carried away.

"Indigo!"

"Huh?" Indy snapped out of her daydream.

"Good morning, sunshine!" Lucy grinned, decked out in a fresh counselor's shirt and jean shorts and sporting a toothpaste smile.

"Sorry, not entirely awake yet." Indy rubbed her eyes carefully. She didn't want to smudge the coat of dark brown mascara she decided to wear today. You know, just in case she ran into somebody in particular.

Lucy grabbed a chair and sat down next to her. "Did you party last night in the bunk?" Indy scooched her chair over. She could feel the side of her own thigh, exposed in a mini jean skirt, make contact with Yvonne's ample hips.

"Nah, I actually got started in the studio. Stayed up way too late working on this still life."

"Seriously? I'm so jealous of your motivation, Hamlisch,"

Lucy said, twisting up her perfect blond waves into a makeshift bun, then stabbing a pen through them to hold her hair in place. "So you spent the whole rest of the night by yourself?"

"Well, not exactly. There were…others." No way was Indigo going to tell Lucy in front of the whole table that she'd been in the studio alone all night with Nick. She smiled to herself just thinking about that notion, and how intimate it sounded.

Lucy took a generous sip of Indy's orange juice. "Hey, listen—I'm on break at eleven thirty. Want to hang then?"

"Sure," Indy said, still a little paranoid that Lucy was arranging some kind of special talk so she could tell her about Nick taking her virginity.

"Attention, campers!" Lillian's goofy, hearty voice boomed over the P.A. system. "After breakfast, please come to the patio of the Main House to receive your adviser assignments. And any adjustments to your final schedules should be made by the end of the day. Thank you all, and have a beautiful day of creating beautiful things!"

Lucy rolled her eyes and smiled at Indy as soon as Lillian's mic popped off, whining feedback that appeared to deafen the seven-year-olds who sat closest to her station.

"So, are you still working with an adviser?" Puja asked Lucy, "or do you get to be somebody's adviser?"

"You can choose! I just don't think there's anything I can teach somebody right now, so Lillian assigned Rashid as my adviser." Lucy had this way of being adorably and convincingly self-deprecating. "I guess I'm also assisting him. Do you guys know him at all?"

"Don't think so. I try not to get too close to the theater people," Indigo joked. "You guys know we think of all of you as zoo animals, right?" A couple of years ago, Indy had come to meet

Lucy and ended up watching the end of one of her experimental theater classes. The students were literally running around in the dance studio howling like monkeys, pretending to pick imaginary lice off one another's backs.

"That's fair." Lucy laughed. "But he's more of a dance guy, actually. He's, like, a big deal in the jazz dance world. He has Ben Vereen's number on his cell under *B*, which is pretty hot."

"I don't know what any of those words mean." Indigo held her fork up to her mouth.

"Well, I'm looking forward to working with a dance dude because I've been really trying to nail the movement side of my acting lately."

Yvonne, still seated next to Indigo, held up the pastry basket and chimed in. "After this bran muffin, let's just hope I'll be able to nail a movement of my own."

Crickets.

The girls bused their trays and Lucy followed Indigo to the patio outside, where Lillian's partner, Debra, sat behind a folding table. "Let's find out who your adviser is!" Lucy squeezed the top of her arm. Indy was wearing a cap-sleeved black Dead Kennedys tee, barely held together with safety pins and a shoelace. She had worn it hoping Nick would notice and be impressed. But he was still nowhere to be found this morning. If she had a choice, though, she would have slept through breakfast, too, considering how late they worked.

They. It was like booze or pot, or a crazy chocolate dessert, the way that word made her feel. Like she and Nick were equals.

"Hi," Indigo said to Debra, who wore a shiny new whistle engraved with some kind of wiccan symbol around her neck. Debra returned Indy's greeting with a blank stare.

"Debraaa!" Lucy butted in. "Love that necklace—is it new?

Help me out?" She beamed at her like she was auditioning for a role. "So, Indy here wants to know who her lucky adviser is this summer...." She leaned onto the table, grinning ear to ear. It was like Lucy thought she had to turn on the charm in order to get information from Debra.

Indy loved Lucy, but somehow a shred of doubt she had about her best friend's loyalty still lingered. She had a glimmer of feeling uncharacteristically annoyed by Lucy's C.I.T. friendliness, her smile—her way of making every head in a room turn when she entered, or laughed, or sang or danced or tossed her hair back, like she was paid thousands of dollars to do in her shampoo ads. It was hard enough to take her seriously when so many of her actions seemed to be for show. As in, there's no business like. But maybe Indy was just overtired. Yeah, that was it.

"Yes, of course. Indigo Hamlisch! Let's find out who you're working with this summer!" Debra replied, with the combined intensity of a major-league coach and a game-show host. Lucy, in a somewhat bizarre new variation on her morning touchy-feeliness, massaged Indigo's shoulders while Debra pulled out a file card.

"And your adviser is..." She blubbered her lips like she was doing a drum roll of some kind. It was gross.

"...Jen Rant!"

Wait. The weird lady Puja had last year?

"Yo. That's me."

Indy spun around to see pretty, petite, twentysomething Jen Rant; a busty brunette in thick eyeglass frames that hid small, sarcastic eyes. Her lips were chapped, and her legs were so short, she cuffed capri-length leggings at her thick ankles. She was dressed in all black, which included a Dead Kennedys T-shirt that was—oh, God—identical to the one Indigo was wearing.

"Well, isn't this a match made in whatever you choose to believe represents heaven!" Debra exclaimed.

"Thanks, Deb. I'll leave you guys to get to it," Lucy chirped, then peeled off.

Indigo gave Jen what could best be described as a cringey half-smile. Jen offered her hand.

"I've seen your portfolio, and you've got a lot of talent," she said awkwardly. "I'm a performance artist—I do conceptual pieces, video installations, multimedia monologues, that kind of thing. But I come from a visual-arts background, so going forward, I think we'll have more than our taste in T-shirts in common."

"Thanks," Indy said. Who was this woman wearing her clothes? She was totally trying to do that thing where adults treat teenagers like adults, almost for the sake of being noticed and appreciated for doing exactly that?

"So, between now and our first session, maybe you can prepare a rough mission statement of what your goals are this summer," Jen continued.

"Okay, sounds good." Indy checked her phone, hoping she'd have enough time to run back to Ferlinghetti to change shirts before her first class.

"Cool. I'll let you go to your first class." Jen looked past Indy's shoulder, as though she, too, was eager to end this awkward interaction.

"Nice meeting you," Indy said, politely enough. But Jen Rant was staring at something far off into the distance. Indy craned her neck to see what she was looking at.

Nick was walking on the pine-lined path that connected the staff cabins to the dining hall. His hair looked like it was still wet from the shower, and half of his perfect face was hidden behind vintage Ray-Ban aviator sunglasses. He wore faded jeans with holes in them and a plain gray pocket tee that hugged his lean body. Just the sight of him made Indy's whole body tighten up like a spring. He sipped from a massive portable coffee mug as he trudged up the path toward them, staring down at his filthy, formerly white Chuck Taylors.

There it was again. That lightning bolt of anticipation and excitement she got only when she saw Nick. Indy quickly ducked back into the dining hall—she did *not* need him to see her and Jen Rant wearing the same shirt; the poseur punk-rock twins on parade. But as she made her way through the doorway she couldn't resist sneaking one last look.

It was going to be an awesome day. She could just tell.

7

Jim Dybbs, the hippie-dippie sculpture teacher, was lecturing the girls about clay.

"There's more to terra cotta than meets the eye," Jim said with a straight face, which was otherwise adorned with sleepy eyelids and a bushy gray beard. His shoulder-length hair was pulled back into a neat ponytail, and he stood behind the crotch-height worktable in the ceramics studio, kneading a ball of red-brown clay with his long, slender fingers—one of which, inexplicably, had a wedding band on it.

"Certain clays are more malleable than others, you know." He added, "It's a lot like flesh." *Gross*, Indy thought. She really didn't want to associate Jim Dybbs with flesh.

"Terra cotta, which translates to 'baked earth,' goes back to cultures that predate history. And when it comes to the first known sculptures of all time, what do you think those ancient people used clay to create? That's right—the naked form. Flesh!" Indy cringed again. "And is it any wonder? Is there a more appropriate material from which to craft the human form, with its rippling folds of skin, fat, and muscle?" Jim pulled down a retractable screen from behind his desk. "Behold! *The Venus of Willendorf*!"

Indigo and the other girls who sat around the long clay-streaked table couldn't help but giggle at the six-foot photo reproduction of a sculpture of an obese lady with pendulous breasts, no face, huge thighs and belly, and a poonanny that looked like an elephant's in heat.

"This female nude was, at one point, and arguably remains, the ultimate fertility symbol. Look at those folds of flesh. Look at the way her hips drape over her legs. That is clay at its most sensual and virile."

"Actually, Mr. Dybbs?" Erin O'Donaghue, a redheaded over-achiever from a New England family that owned sailboats named after each of the chapters of *The Iliad*, raised her hand. "I'm pretty sure *The Venus of Willendorf* was carved from limestone, and tinted with red ochre. It was sculpted in 22,000 B.C. If it was made out of the same crap my dad uses for tiles in our house in Kennebunkport, I highly doubt that fat bitch would still be around for us to look at."

The class stifled its snickers.

"Thank you, Erin," Jim responded politely. What was he going to do, reprimand the girl whose dad was responsible for half of the instructor salaries this year alone? "And now let's go around the room and talk about what your artistic goals are for this summer and how they will involve sculpture. Please also mention what materials you enjoy working with and why. Oh, and your favorite flavor of ice cream. Just to keep it fun!"

Jim Dybbs was greeted with a studio full of blank faces.

"Indigo Hamlisch, why don't we start with you?"

Noooooo.

"Uh, hi. I'm Indy…and I can't really digest ice cream." Off her classmates' stares, Indigo couldn't resist adding a joke. "I get diarrhea when I get the full-fat kind."

"Okay, Indigo. Let's get serious."

"Fine, okay. Every once in a while I'll get some Chubby Hubby."

Jim Dybbs glared at her. She wasn't even sure why she was being so contrary. It was probably because Jim was just such an easy target. Plus, they all already knew one another anyway, so this whole introduction was pointless.

"And what are you going to be working on for the summer?"

"I'm not sure yet," she replied earnestly. "I mean, in the past I've done a lot with two-dimensional media. I did a ton of print-making stuff last summer. And some paintings."

"But what," Jim pressed, "is your work *about*? I remember those paintings from last summer, Indigo. They were powerful. Don't lose that."

"Thank you," she replied. Jim was referencing the series of seven oil paintings she'd done in remembrance of her mother. Each canvas was composed of abstract forms in one color scheme, one for each color of the rainbow. The whole "ROY G. BIV" thing. The sixth and final canvas was appropriately indigo-colored, representing that, at age six—the year she'd lost her mother—the color and light had gone out of her life. The seventh canvas was blank.

But Indy also remembered how, after the staff had gone fucking nuts for it, she had gone back to her bunk and sobbed uncontrollably for the rest of the night. In part because she missed her mom, but also because she was afraid that she'd completed the best piece she'd ever do. After that, there was no way to go but downhill.

"This year I do want to work with more multimedia elements,"

Indy finally replied. "Sculpture, technology, audiovisual stuff, maybe? I guess I don't know what I want to say yet."

She looked down at the crisp new sketchpad on her lap and started fidgeting with its wire binding.

"Well, just remember, you only have three and a half weeks until the art show on Industry Showcase Day." Jim Dybbs began to pace back and forth across the front of the room, then stopped right in front of her chair. "If I were you, I'd be working around the clock with my adviser on what exactly it was I, well—'wanted to say.'" Was he was making fun of her?

Erin and a couple of the other girls—the ones with noses their parents bought for them during the school year, based on their new profiles this summer—snickered.

"Let's move on." Jim started walking the room again. "Erin, you're looking terrific as always. Tell us what we can expect from you this summer! And don't forget to tell us your favorite ice cream flavor!" Dybbs proceeded to kiss the butthole of the most influential Irish-Catholic ginger in media next to *New York Times* columnist Maureen Dowd.

Indy tuned him out and felt her cheeks get hot with embarrassment. It was pretty shitty to bring up the subject of her dead mother and then proceed to criticize her lack of direction on her summer project in front of everyone. They had plenty of time. It was the first class, for Christ's sake!

But Jim Dybbs could never cause her to feel any significant sense of being unworthy in regard to pursuing what it is she'd known she was meant to do since she was old enough to hold a crayon. Indy knew she had more talent in the lavender-polish-adorned pinky toe of her left foot than in all of the O'Donaghues you could fit inside of a Kennedy wake. She couldn't let these tittering morons—bursting with more ambition than ability—make her feel panicky and awful.

Erin gave way to Megan Stein, who sang the praises of mango Pinkberry, then launched into an enthusiastic account of her goals around her summer project—an exploration of the indigenous ferns of the Berkshire region, done in an impressionist style.

Indy rifled through her camouflage bag for her cell, where she found a text from Lucy.

Hey gurl—I M BORED! Meet me by the lake for a j? ;)

The stand-alone merit of smoking pot with Lucy didn't really appeal, but in comparison to this nightmare of a sculpture class, Indy couldn't agree quickly enough. She texted back.

Omg. YES. C U in 5.

She collected her things and interrupted Suzie McLandish, a blond with short, spiky hair and brand-new breast implants her parents bought her to "offset her dykey 'do," to tell Dybbs she wasn't feeling well.

"Maybe it's all this talk of ice cream. I think I should go to the infirmary to make sure I don't have any stomach cramps by association." Indy stood up and put her bag over her shoulder, then walked toward the door. "I'll keep you guys posted either way."

She headed to the lake.

The dry sun felt good on Indigo's freckled arms, and the farther away she got from the sculpture studio, the better she felt. She took in the fresh air and closed her eyes, letting the breeze graze her hair and her skin underneath the silky, patterned Urban Outfitters top she'd changed into after that morning's matching-T-shirt debacle.

Her canvas shoes treaded on the manicured grass, then onto the dirt path that wound around the lower-grade bunks, the dance studios, and the outdoor Shakespearean theater that was built around a patch of elms. She hopped up onto the stage for a quickie shortcut, then dove into the brush where a secret, fern-lined hiking path led her to the lake. And like a hokey device from an old animated movie to introduce its main character, the leaves in Indigo's eye line seemed to magically part, revealing Lucy in the clearing.

She had already taken off her staff T-shirt to tan in her bra and jean shorts, and was sprawled out on her back on a rock—her shiny blond curls tumbled down toward the water.

"Hey." Indigo kept her voice low, so as not to disturb the fairy tale–like setting she was suddenly trespassing onto.

"There you are! I was starting to worry."

Lucy sprung up from her reclining pose like she was a cat. She smiled so big her dimples appeared. Indigo, meanwhile, was half incredulous that in the quick, feline action of Lucy's going from lying down to sitting upright, she managed to bare no belly fat at all. Not even a tiny roll of flab.

"Are you cutting class already?" Lucy asked, patting the space on the big, flat rock next to her. She moved her shirt and slipped it on, making room for Indy, who navigated the path as gracefully as she could, and climbed up to the rock.

"Sort of." Indy crossed her freckly legs. "I walked out. I couldn't take it anymore. Jim—you know, the sculpture teacher with the beard and the ponytail? He was giving me unnecessary crap about my summer project." Indigo noticed a mosquito bite on her ankle and scratched it with her short nails. "Whatever. Have you seen how high up on his body he wears his jeans? Beyond."

"Doesn't he belt them with, like, yarn or something?"

"Probably." Indy picked up a tiny stone and threw it into the water. "So, how's life as a staff member?"

"Thrilling," Lucy said sarcastically. "So far I've wrangled a group of seven-year-olds, restocked the dance studio's Purell supply, and then I got to watch Rashid demonstrate the difference between jazz hands and spirit fingers." She tucked her hair behind her ear with one hand and slid her other hand down to her hip. "Do you wanna smoke this?"

Lucy produced a hand-rolled joint from the teeny pocket on the inside of her jean shorts and twirled it nimbly between her middle and index fingers.

"Of course," Indigo replied.

Lucy found a lighter from what seemed like thin air and lit the pinched end of the joint that dangled from her lower lip like a single tusk. She inhaled, then passed it to Indy, who gazed at the water, her hands resting atop her thighs.

"Your turn." Lucy exhaled a triangular cloud of sickly-sweet marijuana smoke. She gestured with her hand again for Indy to take the joint.

"Thanks." Indigo lifted the joint to her mouth and took a conservative puff, tasting Lucy's strawberry lip gloss as she did. They sat in silence for what seemed like a full minute after that, looking at the water and sitting under the sun.

"Um, Indy?"

"Yes?"

Lucy laughed.

"Pass it along, kindly?"

"Oh, God, I'm sorry. I totally spaced."

"Yoink." Lucy brushed her slender fingers against Indy's, stealing the joint out of her hand as she did. There was another pregnant pause as they both sat on the rock not looking at each other, just getting high together in what sufficed for nature.

"Luce?" Indigo felt herself ask.

"What's up?"

"I think I may have been acting a little weird so far this summer. Unless I'm imagining it, in which case, I should just shut up."

Was the weed to blame for her babbling, or the environment? Or was Lucy seducing her into saying what was really on her mind, just like she seduced audience members she got onstage in front of?

"No, go on." Lucy turned her head of doll hair to look at Indy with her cornflower-blue eyes.

Indy felt her neck get hot and started sweating from her scalp. She realized she was stoned. Why did she say anything just now? Why did she even get high with Lucy? Why didn't she eat more for breakfast? She was suddenly starving and panicked and rootless. If she were a boy, this would have been the time to lean in and go for a kiss, if only to shut off her mind from taking over entirely.

"Okay." Her own voice sounded weird to herself. "Well, first of all. I wanted to tell you something. Remember that secret?"

Lucy straightened. "Yeah?"

"It was about Nick…." She looked Lucy in the eyes, pacing her words slowly and dramatically in order to give Lucy a chance to react or to give her some kind of indication that Eleanor's rumor was true or false. But Lucy didn't even flinch.

"Oh, yeah? Out with it!"

Indy took a deep breath and tried to shake the not-high into her body. Maybe the more oxygen she breathed into her brain, the less she'd be stoned. She continued after she cleared her throat.

"He sent me an e-mail a couple of months ago," Indy said, looking at the water.

"Are you serious? Indy, that's *awesome*." Lucy crossed her legs and scooted closer. "So, what did it say?"

"It doesn't matter…." Indigo trailed off, then suddenly turned her gaze from the lake back toward her friend. "Look, is it true that you and Nick hooked up? Did you lose your virginity to him?" She was shocked at how fast it had all come tumbling out. Her cheeks flared again. She stared down at the rock visible between her crossed knees and scratched her mosquito bite once more, dreading Lucy's answer.

"What?!" Lucy's voice was a loud bell of incredulity and friendly surprise. "Is that what's been bugging you?" She put her hand on Indy's leg. "You've gotta be kidding." She made sure she caught Indigo's eyes once she looked up. "Don't be nuts. Nothing has ever, ever, ever happened between me and Nick. I mean, you've had a super-intense crush on him for how long? Forever? You're my best friend. I'd never hook up with a guy you liked. And I'd *never* not tell you if I'd lost my virginity!"

"I'm sorry." Indy looked down.

"Don't be sorry!" Lucy said, still sounding—not angry, just shocked. "I'm just glad you said something. Where the hell did you get that crazy idea in the first place?" Her kind eyes seemed to look through Indigo.

"Eleanor," Indigo said, shaking her head. "I should have known better." Lucy scootched over on the rock to give Indy a sincere side hug, squeezing her friend's body close to hers and resting her head on Indy's shoulder. "No kidding."

They sat like that for another five minutes, staring at the lake in silence, peacefully stoned, watching the clouds move in the reflection of the water below the perfectly blue Massachusetts sky.

It was around this time when Indy finally remembered why she didn't partake of weed more often during the school year—it made her really anxious and paranoid. She tried to observe her mind racing instead of letting her frantic thoughts run away with her like a doomed train. But her ankle was itchy and her nails were too short and the sun was feeling too hot for the minimal amount of sunscreen she'd put on early this morning. Beyond the matters of physical comforts, Indy couldn't help but wonder: *Was Lucy telling the truth?* She seemed sincere, but she was also really good at acting. "Acting." The word itself made Indy cringe. So did the word "drama," or "theatre"—with an "re," not an "er."

Indy, suddenly and completely, felt like a huge fraud. What was she doing at this sleepover conservatory when real artists paid their dues eating whatever they found in Bushwick Dumpsters and shoplifting art supplies from Lee's? Nick couldn't have grown up with a silver spoon in his mouth, and there's no way he was given the privileges she was. He seemed so raw.

Indigo wished she could have hit some kind of fast-forward button, so she could skip ahead to when she was, say, twenty-seven and Nick was thirty-three. And they could live together in a loft somewhere in Brooklyn, where they'd shower together every morning—that would never get old—then head to their respective studios for long, rewarding days of making art.

How she wished she could jump into that reality right now. She looked to Lucy, who sat cross-legged and blissed out, and almost felt safe enough to open up to her. Maybe they were still on the same wavelength after all.

"Do you want me to be like, wing woman for you? Maybe hang out with Nick during staff things and, you know—push him in the right direction?" Lucy asked. Then she began to giggle.

"I would love nothing more," Indy said, then began giggling too. All of a sudden, she was having fun.

Things were fine.

Indy stayed out at the lake, staring at the water, long after Lucy went back to supervising her classes. She ended up missing lunch, much to her rumbling stomach's chagrin, and still felt the effects of the weed long after they'd smoked it.

Her head was fuzzy, but she was lucid enough to feel guilty about missing her second-period class—Principles of Advanced Collage—and she totally phoned in her Drawing Architecture third-period elective. She chose to draft a charcoal-on-newsprint replica of the painting studio from the safe distance of the swing set, yards away, and did a lousy job of it. As she sketched and swung back and forth, lazily, Indy thought less about the work on the page and more about how much she hoped Nick wouldn't find her there, as she was certain she looked sweaty and twitchy since she first got high.

By the time the sun had set and she'd shuffled over to dinner, Indigo had bitten her fingernails down to the cuticles—a bad habit that came and went, despite her stepmom's splurging on manicures for her at Elizabeth Arden. She barreled through the meal—a deconstructed pheasant pot pie with a quinoa crust and a kale and organic pancetta side—and even ate a third portion.

"Oink much?" Eleanor said to Indy, then added "J.K.," even though she totally wasn't kidding. Then Eleanor went back to lecturing Indigo on the subject of her expertise—herself.

"So, *pointe* class went awesome. I can't believe I was ever intimidated by Renée. I mean, she's just a bitter old frog who's only nasty to her students because we're more limber and castable than she is. It has nothing to do with how good we are at a pas de chat. Although this one new girl—have you met Desi?"

"No, of course not," Indy said, with her mouth full. How would she know another dance major who wasn't Eleanor? She hung out with her only because they roomed together. Usually artists and dancers stayed as far away from each other as they possibly could.

"Well, she's a moose," Eleanor said, "and a totes Johnny-come-lately. I think she's one of those girls who saw *Black Swan* and thought she could dance just because she'd hooked up with a girl once when she was drunk."

"Listen, I'm gonna head back to the bunk," Indy said, realizing there was nothing left to eat. She was suddenly dying to get out of the dining hall.

"Well, so am I, dummy. I was just waiting for you to finish inhaling all those portions. Let's walk back together. *Duh.*" Who taught Eleanor her social skills, Temple Grandin?

The walk back to the Beat cabin with Eleanor was interminable, even though it was a perfect summer night. Fireflies speckled the dim sky as the sun set, and Indy listened to Eleanor's smack-talk about the other girls in her classes, all of whom were, apparently, fat and incapable. Behind them, the rest of the campers filtered out of the main house—Indigo heard the treading of various ballet flats and UGG boots and half wished she'd tagged along with the majority of the camp to attend the evening activity. She remembered hearing Yvonne saying something at the table about an outdoor concert that would be taking place after dinner in the lantern-strewn tent that Lillian erected near the ballet studios. That actually sounded kind of nice, but she had already made the decision to go back to the bunk.

By the time Indy changed into the boxer shorts and enormous Kenyon College T-shirt that she slept in, it was only 8:30 PM. She felt dumb for screwing herself up earlier in the day with pot. Indy thought about how she hadn't gotten any work done, she ate too much at dinner, and her fingernails were all short and gross. But camp had only just started. There was a ton of time left to turn things around and focus, especially now that she was positive that

Lucy had not hooked up with Nick. That, at least, was an incredible relief.

Eleanor got out her laptop and logged on to a BitTorrent site to find all the new eating disorder–themed episodes of *Intervention* that she'd missed. Indy climbed into bed, even though she wasn't really tired. She shifted to her side and stared at the wall, while music that scored some family members' tearful testimonials blared from Eleanor's computer. Finally, she squinted her eyes shut, conjuring up images in her mind for what the perfect summer project might look like. But her imaginary canvases were all filled with Nick's face. Focusing this summer was going to be harder than she expected.

8

A week had passed since Indy had gotten stoned with Lucy by the lake, and even though she no longer had pot to blame for her fuzzy head, she still had a hard time producing anything in her classes that she was particularly proud of. She showed up every day and did what she was supposed to, but her hand wasn't shaping the clay or guiding the paint into any sort of shape that made her feel good about looking at it. And she had no idea what she was trying to say.

That's partially why she was dreading her first session with Jen Rant. She had no idea how Jen was going to "advise" her. Camp had barely just begun, and apparently, Indigo's dry streak was already a hot topic among her fellow visual arts majors. She'd even overheard Megan Stein telling Suzie McLandish that she had "completely lost her voice," which was a little extreme. Plus, Indy had seen Megan Stein's indigenous-fern sketches hanging up in the drawing studio. They were bland and uninspired, so Megan didn't really have the right to criticize.

On the hottest day of the summer so far, Indigo headed toward the Theater Row complex of acting studios, which was next to the Performance Art Center, where Jen Rant kept office hours every other day between 9 AM and noon. Indigo scuffed her purple Converse on the shale steps that led into the building. Her black skinny jeans and tank seemed to cling to her skin like a wetsuit, and Indy found herself wishing she'd worn something looser, or lighter, or had just stayed inside her air-conditioned bunk all day. But hiding out would have only prolonged the inevitable. She was required to meet with Jen, and if she didn't go, she would get in trouble.

The Performance Art Center was a boxy, modern building that was situated both geographically and ideologically between Theater Row, the cluster of stages and studios in which drama majors took their acting classes, and the art studios, where Indy was during most of her day. As the center's glass doors opened automatically with an unnerving beep, Indigo made her way toward the Karen Finley Yam Wing, where Jen Rant waited for her in her tiny office.

"Hello?" Indigo called out from the hallway. She was outside a room labeled with the nameplate RANT. That struck Indy as funny—like Jen's office was a designated place to bitch about things.

When she walked in, Jen was sitting on the floor, her head tilted back, making gargling sounds. She stopped as soon as Indy cleared her own throat.

"Indy! Perfect, you're right on time. Come in," she said, seeming not at all embarrassed to be caught in the act of some kind of bizarre warm-up exercise or whatever that was.

Performance-art people.

"Hey." Indy nodded, settling in on one of Jen's folding chairs.

"Are you sure you don't want to join me on the floor?" Jen asked, from below her.

"Yes. Yes, I am." This experience was already uncomfortable enough without having to crouch down like some kindergartener during circle time.

"Okay, no prob." Jen, in black leggings and a black tank top, sprang up from the floor and cracked her knuckles, then took a seat across from Indigo at her desk in a rolling chair. "So, how are you doing?"

"Fantastic," Indigo lied.

Jen pulled out a folder with her name on it.

"Have you had a chance to write up your mission statement?" Jen leafed through Indy's file, which documented the extensive time she'd spent at Silver Springs, from her administrative records to reproductions of her own work. She saw Jen pause on a color photocopy of the third panel from *Epilogue to Rain*, the abstract color series she had done about the death of her mother.

"You know, I haven't," Indigo replied, surprised at her own defiance in admitting to her own failure. She looked down and began to play with the snaps on her black leather wrist cuff.

"Why not?" Jen wore her best "concerned" face.

"I just haven't felt very inspired lately, to be honest."

Jen shuffled more through the folder, as though she were looking for a clue or something else to respond to besides Indy's flip answer. Indy looked around the room at the posters on the office wall. Eric Bogosian live at the Public Theater. A huge black-and-white photograph of Yoko Ono. Clippings from what must have been Jen's hometown paper, *The Scarsdale Inquirer*, featuring photos of Jen covered in mayonnaise, wearing a leotard, under the headline "Local Girl Makes 'Art' Onstage."

"You know, I've personally found, in my work, that inspiration counts for very little. Most of the time, it's just showing up in the morning that gets me to where I need to be, productively."

"Well, I do show up in the morning," Indy responded slowly. "I showed up at sculpture class this morning and I left with a lump of clay that I'm ashamed to put my name on."

Jen looked up from the folder and straight into her eyes.

"What's up, Indy? Is there anything that's been bothering you since you got to camp? I saw in your file that you might be at risk to—"

"I'm fine." Indy cut her off.

What was she, a therapist? There was no way she was going to spill her guts out to Jen Rant about her problems, her lack of a mission statement, how sucky it was rooming with Eleanor, or her unrequited crush on a staff member. It would be better to just end this meeting as quickly as possible.

"Because, you know, sometimes art can be a cathartic way of dealing with things that are tearing us down in our lives. And sometimes, if we can't deal with life, we can't make art. So, I just want to make sure you're, well, dealing with life."

"Everything's completely fine. I'm sure I'm just stuck. Something will come to me." Indy looked to the door and thought about what would happen if she made a run for it. "It always does."

"Okay, good," Jen said, backing up her chair to its original position behind her desk. "It's okay that you're running a little late coming up with your mission statement. Maybe together we can work through whatever this block seems to be. You might just be suffering under the pressure of having to deal with the big picture too soon."

She was probably right. Indy was probably just overthinking everything.

"Yeah" was all she could say. She acted like such an annoying teenager around others being generous. She even shrugged off the helpful stuff, like she was entitled to good advice from people who cared about her well-being.

"So, let's just start right now," Jen continued, like she was used to dealing with standoffish fifteen-year-olds. "How are you going to use your studio time this afternoon?"

"Well…"

"What have you been thinking about lately?"

Honestly? She'd been wondering if she could get away with deleting Eleanor's music library so she didn't have to listen to any more Bieber. She'd been worried that even though she and Lucy were getting along, things would one day change. But most of all, she'd been thinking about hiding out in the backseat of Nick's truck and begging him to take her virginity, then take her far away from here, and years into the future when they'd both be grown-ups and they could have sex and make art and nothing would ever get in their way again, either from the world or from her own head.

But she couldn't say any of that, so Indigo looked around Jen's office for inspiration. The spines of Jen's big art books glared at her. One had the word "PERFORMANCE!" on the spine. Another, called *L'Art Nouveau*, was hunter green and looked so boring that it was practically invisible. Then her eyes landed on a book that vaguely pleased her. *Pop Art*, it read, in yellow on neon pink in a sans-serif font.

"I've been thinking about pop. Pop music, pop culture…how it ties us together, how our tastes connect us to each other and also tear us apart. Like *American Idol*, or how you can say you like this band or that movie on Facebook, and that's supposed to decide what you have in common with your friends."

"Cool, okay." Jen nodded enthusiastically. "And what else would you want to deal with? I mean, what other themes could you connect to that?"

"Gender disparity," Indy answered, falling back on her old mainstay. "How men are perpetuators of the status quo, and women are just objects of the male gaze, basically."

"Awesome! How do you think you'd want to work on a project about that stuff?"

"Maybe an installation?" Indy shrugged.

"This is great!" Jen smiled. "So let's plan on meeting up this Friday to see how that's going so far. Sound good?"

"Yeah. Sounds great." And then, finally, she was released.

Indigo stood and extended her hand for Jen to shake, then got hugged. The smell of Marlboro cigarette smoke in Jen's coarse, dark hair almost choked her. She disengaged before it got even more awkward.

Indigo headed out of the Performance Art Center and through the automatically closing glass doors into the sticky, sunny day, deciding to take the long way back to the dining hall for lunch. Maybe she'd be inspired along the way. Jen was right. If she just kept showing up to the studio every day and putting in the work, piece by piece, she'd figure out what she really wanted to do.

9

The sun blended into the breeze into the iced tea and lemonades Indy sucked down at lunch, into the fireflies and the swimming classes and the sunburns and the shouts of the younger campers playing jacks on the steps of the main house. She got frequent, cloying letters from her dad and stepmom (Yoshiko would collage pet and creamed corn photos from the coupon section of the paper onto her handmade envelopes) saying how much they missed her on Nantucket this year, and how they hoped she was making lots of wonderful stuff.

Meanwhile, the other girls of Ferlinghetti were chipping away at their summer projects. Yvonne rehearsed her hour-long stand-up set in the shower; Puja storyboarded her new play onto the bulletin board in the hallway, obscuring the never-used "chore wheel" with index cards for acts one, two, and three written out in her illegible handwriting. Eleanor practiced her pliés in her and Indy's room, and Lucy flitted back and forth from her acting studio to her quarters in the staff cabin on the north campus.

Sometimes, when they needed a break from working, the girls would sit together on the porch of the cabin and quietly poke fun at the younger campers passing by. Those mini-superstars looked like they owned the world, walking around in their little cliques, chattering about their auditions for *Godspell* and what they got in their care packages. Listening, Indy was reminded of the summer she and Lucy were twelve and thirteen and snuck out of their respective bunks with a bunch of other girls to toilet-paper the Degas cabin. The next day, when they were inevitably sent to Lillian's office, Rachel Silvera, another visual-art major, claimed the prank was her installation piece and that she was trying to make a statement about crappy dancers. The girls had found it all hilarious even though Lillian did not, but they still got away with just a warning instead of being sent to Fairness Committee. Indy remembered that Nick, who'd been her teacher at the time, told her he thought it was awesome, too.

Nick. As hard as she tried to run into him, the night they spent in the studio together was starting to feel like a distant dream. Since he taught introductory drawing and painting classes, Nick shared space with Indigo only when they happened to be in the studio at the same time. But he was either leaving when Indy was coming in to work or coming in to work when Indy was leaving.

What was also frustrating was that Indy was still having a hard time producing anything she felt good about. The still life she'd worked on during her first night at camp collapsed beneath the labor she put into it—she overdid the brushwork that had, at first, made the rotting fruit so compelling. Since then, she'd painted over the whole thing with white gesso, penciled a self-portrait onto the canvas with a light, hard-lead pencil after looking into the mirror and back for three hours, hated what she saw, and painted over it again.

Tonight, she'd give herself a break. She decided to attend that evening's activity, whatever it was. So when Eleanor dragged Indy back to the cabin as soon as they finished their dinner of yellowtail and jalapeño sashimi with profiteroles for dessert, Indy didn't mind. She felt like she wasn't going to miss another dry evening in the studio or a chance at another interaction with the guy who turned her into cream and pastry with his voice alone.

"Where have you been lately?" Eleanor snapped at her, on the path outside the dining hall, handing off a napkin with her profiteroles inside it. Indy took the pastries and gobbled them up, feeling a little sick as she did. Maybe it was the dairy and maybe she was eating her feelings.

"The studio," Indy answered once she swallowed, passing the bench by the stone vases blooming with rhododendrons that lined their picturesque walk back to the Beat cabin. "I'm not thrilled with the work I've been turning out lately, but I've been putting in the time, at least. I feel like I could be on the brink of something."

Eleanor ignored her completely. "Well, you haven't missed anything good, evening activity–wise. The other night, they set up Ping-Pong tables in the jazz studio, can you believe it? Like, rec-room chic? Just because Susan Sarandon owns a table tennis place in the village, it's, like, three years later, and Lillian thinks it's the new hot thing. Like cupcakes or James Franco."

"Uh-huh." Indigo listened to Eleanor describe and berate the other events she'd missed in the last week, from a "build your own medley" workshop led by the executive producers of *The Voice* to a visiting Cirque du Soleil production of *Zarkana* that took place in both the cafeteria and the Harpsichord Room once the main house had been cleared and rigged for the acrobatic elements. "The acrobats looked pretty fat, actually. Or maybe those were muscles." Eleanor yawned. "Either way, it was gross."

"Uh-huh." Indy realized *she* felt pretty fat in that moment, since she was stuffed to the hilt with flaky pastry and vanilla crème. Her stomach mumbled its disapproval, and she found herself grateful that they were steps away from the porch of Ferlinghetti, so she could sneak into the bathroom before whatever activity commenced.

But as soon as they got inside of their bunk the smell of shampoo, perfume, and blow dryers on hair hit their nostrils with the force of a spiked tetherball.

"Shit!" Eleanor exclaimed. "We only have an hour and fifteen to get ready for the social. Dibs on the outlet near the vanity."

Indigo remembered wearily, with the letdown of a sad trombone note, that tonight was the annual social between Silver Springs and its "brother camp," Kinnetonka Heights. At the very least, this meant she'd have no privacy in the bathroom area, where the Beat cabin girls would be grooming themselves within an inch of their young lives.

"Do I *have* to?" She groaned.

"Yes! Now hurry up and go get all hot," said Puja, who happened to be shuffling by, carrying a flat iron and an armful of hair products.

Indy was in no mood to pretend she felt anything besides contempt for the array of fourteen- to sixteen-year-old zit-plagued wankers and Young Republicans in Training that constituted the camper population of Kinnetonka. It was western Massachusetts's premier summer destination for aspiring young male screenwriters, entertainment lawyers, novelists, news reporters, show runners, and agents. If their parents dined regularly at Robert De Niro's restaurant with New York heavy hitters like Arianna Huffington and Anderson Cooper, the odds were that they sent their kid there.

The facilities were of the same five-star quality as Silver

Springs's—central A/C in each bunk, Michelin star–appointed chefs in the kitchens, Fulbright Scholar instructors—but the maturity level of the average Kinnetonka guy was decidedly lower than any Silver Springs girl's. Not only did that fact confirm the "girls mature faster than guys" axiom—but there seemed to be something about creative guys that made them infinitely more stunted than their female counterparts.

Indy finished in the bathroom and slogged back to her and Eleanor's bedroom to get ready for this thing. Socials were mandatory—Lillian's obligation to the Silver Springs parents to expose their daughters to acceptable marriage candidates from as young an age as possible outpaced her desire to please the campers.

Indigo grabbed her shower caddy from her room and dodged the manic bodies of her fellow bunk mates—Yvonne, Puja, and various actresses, dancers, and singers, including one Asian soprano that reportedly made Lea's Michele & Salonga both burst into sobs when they visited last summer as guest critics on Industry Showcase Day. All of the girls scurried around the common area of the enormous bathroom, setting, straight-ironing, and blow-drying their hair; priming, exfoliating, and toning their skin; and shaving, curling, clipping, tweezing, squeezing, spraying, and applying various other creams and shellacs to various nooks and crannies hidden around their young, hysterical flesh. Yvonne stood in the corner by the toilets doing a desperate jig, trying to pull on a giant pair of Spanx. It looked like the strange Picasso painting Indy always liked—*Guernica.*

"Okay, new plan," Yvonne yelped. "Somebody hold these, and I'll get a running start and jump into them." No one volunteered.

Indy slipped into one of the shower stalls and let the water run until she could inhale the steam that rose from the tile beneath her, then slipped off her flip-flops and jeans, then her tank top, before hanging it up next to the stack of high-thread-count towels the camp provided. She stepped underneath the showerhead and let the water stream over her nakedness, being careful not to look down at what she imagined was her huge, post-pig-out belly.

As the shower head pulsed, she closed her eyes and let herself float far away from the chaos around her, drowned out the sounds of the blow dryers, the requests to borrow so-and-so's spray gel, and Eleanor's alternating shrieks of "Where are my pewter Ferragamo ballet flats?" and "Who the fuck took my goddamn pewter Ferra-fucking-gamo ballet flats!" Indy took deep breaths and then squeezed out the excess water from her long, damp hair, wrapping a towel around her body before slipping on her flip-flops and schlepping her stuff back to her and Eleanor's room. She caught her reflection in the makeup mirror on the vanity that stood directly in front of the door of their bedroom. Eleanor sat in the chair before the mirror with her hair pulled tight into pin curls, applying some kind of thousand-dollar under-eye concealer on her face that was marketed to women four times her age. Indigo, wearing a puce towel and holding two armfuls of shower caddy supplies, caught her reflection. She saw how flushed her cheeks were and how lazy and wet her eyes looked.

"What are you, going for the natural look?" Eleanor said as she applied mascara on the fringe atop one of her darty, snakelike eyes.

"I was thinking of wearing my long black dress." Indigo ignored the no-makeup crack and pulled her favorite ankle-length vintage silk black maxi-dress from her closet. She held the dress up to herself in front of the full-length mirror on the wall between their beds.

"All right, Morticia," Eleanor replied into the magnifying side of the mirror. She'd begin examining and squeezing her pores, and seemed to be having a hard time even pretending she cared what her roommate was going to wear for the boys who were coming to their campus in T minus one hour. She had to take care of herself. "Has anybody seen my fucking Chanel padded clutch!" she screamed to no one, mid–blackhead squeeze. Indy smoothed the diaphanous fabric that graced the neckline of her dress over her bust. She adjusted the fit in the hips and tried not to scrutinize her body too intensely when she stood to the side, checking out her silhouette in profile.

Indy did *not* look anything close to how she'd hoped. She grabbed her meager assortment of makeup items and hoped she could at least figure out something that wouldn't make her look like Sylvia Plath next to these girls.

In the bathroom, all of the girls staring into the mirror looked like circus ponies or dolls made out of candy. A row of them expertly swiped glosses, brushes, wands, and combs across their lips, cheeks, brows, and eyes like they'd been born knowing how to gussy themselves up. Even Yvonne looked like a burlesque superstar; Puja, a Freida Pinto–esque leading lady.

"What's up?" Tiffany Melissa Portman, an aspiring actress who claimed to be Natalie Portman's Protestant second cousin—smiled her powder-pink, barely there lips at Indigo in the mirror.

"Hey—I hope this isn't weird to ask." Indy looked back at her in the mirror. "But can you help me with your makeup? It's just you always look so great."

"OMG, of course!" Tiffany, like most actresses, was thrilled to help as long as the request for her assistance was couched in a compliment of some kind. She pushed Indy into the spotlight of the tracks set up behind the sink and scrutinized her skin like some kind of Clinique counter saleswoman in one of those dumb lab coats. Tiffany smeared on some cold, gooey stuff, then some dry, pasty stuff, then powder. Then she told Indy to look up, then down, then to "go like this" with her lips, then to smile, then make a fish face. When she stepped aside, Indigo saw a version of herself in the mirror unlike any she'd ever seen in her life. She sort of looked gorgeous and she sort of looked like a Lisa Frank folder had exploded onto her face. It was hard to tell if leaving the bunk in this condition was in any way socially acceptable. But the sight of her surely excited Tiffany, not to mention the mini–flash mob of bunk mates that had gathered around her mid-makeover, eager to witness the real-time effects of a generous application of another girl's enormous makeup selection.

"Wow!" Yvonne exclaimed, genuinely impressed.

"You look beautiful." Puja smiled behind her own rosy, glossy lips.

"So, what are you changing into?" Tiffany asked, clearly eager to complete Indigo's transformation.

"Oh. Well, I'm not sure if I…" Indigo glanced down at her dress, embarrassed that she was actually planning to wear what she had on. The silk that twirled around her as she walked had always made her feel beautiful. Now, looking around at the miles of skin exposed among the girls who circled her in the bathroom, she felt like a nun. "Can one of you guys maybe lend me something?"

And that's how Indigo Hamlisch ended up wearing skintight hoochie jean shorts and a too-small wife beater that Tiffany assured her "really flattered her cans." She was also sporting enough jewelry to set off the metal detector at the closest airport, Jimmy Choo stilettos "almost in her size" from one of the Greek girls in the bunk over who sang opera, and so much hairspray in her giant updo that if a bullet were to graze her head, her brain would be perfectly safe.

The other tenth-year girls teetered down the path from the upper bunks to the Kurosawa Screening Room and Mocktail Bar, where their intercamp socials were held each summer. Indy still felt like a sausage stuffed into trashy casing. It was a weird price to pay for fitting in. That's what these socials were more about than anything else—impressing the girls, not the boys, was what mattered most. Even Eleanor seemed impressed when she saw her roommate gussied up like a blowfish that survived a crayon-factory accident. "You look hot," she said, without any audible irony in her voice.

Indigo had to hold on to Yvonne's sturdy forearm, which was draped in the bell sleeve of a form-fitting, cleavage-flattering aquamarine top, as she inched along at a stuttering pace, trailing behind the other girls but trying to keep her head up high, even though she felt weighed down by Puja's loaned-out dangly chandelier earrings and Tiffany's masterpiece of a hairstyle. Indy may have felt like a drag queen, but everybody in her bunk swore she looked great—her body looked "amazing," she didn't look "the least bit fat." In no way was her makeup "clownish." So, that was something, right?

Maybe there'd be a cute boy at the social—a new one, not Jay Stegbrandt, a faux-hippie nerd with a Jew-'fro who was, for some reason, best friends with Andrew Cook—a creepy entertainment lawyer wannabe who really seemed to hate girls. At least there was always Evan Zander, the alpha tennis pro from Kinnetonka, to stare at. He wasn't Indigo's type—he was too young, and jocky to boot—but he was an undeniably handsome spectacle. In fact, Indy once sketched a statue of Perseus at the Met and later realized it looked exactly like Evan was staring back at her from the page.

Then, as she finally hit her stride, walking without Yvonne's help and even flipping her head back in music video–like divadom, Indy saw something in the distance that made all of her confidence, all of her mojo, her steez, her moxie, grind to a halt with the bluntness of a record scratch.

Nick, Lucy, Jen Rant, and Jim Dybbs, all dressed up but not wearing anything much fancier than jeans and T-shirts with jackets, were in front of the art studio, walking together in the direction of the staff parking lot.

"Indy!" Lucy shouted, before Indigo could pretend she didn't see them and they didn't see her. Lucy waved, and Indy felt like she was crumpling up like a piece of scrap paper. Her posture changed.

Lucy bounded toward her. She wore skinny, dark-wash, expensive Seven jeans with a flowy, heather gray top under a cropped leather moto-jacket that fit her perfectly. She looked effortlessly chic, pretty, tiny, and grown-up at once. Indigo cringed when she noticed how little makeup she had on to boot. Even her dimples glowed with the wattage of some ultra-bright natural quality of something that just exists with no work behind it, like how the sun just comes up and goes down every day without anybody putting muscle into the process.

"Look at you! You look…" Lucy chose her adjective carefully, "…amazing!" Indy could tell her friend was weirded out by her crazy makeup and skintight outfit.

"I know, right?" Indigo figured she might as well poke fun at herself. As the girls she was walking with receded into the background, she saw Nick, perfect Nick, approach her and Lucy as they stood in the all-too-appropriate space between the staffers and the campers on the grass. Indy's heart raced as he got closer.

She was outright slutted up. But part of her was glad that Nick would finally see her body.

"Where are you guys going?" Indy asked Lucy, trying to shake off the attention she could feel on all sides of her.

"We're going to see Bob Dylan! He's playing some outdoor festival at Wildwood."

"Westwood." Nick's deep voice arrived before he did, approaching the two girls with a bemused correction of whatever Lucy said was the venue they were going to.

He half smiled and then looked Indigo directly in the eye. It was like he could see right through all her makeup and hairspray. She made up her mind: she was in love with him. More than anything else—more than she wanted to be a famous artist, to be the youngest-ever participant in the Whitney Biennial, to make enough money to afford places in Paris, Amsterdam, and New York, she wanted to make Nick Estep fall in love with her.

"Hey, Indy." Nick was wearing a checkered button-down shirt over jeans, and he smelled like Ivory soap and sawdust. His longish dark hair was combed back behind his ears, his face had a day of stubble grown in, and he wore a battered suit jacket over his shirt with the sleeves rolled up. He looked incredible. Indigo couldn't help but notice, with a sinking heart, that, as he stood there next to Lucy, they looked like a perfectly matched couple.

Lucy winked at Indy, encouraging her to talk to him.

"So, Dylan is playing Westwood?" Indigo said, trying to sound really cool and "whatever" about the fact that an ancient rock icon she knew she was supposed to care about was going to be singing folk songs in his horrible, nasal voice at the Westwood Music Festival, five miles from town. She figured Nick was a big fan and nodded as though she was really absorbed in the news that one of his favorites was in town. "Man, I wish I could come with you guys." She winced at her own words as she spoke them.

"Oh my God, me, too. I know. It's so stupid that you can't." Lucy frowned. "I guess you guys have the social tonight?"

Indigo couldn't make out a single word her best friend said at this point, because all she could think about since Nick said hi and stared at her was how intensely she could feel his eyes on her body. There's no way she was imagining that. Right? As wrong as it sounded, she wanted to feel like an object, like a masterpiece. That must be what Lucy felt being onstage, but the attentions of an audience seemed useless compared to the undivided, adoring gaze of one person.

Indy staggered a bit on her shoes but caught herself before she actually tripped.

"You falling for me again, Hamlisch?" Nick smiled. "I thought I told you to be careful."

Omigod. Indy's face flushed red.

"Haha, I think *somebody* may have started the party earlier than the rest of the girls," Lucy said, smiling and probably wondering what Nick was referring to. Indy had never told Lucy about how he had come to her rescue during Pollock.

"Nick, you ready?" Jen Rant interrupted the chatter with characteristic bluntness.

"Yeah, relax, we were just saying hi to Indy for a sec," Nick told her, and Indy knew that she wasn't imagining the jealous look Jen was throwing her way.

Jim Dybbs stood grinning to the side, completely oblivious to everything going on. He was probably just excited at the chance to be included in a social outing with staffers who were way cooler than he was.

"I guess we should hit it." Lucy looked at Indy with an apologetic smile.

"Yup," Nick said, his eyes scanning her body for one last time, landing on her eyes for a quick smirk. "See you later. Have fun tonight."

"Bye, girl!" Lucy said, hugging her friend and infusing the air with the fresh pow of her fruity shampoo scent as she did.

"Have fun." Indigo stood still as the group walked off into the dusk toward Nick's Chevy truck. As they piled in, Indigo felt horribly abandoned and suddenly foolish. She looked around for Eleanor, Puja, Yvonne, and the rest of her bunk mates, but they were gone, too. She'd have to trudge off to the Kurosawa Screening Room in those stupid shoes all by herself. Maybe she'd make out with a guy there just for the hell of it—just to, perversely and in her own mind, teach Nick a lesson. For what? For not scooping her up and taking her with him to the Bob Dylan concert? Fuck Bob Dylan. But really, what was he supposed to do, kidnap her? Get fired? Take her away to some place far from here where he could eat her alive with his eyes and maul her naked body with his hands before roughly taking her virginity on a motel bed somewhere?

Well, yeah.

Indy looked up from her shoes on the path she was teetering on and realized she was directly in front of the Kurosawa Screening Room and Mocktail Bar. She'd somehow made it there without even knowing it. Her fantasies had floated her to this stupid social, and her feet already hurt like hell before it began.

The sounds of thumping hip-hop and pop vocal mashups, combined with the amped-up, high-volume/low-content chatter of party conversation, wafted through the front door of the low-slung, modern building. Indy tried to shake off the feeling she felt watching Lucy get into Nick's truck for the night, and readjusted her posture so she at least *looked* confident, as she made her way inside the screening room to socialize with boys her own age.

10

As soon as Indigo walked into the Screening Room, she knew her night was going to be disappointing. The awkwardness hit her in the face like the foul stench of garbage on a New York City sidewalk. The girls were on one side of the mocktail bar, sitting on red leather stools while they twirled hairpieces and virgin mojito stirrers. They flirted with one another and threw glances across the room, where clumps of preteen boys stood at a suitably not-gay distance from one another and traded quick spurts of derisive laughter with awkward, darting glances at the tween sirens at the other side of the lounge.

"Seriously?" Indy said, sidling up to her bunkmates. "We're still doing the whole boys-versus-girls thing?"

"Listen, sister. You can take the kids out of junior high, but you can't take the junior high out of the kids," Yvonne said, chewing on a straw. She opened a tiny cocktail umbrella. "Looks like rain!" she added, looking up at the vaulted ceiling. Yes. Obviously, Yvonne knew a *lot* about maturity.

"Indy!" Eleanor, wearing a crotch-length gold spangly minidress that could've passed as a leotard at a certain angle, approached Indigo with an extra martini glass full of whatever it was she was drinking in her other hand.

"Shh, don't tell," Eleanor said. "But I snuck some Campari into this."

She held up her glass, smiling like they were best friends.

"Guess it can't hurt," Indy said, looking around at the room full of nervous teenagers. She took the glass Eleanor handed her.

"To nonvirgin drinks for virgins. Or, you know, not." Eleanor cheers'ed Indigo loudly, as though she was performing for both sides of the room. She must have been buzzed already—she was acting out and being almost nice to people. But Eleanor had a point—maybe these socials *would* be a lot more tolerable if alcohol was actually served.

The guys on the other side of the room kept glancing over at Eleanor and Indy. They were in the middle of the space and making more of a scene than the rest of the Silver Springs girls, who clung to their stools and stared at Lillian, who was doing bartender duty that night. She wore an old-timey scrunchy thing on the white shirtsleeve of her left arm and a tilted derby hat. *Cute look, Lillian*, Indy thought. *Only the opposite.*

Indigo sipped her mock—er, cocktail—slowly, and tried to assess the guys as inconspicuously as she could. Right away she noticed Jay Stegbrandt, who she'd hoped wouldn't be at Kinnetonka this year. He was, of course, alongside his bunk mate/best friend, Andrew Cook, who actually looked really hot in his crisp suit and skinny tie. Jay and Andrew had both gotten taller since the year before, and some of the baby fat had disappeared from Jay's doughy face, but he was still sort of soft-looking in a way that made Indy kind of nauseated. His leather corded necklace with a bead in the middle of it wasn't doing him any favors, either. Was it some kind of unwritten law that every affluent artistic Jewish person had to go through a hippie phase?

"Indigo Hamlisch! Just the person I was hoping to see…." It was too late—Jay had seen Indy looking at him and approached her and Eleanor, who was eating Andrew Cook alive with her eyes. Eleanor took a huge swig of her drink, and Indy followed suit. This was going to be painful.

"Hello, Jay," Indy said, forcing a smile.

"Last time I saw you, you weren't sure if you'd be coming back to camp this year." His tone seemed to suggest they were much closer than they really were. Indy cringed.

"Yeah, well, I wasn't sure. But I did, so I'm here now."

She'd completely blocked the last time she'd seen Jay Stegbrandt from her memory. It was about five months ago, and Indy's parents had dragged her along to some random charity benefit on the Upper East Side. That event was not Indy's scene—lots of middle-aged couples milling around, drinking wine and boasting about their new vacation homes in Gstaad, at an event that cost a couple of hundred dollars a ticket for a charity they knew virtually nothing about.

Jay's parents had brought him, too, and they were pretty much the only teenagers there. Indy didn't really want to hang out with him, but there was no other option. So she'd spent the entire evening with Jay, people-watching and shooting the shit, while he periodically stared down the front of her low-cut teal cocktail dress (chosen by Yoshiko). They'd stolen a half-empty bottle of champagne and snuck up onto the roof to look at the city lights, even though it was freezing cold outside. And there they talked about camp, and parents, and making art, and Indy's temporary doubts about coming back to Silver Springs. It was actually sort of fun.

But then Jay tried to kiss her—and stick his tongue down her throat. Indy had dodged his adolescent, stubble-free face, and the whole thing turned incredibly awkward. She hadn't talked to him since, despite his continued efforts to contact her.

To be completely fair, he wasn't so horrible. But Jay Stegbrandt still represented so many things she couldn't stand about guys her age. He was so yearning to please, so malleable, so polite. There was no sign of a backbone, until the tongue move, which suddenly made him seem like a pervy lizard. His move on the rooftop had been abrupt—he'd never lean her back and make out with her artfully, as Nick would, based on an inspired scene Indy fantasized about last night before falling asleep.

Based on his look (thick, wavy, chin-length hair and a button-down shirt made out of hemp over cargo capris and sandals), Jay was trying to go for "the artistic type." It worked—he was absolutely catnip to the Silver Springs girls who liked "creatives" who played guitar and came from wealthy entertainment parents. Jay's dad was a famous film director and habitually adapted his schlocky eighties comedies for the Great White Way for easy royalties. His biggest success had been *She's a Robot: The Musical*, and the profits from it were enough to keep Jay's hairy toes in expensive Birkenstocks all summer at the priciest boys' camp on the East Coast. But he was so far away from being a real artist that Indy was literally baffled when she first met him and he referred to the derivative, thirty-second instrumental songs he composed on his Gibson acoustic guitar as "his art." What did Jay know about putting in the work needed to funnel that first flicker of inspiration into a full-blown masterpiece?

"So, I have a new CD, in case you want a copy," Jay said to Indy as he tucked a lock of his hair behind his ear.

"Oh, really?" Indigo replied, scanning the room for some-body—anybody—to save her from this conversation. Thank goodness for Puja, who approached them both, just in time.

"Yeah," Jay continued, oblivious to losing his audience. "It's all instrumental tracks I put down at my dad's recording studio. There are four of them. Some songs are even a minute long."

Jay produced a disc from one of the giant pockets of his shorts. There was a tree on the cover. "The booklet inside also has some poetry that I've been working on. I haven't really figured out yet how to convert the poems into lyrics, so right now the music and the words are separate. Hope you like it."

"Thanks, Jay. But actually, I don't have a bag with me, so I don't know how I'd really carry it back…."

"Oh, I'll hold on to it!" Puja chimed in, suddenly wedged between Indigo and Jay, and smiling with every muscle of her pretty face, like a nervous beauty pageant contestant. Indy noticed that Puja had put in her contact lenses and was wearing a lot of cherry-blossom essential-oil perfume.

"Hi," Puja said to Jay, amped up and going for it. "I'm Puja Nair. I've met you a few times in the past, but. Anyway, I'm a fan."

Of course, Indy thought.

Puja wasn't interjecting to save her from Jay—she was totally into him, just like every other Silver Springs girl who went all gooey-kneed around the sight of any guy who wasn't a total lacrosse stick–slinging, gay slur–spouting, white baseball cap–wearing bully.

"Pardon me," Indigo said, excusing herself so Puja could flirt with Jay. Across the room, Eleanor's eyes were locked like headlights on Andrew Cook's.

"Hey," Indy whispered into her ear. "Can you top me off?" The last few minutes talking to Jay had caused her to suck down her drink way faster than she intended. Indigo couldn't help but notice a relieved expression on Andrew Cook's sharp-featured, tan face as she interrupted their conversation. Eleanor shot Indy a homicidal look, then transitioned at once into her phony shark smile.

"Oh, In-di-go!" Eleanor grinned behind bared teeth. "You remember Andy Cook, obviously?" Eleanor tried flipping her hair back, forgetting for a second that it was tightly shellacked into pin curls. She just looked like she had a tic or a mini-seizure instead. Andrew's jaw tightened in a full-on grimace.

"Yes, of course," Indigo said. "The mini–Patrick Bateman–cum–entertainment law prodigy?"

"Don't say 'cum,' dear," Andrew said. "It makes you look cheaper than you are." Eleanor laughed way too loudly, touching Andrew's arm as she did. He flinched.

"Listen," Indy whispered in Eleanor's ear. "I really would love some more booze. If I'm going to make it through this social, I'm going to need something stronger than a Shirley Temple."

"Here, here. Go. Thanks. Bye." Eleanor smuggled the remainder of the bottle into Indy's empty glass while maintaining aggressive eye contact with Andrew, who did share the same predatory animal-like facial features and affinity for hair gel that she did. Maybe they really were a match made in hell.

As Indigo stood off to the corner alone, giving room to Jay and Puja and Andrew and Eleanor, she noticed Yvonne and her twin brother, Dean Bremis, sitting on bar stools and making fun of the crowd together, like junior roastmasters. It was sort of cute.

"Look at that gargoyle over there. The one with thighs you could fit through a pencil sharpener?" Indy heard Dean lisp through his braces.

"Eleanor?" Yvonne said. "What about her?"

"I wouldn't screw her with Lillian's penis."

They both laughed.

At the end of the bar was Evan Zander, the hazel-eyed tennis star who recently had the opportunity to study the art of TV show–running alongside *Breaking Bad*'s Vince Gilligan in his villa on the south of France. He was chatting with Tiffany Melissa Portman, who was playing the part of a femme fatale–looking seductress as she leaned in to seem interested in whatever Evan was saying. She *was* a good actress, after all.

Lillian, who grinned as she wiped down the bar, lifted her eyes to meet Indigo's. Indy turned away in paranoia that her tipsiness would be visible, but Lillian didn't notice—she used her hands to approximate a drum roll on the surface of the bar.

"Attention, ladies and gentlemen!" Lillian bellowed.

The music in the background faded out completely. In the ensuing silence, the campers looked up at Lillian, who cupped her hands on either side of her mouth.

"If you would kindly retire to the screening room, we can begin the main event of the evening! Tonight, we're showing all of this year's best foreign animated shorts Oscar nominees! And a special thanks is due to Jay Stegbrandt, whose father generously provided his screeners for the occasion."

The campers clapped, and Puja beamed at Jay.

Oh, Jesus, thought Indy. She almost forgot about the movie portion of these bizarre socials. When lights went down, it was either snoozeville or make-out city, depending on which kind of awful you were up for on that particular evening.

Debra stood at the entrance of the screening room wearing a red-and-white checkered apron while campers trudged in, alone and in pairs. "Enjoy the show!" she said, handing out single-serving paper bags of organic popcorn. "No coming attractions!"

Indigo took a seat in the middle of the last row and checked her cell for any texts from Lucy. Zero. She must be having a great time at that concert. With Nick. Indy finished the last of her drink and caught a quick glance down at her body in those clothes. She could see her tummy rolls when she looked beyond her huge boobs in that tight top, and her exposed thighs rolled out and stuck to the red leather seats. She crossed her arms over her body, concealing it from her own critical gaze, and put her glass in the cup holder on the seat next to hers.

Eleanor walked down the aisle leading Andrew by the hand like a dog on a leash, and settled next to Indy on her right. Eleanor didn't even look up to say hi, as she was locked into focus on the creep she was courting. Who would be the one to tell Eleanor that Andrew was obviously gay? And that he wasn't, like, the fun kind of gay guy, like Harry Glibbe or Rashid "Jazz Hands" Beatts.

The lights began to dim, and just in time, as Indy was beginning to notice out of the corner of her eye that Eleanor's hands were migrating down to Andrew's zipper. As soon as the screening room became totally dark, Indy's body twitched with the presence of a new body that pulled up next to hers, and the scent of dirty feet, Aveda shampoo, and clove cigarettes that wafted in along with it.

"Hey you," Jay said, leaning in very close to her.

Oh, God. Poor Puja would be crying into her journal that night, fueling Jay's rejection of her into some new play.

"Shh," Indy shushed him. "The movie is starting."

As the screen flickered with abstract animation of amoebas transforming into Rubik's Cubes, jazz played under German narration that filled the tiny screening room. And as the intermittent moans of her bunk mates joined the chorus of things Indigo would rather not be listening to, she also realized three different things, at exactly the same time.

1. She was much drunker than she thought she was moments ago, when she was standing on her feet—in those horrible shoes. 2. Jay Stegbrandt had his hand on her bare thigh. And 3. he was gliding it up toward her crotch slowly and deliberately, and all of it was horrifyingly in time with the jazz soundtrack of the movie.

Indigo closed her eyes, hoping the wave of nausea she suddenly felt—which could have been indicative of any of the things she'd just realized—would pass.

And it did, which was nice. But then the music changed into an electronic "beep-beep-boop" kind of thing, which accompanied a new short with no narration, only subtitles. She took a deep breath. Jay, confident from the fact that Indy wasn't actively rejecting his massage moves, finally leaned in for a kiss. And to her surprise, Indigo found herself, flush from the warmth of the booze and the recentness of all her latest sexual fantasies about Nick, open to his mouth on hers. *Why the hell not?*

She tried hard to think about Nick while kissing Jay but found herself easily distracted by the sound of Andrew Cook to her right, slapping Eleanor's hand away from his groin and refusing her advances repeatedly. The gross smell of Jay's hair wasn't helping, either. Indigo cringed as he sloppily pawed her boobs over her top, and recoiled at the sensation of Jay's turgid tongue piled atop of hers. This was just so…wrong.

She wasn't having a good time, but what was she going to do—watch the movie instead? They were up to a point in the screening program where cartoon muffins were singing Russian ballads in a bakery window. Indy did *not* need to see how that story played out.

So she let Jay paw her some more, and, in a way, enjoyed the closeness of a body pressed next to hers, even if it was the body of a poseur hippie who couldn't tell you the difference between Ben &

Jerry's and Simon and Garfunkel. And as Jay grunted and breathed so loudly in her ear that she wondered if he was hyperventilating, Indy's mind wandered to Nick at that concert with Lucy, and what it was that they could be doing that would make Lucy unavailable to check in on text. What if tonight, once Nick saw Lucy in the light of adulthood and peerdom and all the other bonding stuff that Indigo assumed took place over the course of a staff night out, he decided to make a move on her—to lean in for a kiss, as Jay did?

Just then, at the peak of her distress, Jay, in a phenomenal display of his lack of intuition, decided to take Indigo's hand and place it gingerly on the crotch of his pants. And like she was touching a flame by mistake, as soon as she grazed the re-volting, upsetting territory that was Jay's boner underneath his stupid cargo shorts, Indigo snapped her hand back like it had been burned badly.

"I can't do this. I'm sorry."

She made her way out of the row, bumping into Andrew and Eleanor as she did, muttering apologies as she clumsily darted out of the screening room. She ran, trying to shake off the shame of what had just happened, but slowed down once she hit the fresh air of the outside world. As she gingerly descended the steps to the path leading back to her bunk, it took a minute for Indigo to notice that her feet felt like they were in glass-box torture devices. She also realized she'd look a little conspicuous dashing around campus half drunk in hooker shoes. So Indy steadied herself on the banister and took a deep breath. *Slow down*, she told herself. *Everything is fine.*

But then she had company. Lillian, who'd come running after Indy as soon as she saw her leave, joined her outside of the screening room.

"Indigo! Indigo."

Shit. Indy turned around reluctantly to see what the camp director had to say.

"Are you okay?" Lillian asked. "Did anything happen in there that made you feel violated or unsafe in any way?"

"Other than the dancing muffins? No, no. I'm fine."

"Are you sure? Because, you know, you can always come and talk to me. Or you can write a poem about it, if that kind of expression befits your state of mind, and slip it under my door, anytime."

"Thanks, Lillian."

"I understand if you want to return to your bunk early. Get some rest and let me know in the morning if you want to talk. My channels are always open, communicationally and emotionally."

"Okay." She began descending the stairs again, hoping Lillian would get the hint and leave her alone.

"Oh, and Indigo?"

What now?

"Jim Dybbs told me that you might be struggling a bit with your mission statement."

What? Where did Jim get off telling Lillian *anything* about her creative malaise—it had barely even begun.

"I just want you to know," Lillian continued, "that I believe in your abilities and your talent. It's a question of your being able to circumnavigate the obstacles you create for yourself in your own head that could be your undoing. So please be mindful."

"Um, okay." What was she even talking about? Was she giving her a compliment?

"Good night, Indigo."

"Night."

She slipped off the demon shoes as soon as Lillian was out of sight and carefully stepped onto the path back to Ferlinghetti, barefoot, shining her cell phone's light on the pebbles in front of her so she wouldn't step on anything "hurt-y." She couldn't help but check it one last time for any updates from Lucy.

Not a peep.

Later, when Indy was tucked in bed, her makeup scoured off and the hairspray rinsed down the shower drain, Eleanor finally stumbled into their suite. She was gushing to Indigo about how "respectful" Andrew was to her. "He didn't even try to kiss or touch me! And he comes from such a good family and knows every shoe designer by his first nameeezzzz." Then she collapsed—makeup, gold dress, Campari breath, and all—into her pillow.

Indigo turned off the light and tried to shut herself off, to no avail, to the distracting sounds of all the other girls coming back in from the social. She couldn't sleep, even after the ruckus petered out from the adjoining bedrooms of Puja, Tiffany, and Yvonne. She stared out the window.

And that's when she finally heard from Lucy, although it was in the form of a distant yelp. "Woo-hoo! Bob Deh-LAN!" Indy saw Lucy outside, stumbling around drunk with her leather jacket wrapped around her small waist, hollering at the stars. Jim and Jen, who trailed behind Lucy, tried shushing her—and then, Indigo saw Nick appear on the hill.

He put his arm around Lucy and seemed to prop her up like she was a pretty scarecrow. He put his hand over her mouth and took tiny steps with her, guiding her feet one in front of the other. Nick and Lucy disappeared from Indy's window, into the distant direction of the staff housing. Indigo felt sick to her stomach again. She hoped that she was already asleep and dreaming, because seeing Lucy lean on Nick felt like she was being tortured. Indy suddenly felt hot tears on her cheeks as she sank her head back down into her pillow. She was definitely awake, and it was definitely real.

11

Indigo slept through breakfast the next morning and stumbled to her first class in the stifling heat, after enduring an actual dream in which she watched, naked, while Lucy and Nick were onstage together at Westwood, jamming out with Neil Young. She guessed Neil Young was a stand-in for Bob Dylan. Duh. Her subconscious could be so uncreative. What was the point of dreaming when her sleep brain came up only with derivative ways of reminding her of her jealousy? Indy wished she could have dreams about flying, or being in Hawaii, or eating a Cadillac made out of brownies. Anything but a clichéd reminder of the crap she had to deal with in her waking life.

Indy tried to shake the Lucy nightmare by recalling the events at the social, but she'd momentarily forgotten how nightmarish those were, too. Everything, from making out with Jay Stegbrandt to the humiliating outfit she'd allowed herself to be convinced to wear, was a complete disaster. Why had she worn that, again? Indy remembered how when she looked down, her tummy rolls bulged over the waistline of her jean shorts. Now her feeling of disgust was pervasive, and skipping breakfast seemed like an immediate way to punish herself. She went right to the ceramics studio from the Beat cabin after taking a hot shower. By the time she arrived, she was already sweating.

Her first class was sculpture with Jim Dybbs, who came in moments after Indigo and the other girls arrived. Jim looked bleary-eyed and hungover, like he'd had a "crazy night." Maybe he had, considering he had a stunning young woman on his arm when he entered the studio. But the notion of Jim picking up that girl at the Dylan concert last night made Indy smile to herself. Yeah, right. In *his* dreams.

His companion was a tall, thin redhead with full crimson lips, who had no visible fat on her upper arms or thighs, both of which were visible in her sleeveless, skintight minidress. Summer camp sculpture class seemed like an unlikely environment for somebody that gorgeous. She looked like a giraffe in a Walgreens, she was so out of place—and next to Jim, in his crumpled-up hippie plaid shirt and nerdy chinos, that woman looked like a member of a different species.

"Class, today we are going to be embarking upon a most ancient art indeed—rendering the nude human form in clay."

Oh, Christ, Indigo thought. *This lady is going to get naked for us?* She already felt shitty about her body, and now she was going to have to be eye level with this random model's "entertainment system" before noon.

"Help yourselves to slabs of clay and potter's-wheel platforms," Jim confirmed. "You should all be turning your platforms as you sculpt, to get all three hundred sixty degrees of Rebecca's lovely body."

"No. Did he just say the phrase 'Rebecca's Lovely Body'?" Indy whispered to Erin, whose face was screwed up with a similar look of incredulity.

"That better be the name of a folk song or something," Erin replied as they stood up to go get their supplies. "Otherwise, I think I'm going to vom."

"Which brings me to introductions," Jim continued, now beginning to half smile under his shaggy beard, which crept down his neck like ivy down a brick wall.

"This is Rebecca, who will be modeling for us today," Jim said as the girls stared at her. "And," he added, "a fun fact about Rebecca is: she also happens to be my wife."

"Shut *up*," Suzie McLandish said out loud.

"This can't be real," Megan muttered, exchanging a look with Erin.

"She got in late last night!" Jim either didn't hear the side comments or didn't care. "Though she doesn't look any worse for wear because of it, right?"

Indy took notice of everyone in the room. They all stood around the table with their mouths agape, looking at Rebecca, who smiled blankly at no one in particular.

"That's your *wife*?" Indigo heard herself say out loud. Random snickers followed.

"She certainly is," Jim said, starry-eyed. He and Rebecca were staring at each other now, with matching queasy smiles—the kind babies make when they're about to poop—and Indigo looked around the room for some kind of indication that they were all being Punk'd. Nope—just the shocked expressions of her fellow artists.

"All right," Jim continued, "line up and get your clay while Rebecca disrobes. It's a good thing it's such a hot day!"

Indy joined the horde of tittering art girls over by the bagged terra cotta and tried to disengage from the communal glee pinpointing Dybbs as a weirdo with a pervy personal life. She grabbed a platform, then took the wire with wooden handles at its ends from Megan and sectioned off her slab of clay, watching with familiar titillation as the wire zipped through the damp firmness of the clay tower, leaving immaculate ripples in its wake. Indy grabbed the brick of sweaty terra cotta and began to knead and bend it to her will, until her fingers were caked with burnt sienna. Then she made her way back to her station, in time to be face-to-face with Jim Dybbs's naked wife. She plopped the clay on top of the spinning platform and looked up at her model.

Rebecca was in a seated pose, one pale flamingo leg perched over the other, like they have you do in yoga class. But her back was arched like she was soaking up rays of sun, and her pert, round C-cup breasts—which looked disarmingly natural considering her proportions—saluted the ceiling of the sculpture studio.

It was 10:19 AM, and Indigo was staring at Jim's wife's half-erect nipples. How were they that hard when it was ninety degrees outside?

She began to work. Shaping the clay came naturally—she knew where to put muscle into the materials and when to let the clay take control of the shape. She had done enough life drawing and life sculpting classes that she knew, once she got into it, how to look back and forth between her work and the subject like it was a single task, not a balancing act.

But this morning, Indigo found herself mostly just comparing Mrs. Dybbs's butt-nakedness not to the slab of clay in front of her but to her own body. And that was a fool's errand. It led only to obsession and despair. She got up to wash her hands and get a fresh perspective on her piece. While she did, the other girls chattered.

"So, how is your project for Industry Showcase going?" Suzie asked Megan.

"Actually, great so far," Megan replied. "I'm pretty much almost done with my mural sketch. I've just been feeling so inspired this summer, I don't know what it is. You know?"

"*Totally*. Me too. I didn't realize how many finished pieces I had until I counted last night. I thought I had fifteen. I have thirty," Erin said as she smoothed down the clay on her sculpture with her thumbs, flattening its stomach area. "Plus, I heard that an art scout from the Franks-Curren Gallery is going to be there. Can you imagine showing in New York?"

"My parents would *flip* their *shit*," Megan said, shaking her head back and forth as if she couldn't think of anything better in this whole world than impressing her parents.

They turned to Indy at the sink, who just stared down at her soapy hands, listening to Erin and Suzie brag. "How is *your* project going, Indy? You've been so mysterious, we're beginning to wonder what Hamlisch the Great has up her sleeve this year," Erin said in her snottiest voice.

Megan smirked. "Or if she even has anything."

Indigo knew that admitting she hadn't even really started her project would only fuel the fire. The nearer it was to Industry Showcase Day, the more competitive the Silver Springs girls got. Everyone wanted to be noticed by the various scouts and gallery owners who came to see the show each year, looking for the next big thing to pluck from obscurity and brandish as a prodigy. And if that meant psyching out the other contenders, or just making them feel like shit, well, it was all part of the game.

"I guess you guys will just have to wait and see," Indy said with as much confidence as she could muster. She wiped her hands on her jean shorts and made her way back to her workstation. "But it's going really well so far," Indy added. "Thanks for asking." *Bitches.*

After an hour and a half of slagging away at nothing she'd ever want to attach her name to, Indigo covered her shitty sculpture with plastic wrap and headed out of the cool ceramics center into the early-afternoon heat. And as her freckled face baked in the hot sun, Indy finally faced the harsh reality of her situation. She was the only one without a summer project.

12

Indigo tried as best she could to walk only in the shade as she ambled toward Theater Row, but she was sweating right through her tank top. It was probably due to a mixture of the midsummer heat and the unbearable stress. How was she going to attack this supposed installation she discussed with Jen? What had she said it was about, again? Pop. Pop music, pop culture…what else? Pop-Tarts? Ring Pops? Soda pop?

Maybe there was something to that. She could turn a soda vending machine into some kind of "taste robot"? It could tell you what kind of person you were and whether you should have more Nicki Minaj or Katy Perry on your iPod. No, that was stupid. First of all, those two artists were basically the same person, and second, there was no chance Indigo was going to find a vending machine on campus to disembowel.

Maybe she could make some kind of holiday-related object, like a cornucopia, or an Easter basket …or a Christmas tree! That would be perfect, considering nothing seemed more pop culture than Christmas. She could decorate it with tinsel made from Bubble Wrap and cut up soda cans into ornaments, then hang collaged elements of whatever it was she found particularly deplorable about pop culture that day. Photos of *Twilight* moms, clippings from fashion magazines that list celebrities' dieting secrets. Photoshopped pictures of women in bathing suits looking disproportionately thin. She could really make a statement about society's twisted values.

"Hey, Indy! What are you doing around us theater folk?"

Indy looked behind her to see Lucy getting out of one of the small Tudor-style houses that had been converted into rehearsal spaces. Of course Lucy ran into her—Indigo was on her turf. Lucy caught up to her and smiled. As usual, she looked casually great in her staff T-shirt and pleated schoolgirl skirt, and her face had no indication of sweat on it.

Indy wiped her own glistening forehead.

"Oh, I was just going for a walk. You know—I needed some time away from my own kind."

"Ugh, I so know what you mean! I've been going crazy watching the theater kids make faces at each other all day." Lucy smiled.

"So…" Indigo said casually. "How was last night? Anything interesting happen?" Indy hadn't been able to erase the image of Nick with Drunk Lucy from her mind. The way he held her up, the way she'd laughed.

"Well, the concert itself was a snooze," Lucy said. "That guy can't sing for shit. He should replace his harmonica with an oxygen tank, or an Auto-Tune app, something."

Indy smiled.

"But, yeah, otherwise it was pretty fun. We snuck in some wine, so I was pretty drunk by the end of the night. Jim Dybbs was a huge disgusting dork. He'd, like, get up and dance to the songs he knew? He'd sway back and forth, and then he'd tell us all about his hot wife, who couldn't make it to the show because she was stuck in traffic. I guess they met online?"

"Oh, I got to know Mrs. Dybbs inside and *out* this morning." Indigo said. "She posed nude for our sculpture class."

"*She did not!*" Lucy screeched, jumping up and down. "I can't believe she *exists*. God, she must be some kind of mail-order bride. We should call the FBI and get him arraigned on human trafficking."

"How was Jen?" Indigo asked, remembering the way Jen had touched Nick's hand.

"Jen was annoying," Lucy continued. "She was *all over* Nick, first of all. It was embarrassing. I actually felt bad for her."

Indy felt the prickly sensation of nervous anger form all over her skin.

"How did Nick react?"

"Cool as a cuke, same as ever. He was just, like, politely ignoring her. He was really nice about it but kind of cold, too. You know how he can be."

Okay. So he didn't *like Jen, right?*

"Did he talk to you at all?" said Indigo, finally asking the question she'd been dying to know the answer to.

"Noooo! No way," Lucy was emphatic as they began walking together. "I mean, beyond being friendly and sharing my wine. He seemed pretty into the show. And—oh, there was one thing he said to Jen around the middle of the night that was kinda weird."

What?

"Jen was muttering all this crazy stuff to him," Lucy continued, "leaning on his shoulder and just, like, touching him a lot. His leg, his arm—it was gross. Then, at one point, Nick turned to her and said something like 'Knock it off, things are different now.'"

"He did?" Indy stopped in her tracks.

"Yeah, I'm pretty sure that's what he said," Lucy said, basking in the shady patch. "I was a little hammered by then, so the phrasing may have been different, but it definitely implied that the two of them had something going on in the past." She shook her head and sighed. "Poor Jen just isn't over him yet, I guess."

Indigo felt the tiny shred of loyalty toward her adviser drain away. She seethed with retroactive jealousy for Jen Rant, who not only got to tell her what to do, even though she wasn't that much older than her, but she also got to hook up with Nick. It didn't even matter that he rejected Jen's advances last night. From now on, her mentor was her rival. And Indigo would do anything to win.

"What are you up to now?" Lucy changed the subject.

"Oh, I'm just trying to figure out this installation." Indy tried to think about her project as she spoke. "I think I'm going to build a Christmas tree out of wire and papier-mâché. Oh, and I have to find some empty soda cans to hang on it."

Lucy was used to hearing her friend's crazy-sounding plans for artwork without blinking an eye. "You can poke around the recycling bins outside the staff break room for soda cans," she said. "Counselors suck down more Diet Cokes in those meetings than I've seen in a year of doing commercial shoots." Lucy, even when she was being super-nice, still had to bring it back to herself.

"Oh, cool, thanks."

"I actually have to go there now, right before lunch, for a dumb staff meeting. Come on, let's walk together." They started toward the staff break room. "So, in other news," Lucy continued, "I'm not sure, but I might have a weird crush on Rashid."

"The teacher you're assisting?" Indy asked. "Isn't he gay?"

"I never really thought about it. But he's such a great mentor!" Lucy gushed. "I may just also have a hard time separating who I have a crush on and who I enjoy getting attention from, when I'm doing my best work." It was probably true—Lucy was an attention whore. At least she was aware of it.

"And I really feel like I'm coming into my own as a performer right now. I was so worried, coming on board as staff. I thought I wouldn't be able to do as much onstage or that I wouldn't learn as much as I had in the past."

Indy couldn't help but sigh listening to Lucy's enthusiastic account of how great things were going so far. Of course things had come easily to her. They always had.

"But now I feel more integrated into the program," Lucy said, hopping over a fallen branch in their path. "In fact, earlier, Puja asked me if I could take a part in this reading she's putting together for a new play she's writing. And I double-checked with Lillian, and I can totally do it as long as Puja insists—and she *insists*. It's such a great role. There are so many talented people here. I feel really lucky."

Keeping up with Lucy's optimism could be exhausting.

"I'm gonna go look through the recycling for soda cans before lunch, okay?" They'd finally arrived at the main house.

"Yes! I'm heading to the meeting. Talk soon! Mwah!" Lucy threw a kiss in Indigo's general direction and made her way into the camp's break room—a converted maid's chambers that now housed a semicircle of assorted 1960s chairs, an antique bookshelf packed with organic snacks from Trader Joe's, and two espresso machines, for staff use only.

Indy followed behind her friend, veering off to the right to go into the recycling room, which connected the staff lounge to the backside of the kitchen. The lunch madness hadn't yet begun, so she went unnoticed. As Indigo dug through the discarded aluminum cans, saving the ones she wanted to use in a shopping bag she found in the "plastic" bin, she heard the sound of chattering voices coming from the room over. The staff meeting was beginning.

"Welcome, everyone," Indigo heard Lillian say. Her job as camp director seemed to entirely consist of saying the word "welcome" over and over again for rooms of different people all summer. "Thanks for coming before lunch. I know you're all starving, so I'll keep this brief."

Indigo peeked through the open door between the recycling room and the staff room.

"First of all, how are we doing on supplies? Have you all put in your requests in writing for what you need?" Lillian continued. Indy stopped paying attention. Why was she eavesdropping on a boring meeting?

She went back to collecting cans until her bags were heaving with all kinds of brightly colored aluminum cylinders, then headed back out toward the kitchen. As she did, she heard a familiar laugh.

Lucy had a million of them, but this laugh was the one she used when she was genuinely amused at something. It was like a low cackle she couldn't fake. Indigo used to hear it when the two of them would stay out in the woods after classes were over in summers past, joking about what one of the gross guys from the social they'd just endured would look like getting a blowjob. Indy would contort her face to impersonate Jay in the throes of passion and Lucy would laugh the way she did now.

Indigo peered through the door to try and see what was so amusing. Lucy was sitting next to Nick in the staff room, whispering and passing him a note, just like the two of them used to do whenever they were stuck at a lame pre-meal grace or a terrible one-woman show they had to attend as part of Industry Showcase Weekend. Lucy tossed her head, and her yellow curls tumbled down the back of her chair. Nick put his hand on her shoulder and brought a finger to her mouth. "Shhhh," he whispered, forming a smile. Then, he exploded into hysterics of his own.

Indigo's heart sank down into her stomach, then went back up into her throat, like on the Big Drop ride at the amusement park her dad used to take her to. Indy stared at Lucy's toned, delicate arm resting on the back of her chair, and then looked down at the vulnerable paleness of her own right forearm. It was fat, she thought. *She* was fat. And ugly. Inside and out.

She hesitated for a moment, then took out one of the empty Fresca cans from the bursting shopping bag. She began to twist the can back and forth until it came apart in a jagged helix. The sharp edge scared and intrigued her at once. She lowered it to the inside of her arm, right between the wrist and the elbow, like she'd almost done so many times before. She wanted to feel something real and be in charge of it.

Keeping her eyes open and feeling as alert as a hunter surging with fight-or-flight adrenaline, Indigo made a shallow, bloody, horizontal cut on her arm. Seeing the rich, velvety red streaming down her arm was surreal. Almost like it was just another day in the studio and she'd spilled some cadmium paint. But it stung; it was real.

Indy gasped—louder than she expected to—and immediately Lucy whipped around to see what was going on. She must have forgotten her friend was still in the room adjacent to the meeting. Lucy stood up, but by then Indigo had grabbed her things and fled through the kitchen and out the door.

She ran, bags of cans in tow, clanging down the hill. She couldn't think about the shame she felt, actually letting herself cut. She'd almost done it so many times before but had never actually been ballsy enough to go through with it. She couldn't think about how hurt she was to see Lucy and Nick flirting in the staff room, safely removed from all the camper/teenager bullshit she was still embedded in. And she couldn't think of how much she hated her body right then, how useless she felt as an artist, as a human being. She was a flabby vessel of nothing but failure and sexual frustration and everything else that made her crush on Nick so utterly stupid. She never had a chance with him. She was foolish to have ever thought otherwise.

Indy didn't think about where she was running; she just ran. And to her surprise, when she arrived at the studio instead of her cozy bedroom in the Ferlinghetti suite, she felt less blocked than she was when she began her journey.

She entered the studio, helped herself to the first-aid kit by the sink, and bandaged up her arm. Then, like it was just a routine part of the day, she emptied out one of her bags onto a large, waist-high working table. As cans rolled onto and off the surface, Indy opened up her sketchbook and began to get inspired by her mood state. She thought about how pissed she was at Lucy, who'd probably be able to hook up with Nick way easier than Indy ever could, because Lucy was perfect and thin and sweet and had hair that looked like a bunch of Barbie heads fused together from behind.

She grabbed a pencil and began to draw what it would actually look like to melt a cluster of blond Barbie heads together. Then she drew fire around the heads. She added crows, which she knew how to draw from memory, all around the borders of the flaming Barbies. When she was perfectly satisfied with the composition of her drawing, she turned the page.

Her mind was going a mile a minute. *This would be the tree's base. Here is what the ornaments should look like.* She scribbled words in the margins as her pencil flew across the page. "Pop-cultured," "Holidazed and Confused," "Mary XXXmas." She scribbled a cartoon of a porn star dressed up like Santa Claus. She drew four examples of what she could do to a soda can to make it look like a flower, a spiral, a bra cup, an elevator.

Then she started making the soda cans into what she wanted them to be. She stacked them, cut them into strips with a box cutter, glued them together, fingerpainted them with acrylics and rolled them in glitter, and otherwise manipulated the pile of aluminum to her liking.

She didn't realize how long she'd been working until hours later when the sun began to get hazy in the middle of the sky. The other girls, who had filtered into the studio to work alongside her within the last few hours, started packing up and chatting about dinner and being starving and what the evening activity was and maybe it would be a movie.

Indigo stopped working and finally assessed what she'd accomplished that afternoon. It was formidable. Before her laid a pile of beautifully adorned, brightly painted soda cans, each festooned with accessories she'd applied with the help of a hot-glue gun. There was a wire frame for her tree that she'd made with a needle-nose plier and the thick, malleable wire Dybbs kept in a drum under his desk. More significantly than anything else, Indigo saw exactly what she needed to do in order to finish the bigger masterpiece she had in mind for each of these elements. It was clear how everything would fit together. She took what seemed like the first deep breath of her life.

She didn't bother cleaning up her work, knowing she'd be returning to the studio once she'd had something to eat. Indy even felt a little pang of sadness, leaving her unfinished piece behind—like separation anxiety. But her stomach rumblings were getting distracting, so she washed her hands and splashed water on her face, then grabbed the hoodie she kept in her cubby and made her way back up the hill for her first meal of the day.

13

Traditionally, before breakfast, lunch, and dinner, a staff member led the girls in an introspective song or chant in the dining hall, or read an inspirational quote about creativity, individuality, or another highly regarded upper-middle-class value. Grace was meant to be secular but spiritually nourishing—Lillian toed the line between church and camp every time she advocated the practice of having campers stand in contemplation before they chowed down. But it was an important part of the Silver Springs experience nonetheless.

As it happened, Lucy was leading the dining hall in a rousing version of "Day by Day" from the musical *Godspell* when Indigo entered the room, sweaty, hungry, and in no mood for show tunes. She crept among her fellow campers, who belted on their feet in confident harmony, like the cast of *Glee*, minus the diversity.

"To see theeeeeee more clearly! To love theeeeee more dearly!" Lucy, who stood in the front of the room behind the standing microphone at which Lillian made morning announcements, had her eyes squinted shut and her hand up to the sky in some

gross "Halle-loo!" gesture, like she was doing a drag queen's impression of Christina Aguilera.

Indy snuck through the hordes of revelers toward her assigned table, and in the process realized she was walking directly toward Nick as well. He stood in the corner of the room next to a staff table, and made eye contact with Indy as she weaved around the other campers. And Indy, who was already starving, felt even more light-headed when she saw him. He smirked at her, but not like he was laughing at her—his eyes twinkled with a conspiratorial friendliness that seemed to say, "We both get how ridiculous this is." But was he reacting to the song? Hearing Lucy belt the crap out of that *Godspell* song, for the benefit of the dinner crowd, *was* pretty ridiculous and over-the-top. But is that what he was smiling at? What *did* Nick think of Lucy, anyway?

As Lucy rounded back for the second chorus and held its final note like it was her last chance to make a sound, Indigo realized that Nick and she were still smiling together, across the room. Indy rolled her eyes as the room exploded into applause once Lucy finally finished singing, and then he broke the gaze, sarcastically clapping along with the rest of the room and putting his fingers in his mouth for a loud wolf whistle. Maybe she'd misinterpreted his chumminess with Lucy in that meeting as something more substantial. He was so hard to read.

Indigo dashed to her table and sat down with the rest of her bunk mates in time for nobody of authority to realize that she was substantially late.

"Indy Five hundred! You're here!" exclaimed Puja. "Where have you been all our lives?"

"Working like a madwoman!" Indy replied as she reached out for the platter of panko breadcrumb–encrusted tofu slabs that one of the servers had just delivered to their table. She helped herself to two and slathered them with red sauce from a sterling-silver gravy boat. "I finally had some sort of breakthrough. Yvonne, could you pass the garlic toast points?"

"Please, take them!" Yvonne said, snatching another one from the platter. "The more you eat, the less I can strap directly onto my FUPA!" She patted her lower belly.

"That's so great to hear. We could all tell you were struggling," Puja said with genuine concern on her face. Indy inhaled the plate of food in front of her in what seemed like no time at all.

"Seriously? How? Pass the greens, *por favor*," she said, then heaped her plate with wilted kale and more toast.

Puja took a huge gulp of her coconut water. "Oh, you know, you were just generally moping around and stuff…like you do right before you come up with something brilliant."

"And is wearing hideous clothing also part of your artistic process?" Eleanor quipped, gesturing toward Indy's full-coverage hoodie. Indigo looked up from her meal to see Eleanor sipping from an ice-cold bottle of Fiji water, judging her. "What's with all the carb-loading? Running a marathon later?"

"I skipped lunch and breakfast," Indigo said bluntly, then took another piece of tofu.

"Welcome to my life," Eleanor responded, picking at her greens. "Though it should be de rigueur to fast on days as hot as this one, even for people *not* looking to shed a pound or two." She shot a look over at Yvonne, who was soaking up the sauce on her plate with the crust of a toast point.

"Aren't you hot in that hoodie?" Puja asked Indy, her big eyes widening beneath her clunky glasses. Indigo realized that everyone at her table, even Yvonne, who favored body-concealing clothes even on nonhumid days, was wearing skimpy, lightweight clothing. But Indigo, who was hiding the cut she made on her arm in a now silly-seeming fit of hysteria, couldn't risk going short-sleeved right now. The bandage on the wound she created was still too conspicuous.

Soon the Silver Springs girls finished their meals, and some began to queue up at the dessert station—an opt-out part of the meal process that was instated after parents called Lillian to complain about their body-conscious daughters being plagued by sweets on the table. Indigo was not planning to miss the Grand Marnier soufflés that Michel was handing out by the filtered water station. She grabbed a plate and waited on line.

"Fancy meeting you here." Lucy pulled up behind Indigo, plate in hand and smiling.

"Hey." Indy played along.

"What's up with the long sleeves?" Lucy asked. "Are you trying to win a sweating competition?"

"No…I'm just feeling a little feverish, maybe. I might be coming down with something."

"Oh, that totally blows. I guess that means you're not coming to the screening room after dinner?" Lucy asked. "Desi's dad sent her all of his Emmy screeners." Desi Rosen—the dancer from Eleanor's class—had a father who was a television agent at a big-deal agency in Los Angeles. There seemed to be an endless supply of screeners available at Silver Springs.

"I think I'm actually going to head back to the studio after this and work some more. I made a good dent in this project today, and I want to keep my momentum."

"NEXT!" Michel shouted as he doled out mini-soufflés. Indigo turned around and got her dessert, then stepped to the side as Lucy did the same.

"And you were so worried! See?" Lucy asked with sincere kindness and enthusiasm. "Remind me of your project theme?"

"It's about soda," Indy said. "And technology. And social networking. And Christmas. And how, like, advertising is an agent of the status quo." What was she talking about? It seemed unnecessary and obnoxious for her to try seeming so superior and intelligent. Lucy had already embarrassed herself in front of the whole camp singing that dumb song like an *X-Factor* contestant right before dinner. Why did Indy have to be such an asshole?

"Cool!" Lucy said. "That's awesome you're on a roll. I'll leave you to it, then. Maybe I'll poke my head into the studio later and check on you. Wouldn't want you pulling an all-nighter if you're coming down with something." She dipped her fingertip into her soufflé and took a small taste.

"Okay," Indy said, looking toward the dining hall's southern exit. She had finished her dessert and looked to dispose of the wooden spoon she'd used to get every last bit of its batter off the sides of the ramekin it came in. Lucy extended her hand for Indy's dirty plate.

"I'll take that to the kitchen for ya." Lucy could be so kind sometimes. It made it hard not to feel bad about envying her or being frustrated by her performative side.

"Thanks," Indy added wearily. "Enjoy the Emmy screeners." She realized she was drawing out their good-bye, like a couple in a black-and-white movie waving from the platform and the window of a departing train. She must have felt guilty, because she added, "That'll be *you* nominated one day."

Lucy grinned. "Best actress in a drama series?"

"You were made for it," Indy quipped, only she wasn't joking.

Outside, it was a starless, hot night. Indy took her time trudging down the hill and back into the sweet, earthy, damp coolness of the art studio. She peeled off her hoodie once she was inside, now that she was alone. It was a huge relief, like unburdening yourself of the weight of the world. The goose bumps on her bare arms felt good, until she looked down and saw the bandage over her cut.

What had she been thinking? Or *was* she even thinking? It was like she'd become a different person earlier. It was some serious Jekyll-and-Hyde shit. But since the first time she'd toyed with the idea of cutting, running an X-Acto blade dangerously close to the superficial layer of her inner arm, she knew that the pull of minor self-harm was something she'd have to fight. Shrink after shrink had tied Indy's pain to the loss of her mom at an early age. But Indy sensed deep down the reason she wanted to try cutting came from the same place that motivated her to make art. It was a way she could control things.

She knew that cutting was not creation—it was just defilement. And now she felt awful. The aftermath of the blood and bandages would be an ugly scar, who knew how permanent. A reminder of her weakness. At least now she was back in the studio, where she'd had a successful marathon session before dinner.

Indy settled back into her space, which was cluttered with half-finished artwork, and fussed with her surroundings. She was full of tofu and bread and dessert, and the "comfort" area of her brain was newly stimulated. She couldn't get started on her art, couldn't really dive in fully yet, until her workstation was properly organized, her chair was sufficiently high or low enough, her pencils were sharpened, and everything she could possibly need was in arm's length of the wire tree sculpture she'd started earlier. And then she decided she was thirsty. She should really get a glass of water before anything else.

She looked in the drawers around the big sink for one of the plastic cups she'd used in the past for paint or thinner and found, next to a stack of them, an unopened bottle of red wine.

"Uh-oh."

Indy turned around when she heard Nick's voice. The sleeves were rolled up on his button-down shirt, his hair was sort of wet-looking, and he stood there unshaven, smiling.

"Are you hitting the sauce already?" He had already seen her looking at the wine.

Indigo blushed and shut the drawer at once. "I was just looking for cups." She held up one of the plastic cups to show him, geekily, as though she had to demonstrate.

"Well, you found 'em." Nick walked over to where Indy was, and she could smell that oddly appealing combination of sweat, B.O., and dirty hair that seemed to spill from his pores in the heat. He was close enough to her now that his hairy forearm brushed her bare wrist when he reached around her at the sink. She spun around as though she'd just gotten an electric shock. Nick took the wine bottle from the drawer and removed the corkscrew that lay beside it.

"This is the stash of cheap-o Côte Du Rhône I keep tucked away for art openings and the occasional long night." He uncorked the bottle and began pouring two cups of dark red wine. "Help yourself," he said, leaving a cup for Indy. She lamely tucked her "bad" arm behind her back, trying to hide it from his gaze.

"Thanks," Indy said meekly. She didn't want to look uncool enough to refuse his offer, even though she hadn't planned to drink anything stronger than water for a long time after her regrettable shenanigans at the social. She took a sip of wine—it was thick and hot, like blood. It seemed to make her warmer than she was before, and she suddenly wanted to splash water on her face.

"What happened to your arm?"

Indigo's paranoia caused her body language to snap shut like a bear trap.

"Oh, I, um, scratched it pretty hard today on one of these wires." She walked quickly over to her workstation and held up the base of her wire tree sculpture like it was a key piece of evidence in a court case she was trying.

"You've got to be careful around the ends of those bastards," Nick replied, setting up his easel. He didn't seem to be suspicious about whether she was bluffing.

"What's this going to be?" he asked, gesturing to her sculpture and lifting his cup of wine to his lips.

"A Christmas tree?" Indy said, taming with a pair of needle-nose pliers the ends of the wires that still curled out like stray Afro hairs. "I thought I'd do an installation about pop art and pop culture, and gender and advertising and Americana, and Christmas. What's more symbolic of American values than a holiday that glorifies consumerism?" Indigo was flush with the confidence that the wine seemed to be lending her as she pitched her idea to Nick. "Plus," she added with a nonpretentious smile, "I thought it would be fun to make tinsel out of soda cans."

She looked up from her half-finished sculpture to see Nick listening to her, rapt. His eyes flashed with a reverential pride, like he was excited to be the only one hearing about her piece before it was done. He smiled with a kind of warmth she rarely saw in his handsome face and drained his cup of whatever wine was left.

"You know," he said, "I'll never forget when you decided to recreate Andy Warhol's 'Electric Chair' series with patio furniture and Christmas lights," Nick said, getting up to grab the wine bottle. He refilled his cup and sat back down.

"Oh, God," Indigo said, blushing as he topped her off. "I couldn't have been more than eleven when I did that piece!" She realized how weird that sounded. She'd known him since she was a little girl.

"What's a nice Jewish girl doing, making all this Christmas-themed art?" He smiled again. Nick really seemed like he was flirting. She prayed she wasn't imagining it.

"I'm only half-Jewish," Indy said, getting back to work on her piece as she spoke. "My mom is Catholic. Well, *was* Catholic."

"The Japanese lady who comes on Showcase Day?" He asked.

"No, that's my stepmom, Yoshiko. My dad remarried after my real mom died of cancer."

"That's right," Nick said, suddenly serious. His eyebrows knitted reverentially. "I saw your series last year. I'm so sorry, Indy."

She smiled, taking a break from wrapping the wire around the base, higher and higher into the branches of the tree. "Thanks. You're not the first person to confuse Yoshiko for my mom, though. I guess when you have long, dark hair like mine, you can pass for half-Japanese. At least from behind." She took another gulp of wine, making eye contact with Nick as she did. His eyes looked kind and deep. She helped herself to another cup.

"So, yeah. I guess you could say I'm only half-JAP," she quipped, then took a drink. Nick laughed.

She was on a roll with this confidence thing—performing for him felt great. She could see how Lucy could find it addictive.

"Oh, please," Nick said, coming around to Indy's side of the room to use the pencil sharpener mounted on the table behind her. "You're the least Jappy girl in this whole camp. I don't mean that in an anti-Semitic way or anything. Hell, I'm a Yid myself, even though my parents were huge commie atheists."

Really! she thought. *All this and a nice Jewish boy to boot?* They really were meant to be together.

"You know what I mean," he continued. "You've just always seemed different from the other kids here."

Swoon.

"You're grounded, down to earth. You never seem status-obsessed or materialistic the way the other girls here have to have their hair blow-dried before breakfast, or need the newest crazy expensive pair of designer shoes to wear to a fuckin' violin lesson."

Indigo practically fainted with happiness. Saying she was different from the other girls at Silver Springs was a declaration of what she'd always hoped to hear. He'd always liked her more. They had a special connection. At least that's what her body told her. And what her increasingly sloppy, infatuation- and wine-addled brain actually heard.

"What are you working on?" she finally slurred, barely able to recover from the compliment Nick had just bestowed.

"Here—I'll show you."

He slid into the bench next to her, his pencil newly sharpened, and reached across the table for his pad. She felt his arm brush against the outside of hers once more, but this time, it distinctively felt intentional.

Indigo rallied the boldness she needed to look to her right, where Nick sat extremely close to her. He was staring down at his pad, sketching furiously.

"Okay," he said, still drawing as he spoke. "So, I'm doing this series of twelve wall-sized paintings about the end of days."

"'Wall-sized'?" Indigo asked, unsure of what else to say in order to seem curious and keep Nick engaged.

"Twenty by thirty feet," he replied without looking up.

"Wow." She tried to imagine a painting that large. And twelve of them? It was insanely ambitious, but that was kind of his thing. He was like the anti–Jay Stegbrandt. Nick had big ideas and got them done.

"So, here." He finally looked up from the page at Indy's face, which flushed with wine and embarrassment. She smiled at him, then got serious immediately, as though to indicate how interested she was in his painting.

"This is the third painting I'm doing of this one particular horse. It's a series of twelve, like I said, so I'm doing three paintings of all four horses of the apocalypse. This one is a Clydesdale. And he's in the background here, with this skeleton riding him bareback."

"This is going to be so awesome," Indy said, pouring herself a third cup of wine. She was officially buzzed. There was no way she was getting any work done tonight.

"Finish me off?" Nick asked. She brushed arms with him again to empty what was left of the wine bottle into his cup.

"Anyway, these carcasses in the foreground," he continued. "Those are littered with the remains of totaled cars and burnt trash. I want to have the side of this car spray-painted with the word 'Mayhem,' in graffiti." He kept adding to his sketch the more he described it. It wasn't her cup of tea conceptually, but the way he described it made it exciting for her to think about. Although it was tough to differentiate how excited she was for Nick's piece coming together with how thrilled she was to be sitting so close to him, talking about art. All of sudden she felt dizzy and put her head down to rest it on the cool table.

"Hey, are you all right?" Nick asked.

"Mm-hmm." Indy nodded into the table's surface, smiling goofily.

"Nick? Do you really believe that the world is going to end one day?" She tilted her head up to rest her right cheek near his pad, looking up at him.

He laughed. "Nah, I don't believe in that stuff. I just think it's fascinating—and horses are fun to paint. Plus, I've seen way too many apocalypse movies." He ran his fingers through his dark, wavy hair. "I'm sort of a sci-fi geek."

"Oh, yeah?" Indy asked, rolling herself back up to sit upright. "Were you a big nerd growing up?" She smiled tipsily and smoothed down her ponytail. She had completely forgotten that she probably looked all disheveled. It didn't seem to matter much now, though.

"Sure," Nick said, smiling back. He finished his wine. "That's sort of the whole reason I began making art. To create my own version of reality when I was growing up in a world that didn't make me feel like it had a place for me inside of it."

"Growing up is hard to do." Indy giggled at how dumb she sounded.

"Oh, boy," Nick said. "You're so gone." She felt the outside of their legs brush up against each other under the table. Every inch of her skin seemed to tingle in reaction to their contact.

"I am fine," Indigo slurred, intentionally shifting her body so her arm could touch his again.

"You better not get me in trouble for giving you wine," Nick said, gently teasing her. "In fact, you're probably over your curfew as well."

"Curfew-shmurfew. We have art to make." They smiled at each other, their eyes meeting. Suddenly Indigo felt entirely lucid. Her boundaries around her teacher seemed to evaporate as readily as her feeling of intoxication.

In a moment of lunatic boldness, Indigo took a deep breath and decided to make something happen. She put her hand on top of Nick's, and, as soon as he didn't pull away, felt herself lean in to let him kiss her.

He leaned in, too, and put his other hand atop hers on the table, stabilizing her. She could smell him even more powerfully the closer her face got to his. Her pulse raced, and her whole body seemed to vibrate in a bold confidence she hadn't felt until that moment. She closed her eyes and felt his strong hands wrap around her waist.

Finally, their lips touched. Indigo felt herself melt into him, completely lost in the moment that she had waited for since practically forever. It was warm, it was real, and it was even better than her imagination had been able to realize. She felt her body completely relax as she kissed him, losing control of time and space and circumstances.

This was it. This was everything.

"Indigo," he said, pulling away and halting all momentum.

Her eyes burst open.

"Huh? Yes?"

"Indigo, you should probably go back to your bunk." He pulled away from her and looked down at the floor.

"Oh," she said, her heart sinking rapidly, like an elevator cut from its suspension cables, hurtling down to the basement. Her throat felt hot and tight, and her whole body seized up with dread for the inevitable onslaught of tears that would soon follow what was about to be the worst rejection she'd ever have to live through.

"I'm sorry," Indy said, frantically trying to clean up her workstation. "I'm so sorry," she repeated, though it didn't make much sense. She didn't do anything wrong, she'd only followed his lead. There had been so many signals.

"It's okay," Nick said, rubbing his own temples. "It's just…we shouldn't have done that."

As Indigo stood up, she felt blood rush down from her head into her wobbly legs. She staggered a little bit, looking down at her shoes and eventually holding on to the table for support. The room began to spin. She shouldn't have stood up so quickly. She shouldn't have had any wine at all on such a hot day, let alone however many glasses that was—three?—in a row, like some kind of experienced drinker. She shouldn't have kissed him. Now he wouldn't like her anymore. What was she thinking, ruining everything?

And just then, she felt Nick's thick hands on her bare shoulders.

"Easy," he said, steadying Indy's wobble. He slid his hands down the back of her arms and held on tight. And then, before Indigo could even react to what was happening, Nick had his arms around her in full, and spun Indigo so they were face-to-face again. She could feel his breath on her cheek, and his strong hands dug into her skin. He looked her in the eyes and seemed to move in closer to where she stood, on barely solid ground.

"Look," he said, his hands still gripping her bare, fleshy upper arms. "Don't think I didn't want to do this. Don't think I haven't thought about it before."

Oh my God, Indigo thought. Was this a dream? Or was Nick really saying these things she'd always hoped he'd say?

"I know you're special. I know you're different. And you're incredible. Mature, talented, beautiful…you're just…awesome."

Indigo stood there, in shock, staring into Nick's eyes. She still felt dizzy but no longer drunk. This was actually happening, and her body wanted her to be present for every last second of it.

"But it's been a tough time for me this last year," Nick continued, releasing his grip on Indy but keeping his proximity to her. "There were some rumors about me…some trouble…none of it was true, but it was still a mess. And now I have to keep my nose clean. And I can't do anything with a camper that could be misconstrued or get me into trouble. Like this. Like you."

Indy exhaled. He was still saying no, but she only heard "yes." Yes, she was different, she was brilliant, she was special, he wanted her. That's all she needed to hear to feel suddenly exhilarated, buoyant, perfect, alive.

"So, go to bed, Indy. Leave your stuff out and go to bed. I'll clean up for you. Sweet dreams."

He kissed her gently on the forehead—it felt like a religious rite the way he did it, like Ash Wednesday at a chapel, with Nick's dry, soft, warm lips on her forehead instead of a priest's ashy fingers—and gently guided her in the direction of the studio door. Indy looked back at him and smiled, then took slow steps out of the studio and toward her bunk, floating home the whole trip. She no longer felt drunk—what she felt was a different kind of intoxication, a weightless, euphoric sense of being high and in some kind of limbo between your own fantasy life and actual reality.

But what was he actually saying to her? What did he mean? He said she was special and different; obviously she remembered all of that. He said he wanted to "do this" and that he'd thought about "it" before. Her knees weakened with ecstasy just remembering how he had actually kissed her in real life. Right? That's what happened? Of course that was what happened. And the only reason he couldn't have continued making out with her was because she was a camper and he'd gotten into trouble? What did that mean exactly? Her mind got muddy and messy then, like when you forget to wash a brush in between using dark and light paints in a watercolor set.

Indigo snuck into the Ferlinghetti dorm and slipped off her clothes before creeping into bed without a sound. Eleanor slept on her back with an eye mask over the greater majority of her face, her arms rigidly alongside her body like a corpse.

As Indy huddled into her own covers, she touched the bandage on her forearm. Having that intense encounter with Nick erased all memory of her cutting incident and the raw emotions that surrounded her desire to hurt herself earlier. It made her flaws invisible. He really was made of magic—not just in who he was but in what he did to her.

He liked her. That was the most important thing to take away from this bizarre, humid, wine-stained night. He liked her so much, but he couldn't fully act on it because he was a counselor and she was a camper.

It was hours before Indigo finally drifted off into a dreamless sleep.

14

The next day was a cakewalk. Indy sailed through all her classes with the same manic, ebullient energy with which she tossed and turned the night before. Rich, newly layered fantasies about Nick ricocheted around her head. At breakfast she ignored Eleanor, who asked whether she'd even come home last night.

"Maybe you're just a deep sleeper now," Indigo suggested over chai tea and whole-wheat pretzel croissants that Lillian had shipped in from Manhattan's City Bakery. Eleanor seemed confused. Usually Indy spoke to her with some sort of sarcasm or outright agitation. Now her roommate was just shrugging her off with low-key cheer. Indy honestly didn't care about her roommate's hard-earned attempts at getting under her skin—it was a pleasant change.

It was a cooler, more arid day at Silver Springs, and it felt like a relief. Now that she knew Nick liked her, it was like the whole world was breezier.

Indigo waltzed through sculpture class with Jim Dybbs, shrugging off a nasty splinter she got in the process of sanding down a four-by-four. She sleepwalked through an oil painting elective workshop with a visiting artist lady from an artist's residency in Rhode Island, who guided everyone through a never-ending presentation on the importance of ultramarine blue when achieving perfect skin tone. And she sailed through lunch, barely touching her croque-monsieur and humming with happiness when she passed the pitcher of Arnold Palmers down to Puja's end of the table, making sure to add, "Enjoy!" before she did.

There was no doubt she was giddy and goofy and feeling like a different person today. In fact, it wasn't until she bounded past Theater Row and into the Performance Art Center to take a meeting with Jen Rant when Indy felt a little down for the first time all day. She hadn't dealt with Jen since the night of the social and the Bob Dylan concert, and she hadn't been particularly dying to catch up with her since she learned of her supposed past with Nick. What's more, even though Indigo had eked out some work since they last spoke, she still felt superstitious around her productivity. As though if she talked about it to Jen, her adviser would put some kind of a jinx on her creative streak.

Plus, Indy was still wearing long sleeves to conceal her arm. She really hoped Jen wouldn't notice, because that certainly was a conversation she didn't want to have.

"Come in!" Jen called from behind her office door. Indy turned the knob and cracked the door to find her furiously scribbling into a leather-bound sketchbook.

"Am I interrupting?" Indy was unsure if she'd come at the right time.

"No! Hi, Indy! Sorry, I'm just finishing up my Morning Pages." Jen finished dashing out whatever it was she was writing in her notebook, then finally shut the cover and spun her chair around. "Sorry about that! I usually try to do my Morning Pages, well, in the morning! But I slept in today, so I'm getting a late start on my creative routine. Speaking of which…"

She opened Indy's folder, awkwardly segueing into a new, non–Jen Rant–themed stream of thought. "How is *your* creative routine, Indigo? What are you doing to keep yourself staying inspired and productive since we last spoke?"

"Well, I've made some progress on my piece. I worked on it all day yesterday, and I feel good about what I still have to do."

"So, you're on a roll!" Jen smiled wide. It seemed fake.

"Well, I was yesterday." Indy's mood was starting to stiffen. "I haven't worked on it today yet."

"You know, I find that *discipline* really helps my creative practice." Jen took a deep breath. "Even if you don't *feel like* working on something every day, what separates an amateur artist from a professional is the person who digs into the work no matter how she feels about it."

What the hell? Indy thought. She'd busted her ass yesterday on her project, only to get a lecture that she didn't make it to the studio today? The last time she'd seen Jen, Indy had barely cracked her idea—now she was supposed to feel guilty about not working on it like a factory slave?

"Well," Indy said, looking Jen straight in the eye, "I guess that's not really my process. I work like crazy when I'm inspired, and when I'm not…"

"Then you beat yourself up until you can't take it anymore?" Jen volunteered.

"Sort of," Indigo admitted.

"That's not very balanced," Jen said. Then she brightened on a dime. "But artists are seldom the most balanced people in the world!"

Indigo, realizing she was no longer in trouble, relaxed and allowed her mind to revisit the happy Nick thoughts that kept her aloft all day.

"So, tell me about your piece. How has your mission statement changed since we met last?" She scribbled notes in the margins of Indy's chart.

"Well," Indy said, somewhat dreamily, lapsing into the reverie of her private fantasies about her and Nick, and making sense of them with everything that had happened the night before. Indigo had become such an expert when it came to fantasizing that she knew how to do it in the company of anyone—parents, teachers, doctors, rabbis—without letting on that her mind was on far more intimate matters than what they were actually discussing.

"I guess I'm not sure whether I still want to make a critical statement about pop culture in a society of consumerism anymore, really," Indy said breezily.

She noticed from the corner of her eye that Jen had looked up from her folder.

"I mean, what's the point of exploring themes about the superficiality of social networking or how marketing reinforces economic disparity." Indy felt like she was drunk again on some kind of cheap champagne—or her own tawdry fantasies of Nick ripping off her clothes and ravishing her in some kind of pastoral setting. (A golf course? A barn?) Whatever she had to say about her work right now seemed like the furthest thing from a priority.

"I'm thinking of changing the point of my piece," Indigo concluded, with no prompt from Jen, who seemed to react to what she was saying like it was some kind of sick joke. "I want it to be about happiness and love."

"I mean, at the end of the day," Indigo continued, wondering aloud to Jen with a dopey half-smile on her face, "isn't there nothing more transgressive than romance?" A long pause followed as

Indy came back to planet Earth, her eyes landing back down on Jen's face.

"What," Jen said, without any question-asking inflection.

"Well, I'm just feeling really good right now, and I think that maybe there's something to the idea that it's humanism, not consumerism, that's really the central value of what makes the world run. And maybe my piece should be more about that?"

"I guess I'm just confused, Indigo," Jen said, in a slightly higher pitch. "When we last met, you seemed to be excited about this project. You had a clear set of intentions going into it, and you even made some pretty impressive progress in the studio—even though you didn't show up today." Jen adjusted her chair, then brought it back up to where it was. "Now you're saying you want to change your mission statement?" She fidgeted with her pencil and knitted her bushy eyebrows. "I don't understand why you'd want to undo the work you'd already put into it. Unless…is there something going on in your personal life that's distracting you?"

Indigo finally snapped out of a fantasy about her and Nick swimming nude in—was it a lake or the ocean?—and realized that her adviser was basically reprimanding her. She guessed that was how it went—even if you weren't feeling guilty about getting enough work done, somebody else was always around to make sure you felt a little bad.

"No," Indy said curtly. "Nothing at all."

"Nothing going on with the girls at the dorm?" Jen offered.

"Nope," Indy said, then waited out a long pause to finally throw Jen a crumb. "I mean, I guess I've just been in a better mood than usual lately. But that's not for any reason in particular, really. I've just been feeling…giddy, I guess."

Jen nodded sagely.

"I've been there." She put Indy's file folder in her lap and

137

folded her hands over it. "You know, this might be embarrassing to share, but when I was your age, I had the biggest crush on one of my dad's friends."

"You really don't have to—" Indy started, but Jen continued on. Indy cringed and braced herself for the impending overshare.

"Around that time, I really felt like I was doing some of my best work—I was drawing and painting and writing all day, all night." Jen continued, "I was so productive, it was ridiculous. In retrospect, I don't think the work I was actually doing was all that incredible."

Jen stood up and looked out the window. This was all a little melodramatic for a dumb adviser meeting. Indy wished she would make her stupid point so she could get out of there.

"Anyway, when I had that crush, around your age, all I could think about was my dad's friend."

Ew. She didn't want to picture a teenage Jen Rant lusting over some old dude, nor did she want to entertain the idea that the two of them had anything in common at all, whether it was a creative streak or a penchant for older guys.

"And while artists are really moody, I guess I wasn't really prepared to know how debilitating my 'good' mood would be to my work," Jen continued. "All I could think about at the time, instead of getting my work done, was how I could get this man to take notice of me. His name was Herman." She closed her eyes as she said his name, like she was in pain or something.

Indigo couldn't listen to any more of what Jen was earnestly conveying from the bottom of her soul without smirking. This story had officially become fucking ridiculous. Herman? Like Herman Munster? Wait until she told Lucy....

Indigo suddenly remembered one of the things that Nick said last night. He'd mentioned that any rumors about him from last year were totally untrue. There was absolutely no way anything had ever happened with Lucy. She felt warm with the reassurance that Eleanor was what she always suspected—a liar who only wanted to get between her and her best friend, no matter what the cost was of the bullshit she fabricated.

Indy couldn't wait to come clean to her bestie. She'd tell Lucy everything. About her unfounded jealousy around the concert and the staff meeting...all of it. Then the two of them would laugh at how dumb it all was. Or, really, at how dumb Indigo had been for ever doubting their friendship.

"Anyway," Jen Rant continued, seemingly oblivious to her mentee's mind being one billion miles away, "my dad eventually got transferred to another office, and he stopped socializing with Herman. He never came over to our house after that, and though I was heartbroken at first, I found out that not having him around as a distraction was actually really helpful to my productivity. I got a lot more work done once I got over Herman."

Indy thought to herself that "Once I got over Herman" would be an amazing title for a future piece.

"Then, last summer, I was involved with somebody I was...working with."

Indy's ears perked up. She *had* to be talking about Nick now. She sucked in her breath, hoping her adviser wouldn't notice.

Jen's eyes drifted to the window, visibly hangdog and moist all of a sudden. "I was miserable and heartbroken, and even though I tried to work through it—to funnel the pain into my work—I couldn't make a damn thing out of it. It was a wasted summer of total misery." This sounded familiar. But Indigo didn't want to think that she and Jen had ever kissed the same guy.

Jen snapped back to the task at hand.

"The point is, we all give ourselves emotional inspirations and distractions that can either help us get work done or derail us from the task at hand. Sometimes the stuff that feels good in life can be really bad for our work, and sometimes things like pain, depression, or even plain boredom can encourage us to make art. Your goal between now and the next time we meet is to think about finding balance." She took a seat again.

"Anything is possible with your talent." Jen forced a weak smile, and Indigo returned it, relieved that the sermon had gotten "wrap-uppy."

"See you Wednesday," Indy said, standing up to leave.

"Yes," Jen agreed, her eyes seeming to get misty again.

Indigo hightailed it toward Theater Row, where she hoped to see Lucy in a rehearsal or assistant-teaching a class at this hour. But she was nowhere to be found. She peered into the glass-paneled walls of the huge, modernist movement and dance studios, and around the rehearsal spaces.

Finally, she pulled out her cell to type up a quick text. She and her best friend had lot to reconcile—even though their latest awkwardness had been, until now, entirely in Indigo's head.

As soon as she reached into her bag for her phone, Indy felt it vibrate with an incoming text that was just cryptic enough to be worrisome.

Meet me by the lake. Now.

But it wasn't from Lucy at all—it was from Eleanor.

15

Against her better judgment, Indigo found herself walking toward the lake to meet up with Eleanor, who'd sold Lucy up the river. She decided to meet her only because she was curious about what her text could possibly mean. And, to be honest, it was also too nice a day for her to consider heading back into the studio just yet.

The spring smells and the sensation of the breeze on her skin only added to the sense of giddiness Indy had felt all day. She took off her long-sleeved button-down shirt and tied it around her waist in defiance. It didn't matter if anyone saw her bandage. She'd just blame it on her wire sculpture. It just felt good to have the sun dapple her arms and to breathe in the fresh air.

This must be how normal, happy people felt. The kinds of girls who didn't live at the mercy of their demons and their hormones and their constant desire to make stuff on a monumental scale and leave a legacy behind. Maybe there was something to the notion of balance that Jen was talking about.

Indigo ignored the slight pang of guilt she had walking toward the lake instead of toward the studio, and tried to feel better by telling herself she was going on an "inspirational" walk. Artists weren't always just inspired in the studio. Sometimes they got their best ideas just walking around and letting their minds wander. Indy remembered when Jim Dybbs, her adviser last summer, had given her that very advice. Nothing like a beautiful day and a good mood to make you more vulnerable to the advice of hippies.

The gravel and stray leaves on the path to the lake crunched beneath Indigo's moccasins as she found herself noticing everything. The shadows on the trees and the clouds in the sky above her. The group of eight-year-old theater students rehearsing in a grassy clearing, wearing silly wigs and reading lines from *Hamlet*. The wooden signs shaped like arrows that guided campers toward different parts of the campus. She'd never even bothered to look at those signs very closely, but now she could see that each one was expertly painted with tiny, intricate designs. Her new perspective felt good.

As she rounded the corner past the woods and toward the lake, she stopped in her tracks when she heard what sounded like a rustling in the woods. She'd heard rumors of bear spottings from Yvonne in particular, who claimed (even with telltale blue icing stains on her top) that a teenage grizzly was responsible for clearing out the stash of last summer's birthday cakes from the pantry. Unsure if the source of the noise was a dangerous animal, Indy stood totally still. She waited for another sound but heard nothing.

So, she continued on, until a familiar distinctive giggle caused her to come to a screeching halt. Indy peeked into the woods, hiding behind a large American elm, and moved aside the giant leaves on a fern in front of her to see where the laugh was coming from.

It was hard to see behind the brush, but Indigo could definitely see Lucy's back to her. That head of full, dazzling ringlets was a dead giveaway.

She tossed back her curls in another giggle fit. Indigo maneuvered herself so she could see more clearly.

She almost cried out as soon as her best friend shifted her body weight to her right. It was Nick she was talking to, laughing at, flirting with. He was wearing jean cutoffs and a white New York Dolls T-shirt, running his fingers through his thick hair like he did all the time at the studio. As he had just last night.

"What are you talking about?" She heard Lucy giggle.

Just like that, Indigo's great mood darkened. Her heart sank and her belly ached. Her hands got clammy and her neck began to sweat. But something compelled her to keep watching.

Nick took Lucy's hand and moved in toward her petite frame—deliberately, and with seductive intention—like he had done with Indy only hours before in the studio, right before they'd kissed. It was now becoming clear that Lucy and Nick were going to kiss, too. Indigo couldn't bear watching for a second longer.

She turned around like she'd been hit in the face and ran back toward her bunk. The ground—the dirt and leaves and pebbles—all crashed beneath her feet, which was somehow satisfying. Indy was done with being quiet. No more lurking, creeping, observing. That was for pussies. Now that she was betrayed—hurt, furious—she wanted to make as much noise as she could. Let Lucy and Nick hear her escape. Let them worry.

"Indigo? Indigo, Jesus, wait up!" Eleanor's voice rang out in the distance.

Indy could have been a mile away or ten by the time she let the boiling rage that corked her ears dissipate to allow sound in. She turned when she heard her name to find Eleanor chasing after her, just out of the entrance to the woods by the lake.

"Where did an art student learn to run like that? You're not even out of breath? You guys are supposed to be fatties." Eleanor gathered herself and smoothed down her hair and clothes—her composure had been ruffled by all the chasing. "Did you go to the woods? I didn't see you there."

Indigo just stared into the space an inch or two in front of Eleanor, her face slack with shock and pain.

"Oh my God, what's wrong? Did you just see a ghost?" Eleanor's snotty veneer melted away as she caught the whiff of what could be some potentially juicy gossip that could justify her roommate's expression.

"I…just…" Indy was so mad she couldn't even form sentences yet.

"What? What's going on? What happened?" Eleanor prodded.

Indy tried, but she couldn't keep it in anymore.

"Fuck Lucy, and fuck Nick! I hope they both die in a fucking fire!" She heard herself unravel at a high, shrill volume to her frenemy. She sounded like a hysterical dork, her voice quivering with emotion. She didn't sound bad-assed, the way she hoped she'd sound when she got angry and began to swear.

Eleanor's face lit up like a little girl's on her birthday, surprised by a cake with glowing candles. Now the good stuff—the *real* gossip—could finally begin.

"What happened?" Eleanor asked. The question hung between them like a loaded gun. It was Indigo's turn to talk, but she just started to sob.

Indy wailed and choked on her own angry tears. It seemed to come out of her mouth, not her eyes, which stung with rage. Eleanor just stood in front of Indigo, watching her cry, waiting patiently for the dirt.

"Lucy and Nick," Indigo said again. "Fuck them both."

"Yeah, but what did you *see*?" Eleanor wouldn't let go until Indy had told her something coherent and repeatable about the parties in question.

"They were…" Indigo choked back her tears and hardened a bit. "They were about to make out, basically. He was moving toward her …" Indigo got freshly angry just hearing herself say out loud what she'd just now seen. "Oh, fuck it. Fuck them. Who cares. I'm done."

Eleanor nodded in rapt solidarity and handed Indy a cigarette. Indigo took it and lit up, even though they were perilously close to campus. She didn't care anymore if she got caught and sent home. She wanted to get away from camp—she wanted to get away from Lucy. She wanted to make sure she never saw that two-faced bitch again.

"Not to be like 'I told you so,'" Eleanor said softly, "But didn't I mention that the two of them had a thing on the first day?" She put her hand on Indigo's shoulder—her fingers felt like ice.

This is my ally? Indy thought to herself. It was too much to think that this psycho was telling the truth, and that Lucy was the liar all along.

"Lucy and Nick were totally hooking up last summer," Eleanor continued, piecing together the story as she spoke. "Now it's just trickling over." She watched a shattered Indigo stub out her hardly smoked cigarette with barely a trace of empathy. "This must be so hard for you," Eleanor said, with fake concern knitted into her severely thin eyebrows. "Your best friend basically lied to you."

Indigo briefly dipped out of the rage-fueled self-pity that swirled inside her head like a mucky tornado and saw Eleanor for who she was—a bottom feeder who thrived on the misery of others, no matter what their allegiance. The only good thing to say about her was that what you saw was what you got. There were no illusions when it came to her character—at no point was she trying to fool you into thinking she was your BFF. Not like Lucy. Indy clenched her fists, imagining pulling her blond ringlets out by the roots with her bare hands.

"See you later, Eleanor," Indigo said, then walked off toward—toward what? She had no idea. She didn't want to go back to the bunk, she had no interest in going to the studio, and the direction of the lake was obviously a nonstarter.

She'd just walk. Anywhere.

Maybe the more Indy meditated on how angry she was, the more likely some action or clarity would come from the messy sludge stew of emotions that pumped through her body like a toxic spill.

"Don't confront her without me!" Eleanor's voice faded into the background as Indy bounded away with defiance. "I want to videotape it!"

Lucy knew how much Indigo liked Nick since they were actually kids, making lanyard friendship bracelets out of biodegradable craft materials and playing hearts in their bunk together at age eight and nine.

It hurt Indy's heart to think about how Nick crossed her, but she wasn't as angry at him as she was at Lucy—she was just devastated and heartbroken. She still loved him. Even though he was so full of shit with his "I would, but you're a camper" shtick. Was that even what he said? Or just what she heard?

She couldn't bear thinking about him betraying her, so Indy put Nick out of her mind. She focused instead on her hatred of Lucy, and tried badly to spiral her seething contempt for that snake into some kind of plan.

16

Indigo felt like a zombie as she walked to the studio. She just wished she could go back to a time before she saw Nick and Lucy in the woods together. Or somehow change history so it never happened. Her feelings toward him now were fuzzy and conflicted—part of her wanted to hit him in the face and the other part wanted to kiss him again.

But Indy knew at least one thing for sure. She was furious at Lucy.

She pushed on the studio door cautiously, but the room was completely empty. No signs of Nick or any of her fellow art majors. No light, no works in progress on the tables—no signs of life. Indigo was unsure what to do now that she was alone in the studio, so she inventoried the work she'd done on her big project.

A sense of guilt began to overtake her. She had so much more to do in time for Industry Showcase Day, which was in—was it only a week? Less? And what's more, her tree sculpture, which until recently had seemed so well formed and on its way to becoming a finished—even great—piece, now seemed to taunt her with how much she had to do in order for it to be good. She took out her work and laid out her supplies on the drafting table, but she couldn't will herself to do anything.

Indigo felt dizziness, confusion, and frustration all at once when she looked at her piece. It went from unfinished to imperfect under the scrutiny of her gaze. It didn't help that her thoughts kept drifting back to Lucy and Nick and how neither of them could possibly be the same people Indigo had always thought they were.

She couldn't even lapse into the reprieve of romantic fantasies about Nick, after what she'd witnessed in the forest. Thinking about making love to him—losing her virginity to the man whom she had first learned to associate "sex" with—was impossible now that she was this hurt. It was no longer a comfort. All of her hopes and optimism about their future melted like a chocolate bar in a glove compartment. What was left was messy and ugly, and she wanted Lucy to pay. She wanted her former best friend to feel as bad as she did.

Indigo couldn't funnel her rage into her work, even as the idea occurred to her that it was what she was supposed to be doing. It was amazing how she realized exactly what would make her feel better but decided not to do it, then also managed to feel bad about *that* decision at the same time. She was clearly in self-destruct mode.

She thought about Jen Rant, that mousy jerk, and how she had said something about happiness getting in the way of creativity. So, Indy was damned if she was happy and damned if she was miserable?

Her eyes glazed over with fresh tears, blurring the artwork in front of her. She couldn't bear it anymore. It was better to go to bed and end the day before things got even worse. She would just ride the tides of emotion that carried her into the darker recesses of herself until it was all over. If she tried to resist the undertow, she'd run the risk of drowning herself in her own misery.

Indigo was going to leave the unfinished sculpture on the table and just walk away. But suddenly, she had a fit of dark energy. With a burst of rage, she wiped her sculpture clear off the table and listened, satisfied, as it crashed to the floor with a loud thud. Then, she stomped on her tree, warping its frame and smashing the soda can ornaments she'd worked so hard to craft. She hated this piece, and she hated the naive person who made it.

She plugged in the blow torch by the metalwork station in the studio, not bothering to put on goggles or let it properly heat up, and kicked what was left of her piece over to it. She took the torch to her mangled tree and watched in horrified glee as the blue bullet of flame turned the coarse, coiled wire into a silvery, mushy gunk that coated the surface of the wooden studio floor panels. The chaos of it was exhilarating. She felt, for a moment, like the girl who didn't care about the rules—as the rebel she'd always imagined herself.

The sculpture melted into something unrecognizable in a matter of minutes, and Indy scanned the studio for more to destroy. She left the torch on its side, still breathing fire from its spout, and brought back from her locker a heap of her drawings and sketches to feed it. But as she returned to the torch with her arms full of her most flammable works, Indigo found that the floorboards had caught fire. It was small and contained, but the flames were beginning to creep beyond the sculptural remains around the torch.

Her heart jumped.

She wasn't as panicked as she would have been if she weren't already in this bizarre, destructive trance—but she was still aware enough to know to grab the fire extinguisher from under the sink and remove the peg from the spout, as she'd learned to do in countless studio safety demonstrations.

But before she squeezed down on the extinguisher's handle, Indy marveled at the appetite of the creeping fire, and how strangely pretty it looked—how out of place. Indigo grabbed her sketches and drawings and pages from her notebooks and tossed them into the flames, which lapped up the fruits of her labor hungrily and immediately. Then she tested the fire extinguisher. A stream of white foam expelled from the can and splattered all over the tables, making a satisfying *Whoosh!* noise.

She caught sight, in the corner of her eye, of Nick's sweeping, postapocalyptic masterpiece. It was a canvas strewn with skulls, machine-gun shells, soot and ash and sand and nothingness, under a crimson red sky. A world he'd crafted in her company not long before. It stood there like a disapproving authority figure, watching over her maniacal episode, shaking its head in stern reprimand. "Whatever happened to Indigo Hamlisch, Serious Artist?" Indy heard the painting ask, in Nick's deep voice.

"She's burning up her own artwork." Indy smiled to herself. "And yours, too!"

Indy grabbed the corner of Nick's canvas and ripped his piece in half. The sound it made, the feeling of the tearing canvas, the sight of Nick's world coming apart by her own hand, was terrifying and thrilling at once. Indy tossed the chunk of his painting—the bit with the skulls on the moon, or whatever the fuck it was supposed to be—into the fire. She watched in sick satisfaction as the flames lapped it up like a carnivorous plant hungry for blood. Once the painting had completely melted away into the ashes, Indigo put out the fire by shooting powdery white foam all over it. Suddenly she felt at peace.

But that sense of calm didn't last long. Now that her trance was broken, she realized what she had done and began to panic. There was no way she wasn't going to get caught for this. What was she thinking? And why did she have to burn Nick's work, not just her own? Destroying another camper's artwork was grounds for immediate expulsion—she wasn't sure what the consequences were for ruining a staff member's piece, but they couldn't be much better. She started freaking out and tried to clean up the studio, but it was a horrible mess.

Indy wiped the tables and frantically swept up what was left of Nick's canvas with her hands, dumping the ashes into the sink. She grabbed some rags and ran them under the faucet, then tried to mop the white stuff off the floor. But once the debris was gone, the floor underneath was still black. It was no use. She'd really fucked up, and soon everybody would know. Indy's heart leapt when she heard laughter in the distance. She had to get out of there, and now.

When she arrived back at the bunk, Indigo realized that she had absolutely no idea what time it was. The entire Ferlinghetti cabin was silent, which made her think that everyone was either at dinner or an evening activity, or even sleeping. It could have been anywhere from 6 PM to 1 AM. She resisted the urge to check her phone for the time, in case she'd see any desperate, pleading texts from Lucy. She climbed into her bed instead and closed her eyes.

"Oh, there you are!" Eleanor said, bursting through the door, with a convincing display of what seemed like true compassion. "I was worried about you."

Eleanor had a glorious knack for bad timing. She had obviously just come from the studio, as she was wearing head-to-toe dancewear and still smelled of sweat. She plopped down on the foot of Indy's bed and put her bony hand on her forehead like a concerned mom.

"Are you feeling any better?" asked Eleanor, clearly auditioning for the role of Indigo's BFF, now that she'd witnessed the course of events that had left the gig vacant.

"Yeah, I'm just tired." Indy hoped her roommate would take the hint.

"You're warm, but that's probably from the crying. Do you have a headache?"

"I'll take a Tylenol or something."

"Well," Eleanor said, nodding with an Oscar-worthy demonstration of good intentions, "let me know if you need anything stronger. For the pain, or if you can't sleep, or just to take the edge off."

"Thanks?" Indy wasn't sure that any of Eleanor's pills were going to solve this, but it was kind of sweet anyway.

Eleanor made her best attempt at a warm smile. "You know," she continued, "for what it's worth, I think what Lucy did to you is disgusting. And I want to help you feel better about it."

"I don't want drugs," Indy said, stifling a yawn. She felt completely beat—her body had been through so much today. From the jubilation of feeling wanted, to the realization that her best friend was deceiving her, and finally to the rage and guilt she felt in the studio moments before. It was all too much, and now, because she felt so depleted, she was vulnerable to whatever Eleanor was about to say. Indigo was a captive audience of one.

"I think what would make you feel better"—Eleanor offered Indigo a sip of the diet Red Bull she carried—"is to take action."

"'Take action'?" Indy pushed the can away and looked at her roommate, who was already morphing into scheming mode. Eleanor's face always looked more lizardy when she was plotting. Her eyes slitted up like two blips on a TV screen before it went to black.

"Well…" she said, with what seemed like genuine delight, "what if we got Lucy fired?"

"That's insane," Indy said, sitting up against the wall. "What the hell are you talking about?"

"Last year"—Eleanor scootched closer to Indy on the bed, her face ablaze with intent—"when I heard about Nick and Lucy, I got so close to getting that scumbag fired. *So close!* But I learned from my mistakes, and now I'm telling you, we can do it to her instead."

"Wait," Indy said. "That was you who tried to get Nick fired?"

"Well, yeah!" Eleanor said, as in "Duh." She began removing bobby pins from the tight bun at the nape of her neck. Her hair began to fall down in sweaty, blond clumps.

Indy couldn't believe what she was hearing. "So, you forged that e-mail? That incriminating one you said he sent to Lucy from the computer lab? That you 'found'?"

"Of course not!" Eleanor said, a little too quickly. "I didn't make anything up—I just presented the facts as they happened. Nick was having an affair with an underage camper—your pal Lucy—and I was simply kind enough to gather and present the evidence accordingly." Eleanor pursed her lips and ran her fingers through the pile of discarded bobby pins on the bedspread. There must have been about forty.

Indy looked her in the eyes. "I don't get what you're suggesting I do. Send a fake e-mail?"

Indigo's brain was fuzzy, and she didn't feel like thinking about the ethics of Eleanor trying to get Nick fired a year ago. She still wanted him, but she wasn't nearly as protective of him as she would have been earlier, had she heard that her roommate had designs on his job stability.

"No, way better." Eleanor continued. "I'll have my mom

overnight me a few of our old nanny cams, from when she was suspicious of the help."

Eleanor got up and paced, like she was in some crummy soap opera.

"We can install one nanny cam in Lucy's dorm," Eleanor said, "plus one in her acting studio, and maybe one out in the woods by the lake, where you saw her today...kissing Nick." It was like Eleanor was twisting the knife, saying his name and repeating what happened.

"I dunno, Eleanor. Sounds kind of extreme." Indy was reluctant to go along with her roommate's scheme, but it wasn't like she had any other plan.

"This way, we can catch her doing something that could be considered grounds for getting dismissed from camp," Eleanor continued, ignoring her roommate's protests. "Nobody can argue with video footage. It's not like an e-mail that can be misinterpreted or forged...or that people can think is forged, even if it's not." Her confidence around her methodology was mesmerizing and weirdly impressive.

"Eleanor, let me sleep on it, okay?" Indy said, her eyelids at half-mast by now, like a *Garfield* cartoon. "I'm not sure that setting up surveillance cameras to catch my best friend in some yet-to-be-determined, nefarious act is the best—"

"Your FORMER best friend," Eleanor interrupted her. "A best friend wouldn't lose her virginity to the one guy *you've* had a crush on since the beginning of time!"

It was creepy how much Eleanor knew about everybody's personal business.

"How did you know I've liked him for so long?" Indigo asked.

"The way you change around him. How you blush when you see him. A *friend* notices that stuff," she added, clutching her hand. Indigo felt herself squeeze back, against her better judgment.

"It's for her own good," Eleanor continued. "She can't break the rules without learning the consequences. And think of it this way. We're just keeping an eye on Lucy. If she doesn't do anything wrong, we won't have any evidence to submit, and she won't be fired. See? Win-win!"

"Fine," Indigo said, her eyes shut and her head fully down into her pillow.

Eleanor smiled and turned out the light.

And just like that, their unlikely alliance was official.

17

After the fire, Indigo decided, with Eleanor's encouragement, that she would spend the rest of her time at camp working in her bunk instead of in the studio. The last thing she needed was to return to the scene of the crime. She felt horrible about what she'd done that night—especially to Nick's painting. You never touched another artist's work, period. No plagiarism, no vandalism. Those were really the only two rules to live by at Silver Springs—and she blew it. Indy's remorse grew bigger by the minute; she couldn't face herself, and she certainly couldn't face the studio. What if she were to go back there and Nick saw her and confronted her? She couldn't bear seeing him in any context, let alone one in which he exerted his authority or expressed disappointment in her. That would surely push her over the edge.

The night after the fire, she enlisted Eleanor to keep watch outside the studio while she gathered supplies—paints, pencils, brushes, easels, turp—anything she could carry in her arms back to Ferlinghetti, as Eleanor led the way with her flashlight and the lit end of a Marlboro Light. Once they arrived, Indy set up her and Eleanor's room as a single-serving art creation unit.

Over the next few days, things started to get messy. What was once a modern, minimalist room with two beds, two dressers, and a generous closet now held the clutter of Indigo's frantic mind state. There was newspaper and glue everywhere, wire and clippers by the foot of each bed, and canvases and bottles of spray fixative leaned up against the vanity. To enter, Indy and Eleanor had to tiptoe around various charcoals, pastels, and stacks of palette paper.

Their door remained closed in an effort to be discreet about Indy's secret mini-studio, and Indy barely left the bunk, entrusting Eleanor to retrieve snacks and meals for her from the dining hall instead. Indigo knew how she'd probably look to the outside world—like a kook who'd gone off the deep end.

A few days into the madness, Puja and Yvonne innocently poked their heads into Indy's suite to ask if she wanted to join them for a quick game of Dance Dance Revolution in the Cindy Sherman Snack Bar. The look on Yvonne's rubbery face when she saw the mess Indy sat in at the time—she was surrounded by a nest of tin foil and newspaper, like a homeless person but with better skin—was enough to show just how the rest of the camp probably thought of her. Or would, if they had seen more of her. Puja looked concerned; Yvonne looked genuinely horrified and disgusted to see what her friend had since descended into. Madness? Clutter? Heartbreak?

"It's starting to look like an episode of *Hoarders* in here, dude," Yvonne said, picking up a piece of twine and twirling it around. "Like, the ones that they save until the end of the season, to get the ratings up. The real psychos—"

"Yvonne, I think she gets the point," Puja said, and then turned to Indy. "Seriously, though. Come take a break."

"You know, I think you guys are right," Indy said, standing up from the small patch of floor that wasn't occupied by some crumpled drawing or tube of paint. She stretched her arms above her head and heard a few snaps and pops. It *was* getting pretty claustrophobic in there.

She wasn't producing anything she liked, and she smelled like a wild animal. It was frustrating: usually artists endured the pain of creation knowing it was necessary in order to make something worthwhile. But if what had been ruining her life was just a roomful of shitty-looking garbage, was Indy just living like a recluse for no good reason? The idea of all that wasted time was enough to make her want to cry.

"Honey, I'm home!"

Right on cue, Eleanor burst past Puja and Yvonne, who were still standing in the doorway, and waltzed into the room, accidentally kicking over a cup full of paintbrushes as she did.

"Sorry, ladies. No visitors to the crazy ward tonight." Eleanor dropped her bag on the floor. "Indigo has work to do."

Puja rolled her eyes and grabbed Yvonne's arm. "See you later, Indy. If your captor ever releases you." Indy heard Yvonne mumble something about Eleanor being the insane one as they walked down the hall and out of the bunk.

"Sit down on my bed," Eleanor said, "I have something so mind-blowing to show you."

"Wait," Indy said. "What's today?" She was suddenly panicking.

"Tuesday," Eleanor said, kicking some stuff out of the way so she could open her bottom drawer. "But anyway, this thing I have to show you—"

"Shit!" Indigo said, clapping her hand to her mouth. "I'm supposed to meet with Jen every Wednesday and Friday, which means I totally spaced on at least one meeting. If I don't meet with her tomorrow, I'm fucked. Even if I *make* the meeting, what am I going to show her? Everything I've been working on is total crap. Jesus Christ, Eleanor. Why am I even here? I have no idea what I'm doing."

"See, well, that's where you're wrong," Eleanor said, smiling in that authentic, sparkling, sharklike way that indicated true delight, or a plan starting to take root.

"In here"—Eleanor reached over to the floor and grabbed her purse, being careful not to upset too much of the paper matter around it as she did—"is some pretty outrageous proof that the nanny cam project we embarked upon was not for nothing."

"What?" Indy asked. What did this have to do with her work being lousy and having a meeting with her adviser tomorrow?

"Video footage. Of Lucy. Oh, and it is incriminating. It's like we let a fishing line off a boat or something, and we got a white whale to bite it! Does that metaphor work? My family doesn't fish."

"And mine does?" Indy said.

"Well, your stepmom is Asian—right? Don't those people basically rake the bottom of the ocean and serve whatever they find over noodles?"

"Oh my *God*, Eleanor! What's your *problem*?"

"I'm sorry, my bad. Please forgive me. That was out of line."

Indy shut her eyes in exasperation. "So, your point is that you caught Lucy doing something on one of those cameras you set up?"

"The ones I put by the lake and in her cubicle near her rehearsal space were a total bust. But the one in her bedroom? *Jackpot.*"

Eleanor removed a DVD from a case in her purse and inserted it into her MacBook Pro. "Indigo, this is beyond anything we could have ever imagined. There's no way in hell Lillian will allow Lucy to stick around once she sees this footage."

Eleanor hit play.

The footage was dark, for sure, but it was definitely Lucy. You couldn't mistake those curls for anyone else's, and she practically smiled into the camera, all dazzling big teeth practically blinking a row of lights that illuminated the frame.

Then someone stepped into the shot with his back to the camera. It was hard to see whether it was Nick or not, but the idea that it was suddenly crossed Indigo's mind and made her change course about whether or not she could bear watching the footage.

Indy watched the screen as Lucy made her way over to the guy, whose dark, medium-length haircut almost got in the way of the action. And it *was* action. They shared a quick kiss, and then Lucy stepped back and gyrated, lifting her shirt off and showing her perfect, slender figure—her perky breasts barely concealed by a cotton bra. She licked her finger—where did she learn to do that? Stripper class at Crunch gym?—and traced the midline of her body all the way down to her panties, then snapped the elastic on them.

"Gross!" Indigo said.

"I know, right?" Eleanor said, smiling.

Then, Lucy—who really was as photogenic as she was beautiful in real life, thought Indigo, against her will—put her finger in the mouth of the guy, who was, at this point, completely out of frame, safely behind the greedy gaze of the hidden camera.

"I feel weird watching this," Indigo said out loud, if only to break the tension. She noticed that Eleanor didn't seem uncomfortable at all—her eyes danced with a twisted pleasure, either from the delight of having caught Lucy in a nefarious act, or from being genuinely turned on.

"It gets better," Eleanor said with a straight face, not looking away from the screen.

In the shadows of the video footage, Lucy began gyrating atop what was assumed to be the lap of the guy off-camera, moaning as she did, and rolling her head in circles like she was convulsing with pleasure.

"Oh. My. God," said Indigo. If that was Nick she was straddling, she'd never be able to talk to Lucy again.

"Yup," said Eleanor.

Lucy kept at it. Moaning, breathing heavily, feeling her own boobs outside her bra, squeezing them together as she bounced up and down. This couldn't be how people really had sex. Was it sex? Was it a lap dance? Who was the guy? Indy fought every urge to shout "Move the camera so he's in the shot!" Was that or wasn't it Nick?

"Uh-uh-uh-uh-oh-my-God. Oh MY GOOOOOD!!!!" bellowed Lucy, before Indigo could be too distracted by her train of thought.

WHAT? Lucy apparently now had a perfect body, and porno moves to go along with it? Indy would have been jealous of her if she weren't so embarrassed and confused about what exactly she'd seen.

"And now," Eleanor said dramatically, "the climax."

"Isn't that what we just saw?" Indy asked.

Lucy, still in a wobbly darkness, dismounted her partner and skipped off into the next room. She came back with a bottle of prescription drugs and a rolled-up dollar bill, waving them both in the air like goodies she was showing off.

"Ta-da!" She spilled the bottle of pills onto the dresser next to her bed, and broke them up with the palm of her hand, then divided the dust into tidy white lines with a credit card.

And then her head of blond curls went down, nearly out of the lower frame, and all you could hear was a sniff, whoosh, and gulp sound—in that order.

It was shocking beyond anything Indy could have imagined.

Indigo had smoked pot with Lucy, of course, but seeing her friend snort prescription drugs seemed too surreal to process. It was like an episode of *60 Minutes* or something—like something parents warned their kids about. "Don't huff cleaning supplies! Say no to crystal meth! Don't snort prescription drugs!"

But here she was, Indy's towheaded former best friend, her face down in a mess of mystery powder. Ativan, Xanax, Vicodin—who knew? It was hard-core shit, and Indigo felt awful for knowing that Lucy was dabbling in that kind of darkness. She felt even worse for having had to see it firsthand—and under secret circumstances that she couldn't confess.

"I wasn't expecting this at all," Indigo announced.

"I know!" Eleanor squealed. "We couldn't have hoped for a better smoking gun. With this evidence, not only will she get fired, but she'll be thrown into Passages, the Malibu rehab where Demi Lovato tended the smoothie bar for six months last year. Say buh-bye to that Pantween shampoo campaign, Lucy!"

Eleanor rubbed her hands together wickedly.

But Indigo couldn't be happy about it. She felt awful—sick to her stomach with guilt. But it was too late. Sometimes things just couldn't be unseen. And after everything Lucy'd put Indy through this summer, Indy tried to believe with all of her soul that she deserved what was coming to her.

18

"*I was worried* about you, Indigo." Jen Rant was sitting cross-legged on her office chair across from Indy, who slumped in the corner beneath her gray hoodie.

"It's not like you to miss meetings," Jen continued, knitting her thick, Frida Kahlo–esque eyebrows in matronly concern. "I haven't seen you around the dining hall or anything." Jen leaned forward on her chair, for the full "teacher with a purpose" effect.

"I've just been pretty absorbed in the process of making stuff, and I don't really want people checking in with me along the way."

"I can understand that," Jen said, nodding. There was a pregnant pause before she continued. "Nick told me he hasn't seen you in the studio for a while."

The mention of Nick's name sent her into a particular flurried nausea. The guilt she felt for destroying his piece only intensified every day.

"I've been working out of the Beat cabin," Indigo tried to respond without any noticeable emotion.

"Any reason why you're avoiding the studio?"

Was Jen hinting at the fire? Was she trying to get a confession? Indy had been pretty isolated, so she didn't know whether people were buzzing about the missing artwork, the charred floor, and other remnants of her impulsive mistake from last week. But she assumed that if they were, she was suspect number one.

"It's just easier for me to concentrate in my own space." She cleared her throat.

"And what are you concentrating on?" Jen asked, lowering her gross bare feet down to the carpet and using them to move herself, rolling chair and all, closer to Indigo, who winced at the gesture.

"I'm concentrating mostly on the process. The process of creation. The process of the work."

"I'm not sure I follow you.... What does that mean, exactly?" Jen asked.

"Well, I...I don't really know." Indy felt herself let down her guard. She had officially run out of bullshit, and the game of convincing Jen that she believed something she didn't was no longer working.

"I just keep starting stuff and then it turns out looking shitty and awful and then I throw it away. I do that all day. It's like chipping away at a mountain that keeps growing back. I hate it."

Tears formed in the corners of Indigo's eyes. It was not her intention to show her hand to her adviser, but there she was, blubbering like a toddler all of a sudden. All it took was an admission to Jen Rant that she'd been spending her time in bed, scribbling on scrap paper fit for the bottom of a parakeet cage, instead of working slowly but surely on some kind of masterpiece in the studio, the way she was supposed to be doing. Like she had done every other summer of her life.

"Shh, it's okay." Jen Rant opened one of her desk drawers and handed Indigo a travel pack of designer tissues with the words "Steampunk Kitty" emblazoned on the plastic casing. "We've all been there before." Indigo grabbed a mahogany-and-bubblegum-colored tissue from the pack, unfurled it to see an illustration of a Persian cat wearing a top hat and monocle, and blew her nose into her hands so hard, Jen jumped a little bit. Indigo kept sobbing.

"You know," Jen said, pushing her toes into the carpet as she rolled back into her first position in the room. "The thing about artists is that when we're working on something, we're never alone."

Indigo considered this.

"But when we're in between projects, or we're feeling uninspired, or if for whatever reason we're not able to concentrate, it can be the most alienating thing in the world not to have our work to comfort us—to keep us company. When your relationship with your work is awry, your mind can be a hostile place—nothing can grow there." Jen narrowed her eyes. "Your thoughts keep horrible company in that state."

That must be why Indigo felt like utter garbage. She couldn't create art, so she had no reason to like herself. Not only was her best friend a distant alien she didn't feel like she knew anymore, but her crush, who had once taken up prominent fantasy real estate in her mind, had been since recast as an enemy. Her dad was far away with her stepmom, her real mom was dead, and the only person she was speaking to was Eleanor, who was, now that she thought about it, a miserable tiger that couldn't change stripes.

Being out of her bunk for the half-hour it took to walk over and sit down with another human being was all that Indigo needed to remember that. Eleanor, however helpful she'd been to Indy in her distressed mental state recently, was still, by nature, meaner than Indy could be to herself when she was depressed. And that was pretty bad.

"I guess I've also had other stuff on my mind," Indigo admitted. "I saw…well, I don't want to say, because I don't want to get anybody in trouble. But I heard about something that happened between my best friend and…somebody else…that makes me want to avoid the studio. I don't want to say anything more. I hope that's okay."

Jen's face seemed to get even paler than it usually was. "What do you mean?"

"Well, nothing happened that necessarily needs to be reported," Indy said. "But Nick…"

Shit. Did she really just say his name out loud? What was the matter with her? Where was her filter? Getting Nick—or was it Lucy?—fired was *Eleanor's* project. But there was something about being around Jen, whose hungry curiosity about what it was she had to say about this stuff, that made Indy suddenly want to tell her everything.

"Nick what?" Jen asked urgently. She was obviously trying to downplay how intrigued she was by Indy's little slip.

"Nothing," Indy said quickly. "I misspoke. I didn't see anything, and none of this has to do with my doing my work. Which I will do. I swear I will."

Jen stared at her. She seemed colder.

"Well, then," she continued. "You realize the Industry Showcase Art Exhibition is this weekend." She seemed stern all of a sudden. "I need to have a completed project ready to hang in the gallery by then, or you'll be left out of the show. And it's been my experience that when scouts come to Industry Day, they are looking to discover someone. I don't think you want to miss that, do you?"

"Of course not," Indy replied, a little taken aback.

"Good to hear," Jen said, writing some notes down on a pad. "You know, there was a small fire in the painting studio a little less than a week ago."

Shit. Oh God. Oh God.

Indy's heart began to race and her forehead instantly sprouted a line of sweat beads along her hairline. Surely Jen had to notice that she was freaking out.

"Nobody knows who set it or what happened exactly," Jen said. "It was in the middle of the night, so there were no witnesses. Apparently, somebody destroyed another person's work. It wasn't a fellow camper's painting, but it's still pretty serious. I just wondered if you knew anything about it."

"Nope, not a thing," Indy lied, but she knew the blood had drained from her now-sweaty face.

"Or if you were avoiding the studio for any particular reason having to do with that incident?"

"Nope," Indy said again, shifting around in her chair. When did she become so entrenched in scandal? She was a good person deep down—but a bad liar. Surely Indigo was blowing her own cover with all of her fidgeting and darting glances.

"All right," Jen said reluctantly. "I'll come by the studio to check in on your progress. I really can't have you presenting a blank canvas and saying it's a statement on minimalism. That's an amateur-hour prank—*and* it's been done before. I expect more from you."

Indy had to clean up her act. She needed to throw away all the trash in her bunk and take whatever artwork she could salvage to the studio. She'd go during lunch, when Nick was in the dining hall, but she'd still go. Indigo felt herself get nervous, but it felt like the right thing to do—a good step to make.

The silence around the Performance Art Center, along with all the peacefulness that came along with it, soon dissolved like sand through open fingers when the sound of girls around Theater Row exiting their classes after what was the first period of the day crept toward Indigo.

And then, in the distance, like a scent of leaves that evoked fall without forcing you to make the conscious connection, or the first insinuation of a breeze right before it hit your skin, she saw Lucy.

She looked great—happy, rested, tan, toothy, comfortable in her environment. Lucy saw Indigo and smiled at her in the most natural, kind, authentic way. She looked as comfortable as Indigo felt anxious. And then they were next to each other and Lucy was hugging her.

"Where have you been hiding?"

"In my art cave," Indigo tried to joke, feeling like she was about to break down and cry. She wanted to apologize for what she'd done to hurt her, but she was still angry, too. She hadn't seen Lucy since the woods, and the sight of her brought back feelings of rage as well as guilt. Indy was so tired of her stupid feelings. Why did being an artist necessitate riding a nonstop roller coaster?

"Ha-ha." Lucy smiled.

"No, I've been under the weather for real," Indy said. "I think I may have had like a short bout of mono or something? Mono lite. I've just been staying in bed. But I'm fine now. Not contagious or anything. Don't worry."

"I'm not worried." Lucy gave her friend a squeeze on the shoulder. "I just missed you. I'm glad you're okay. You still look sort of pale."

"Yeah, well, what can I say, I'm the original goth." Indy smiled weakly. "So, what are you up to?" she asked, behind a fake grin.

"Well, everything. It's been a crazy week. I told you I was cast in Puja's play, right? I'm starring along with that girl from your cabin, Tiffany Melissa Portman?" Clearly Lucy was just pretending everything was fine, when she must have known it wasn't. She had to be the best actress of all time.

"Anyway, it was supposed to be a reading, but it turns out Puja is actually a really great stage director as well as an amazing playwright, and ambitious, obvs. So the whole thing has taken leaps and bounds in terms of scale, and now it's a wholly staged theatrical production. It's really edgy, completely brave. It's about this girl who's really weak, and she has this mentor she needs to impress, but she crumples under the pressure. Stuff you can relate to, but on, like, a much deeper and more far-out scale?"

Indy cringed as Lucy kept gushing. "Puja is incredible, too," Lucy continued. "She has me stretching my range and pushing my boundaries in ways I didn't think I could ever do. I'm so excited to do it. I can't wait for you to see it. I think you'll love it, I really do. I know how you feel about cheesy theater, and this isn't that, I swear. It's really dark. Are you coming tomorrow night?"

"Oh, is it tomorrow?" Indigo asked, still piecing together her schedule with her newly acquainted perception of the outside world.

"Yes." Lucy laughed. "It's kicking off Industry Showcase Day, technically. I hope you're feeling well enough to come. I'd love your notes on my performance, and I know Puja would die to know what you think."

"I'll be there," Indy said.

Lucy clearly had no idea that Indigo and Eleanor had been conspiring to get her fired, or that Indy had seen her and Nick together in the woods. And did she really think mono lite was a real thing? Maybe she was confusing it with a protein shake.

They walked down the hill together, away from the penny fountain, and veered south toward the Pilates studio and the Esther Williams Pool. "You know," Lucy said thoughtfully, "before this summer, I was worried that I wouldn't be generous enough to teach others how to act. Like, how it was when I interned with that casting director last winter? I hated reading sides with other actors and knowing I'd be ineligible to book the role. It drove me crazy. It was like serving food to homeless people at a soup kitchen when you were really starving yourself."

Indy began to walk toward her bunk, and Lucy followed.

"But assisting Rashid has taught me that helping others doesn't take anything away from myself."

"Uh-huh."

They walked until they got to a fork in the path—the path on the left led to the dining hall; the one on the right led to the Beat cabin. Indy stopped as Lucy began walking to the left.

"Well, feel better," Lucy said, as sincere as a Hallmark valentine. "Oh! What are you putting up for the art show? I can't believe I forgot to ask. I'm so sorry."

Indy was beginning to sweat under the heat of the sun and her long sleeved shirt. "I'm…I'm going to do something really big and really great. I want to keep it a surprise. You'll see."

"I can't wait." Lucy waved good-bye and practically skipped off toward the main house like she didn't have a care in the world.

19

In the time since running into Lucy, Indigo had cleaned her bunk like she was in some kind of housekeeping contest. She used a fresh pair of her own cotton underwear on her face as a makeshift surgical mask while she frantically tidied up all the crap she'd accumulated during her breakdown. There were piles of dust of all different varieties, and the more she Swiffered, bagged, and shook out her linens, the more her eyes watered with residue from the clay, charcoal, pencil shavings, eraser remains, and anything else you can imagine getting in your hair and eyes.

By the time Eleanor came back from dinner with a pilfered napkin full of a single portion of the night's meal—barbequed wild tiger shrimp with farmer's-market arugula and roasted quinoa—Indy was gone. She had already packed up the stuff she wanted to take to the studio and threw everything she wanted to get rid of into two huge garbage bags she left in the corner of their room.

The next morning, Indigo showered and changed into her long black dress and paired it with a jean jacket to cover her arms. She blew her hair straight and even put on foundation with sunscreen in it, and some mascara. If she was going to come back to the studio, she was going to at least look decent doing it.

The first thing Indy noticed when she walked into the painting studio was that Nick wasn't there. The second thing she noticed was that it was really crowded. There were all the girls from her drawing and painting electives, taking time out from chipping away on their ambitious Industry Showcase Day projects to stare at Indigo in slack-jawed amazement the moment she walked in.

"Whoa, Hamlisch! We'd pegged you as a goner," said Erin, wiping sweat from her forehead.

"Hey, Indy!" Suzie yelled from across the room. "Join the party."

"Hey," Indigo said, as casually as she could. She tried not to gape at the part of the floor that was still black from the fire—the only telltale remainder of that night, it seemed—and set herself up at an empty easel. She walked with intention to her workspace, and felt the eyes of her peers on her as she did. Indy grabbed a large pad of Bristol paper and a rubber-banded bunch of colored pencils on the way, and pretended like she was wearing blinders.

But the other artists kept staring at her, as though their eyes were shouting at Indy, "Where the HELL have you been and how the eff are you going to pull off a major project in twenty-four hours or less?"

Truthfully, Indigo had no idea. In fact, showing up at the studio the day before the exhibit could have been the latest and the most public of her mistakes to date, which, so far, included: coming back to camp, choosing an unavailable guy to have an obsessive crush on, setting a fire, destroying the same unavailable guy's work in that very fire, ruining a friendship, becoming an unwitting partner in Eleanor's scheme against that now ex-friend, and, finally, embarking upon a self-destructive course of non-action that landed her with no artwork to show.

She would just have to endure the pain of it. The frustration, the dry spell, the untimely lack of inspiration, the paralyzing anxiety around having to create something Big and Good on an impossibly tight deadline. When the urge to look around and gawk at the beautiful and impressively accomplished works of art in the studio around her got too strong to avoid, Indigo turned and ogled, and saw the heads of her peers whip back around to the fruits of their labor as she did. The stuff they were working on dazzled Indigo—she was intimidated and jealous and felt so guilty for not putting in the hours of inspired work that everyone else had.

There was Megan Stein's twenty-foot mural—a multicolored, enormous, sprawling, heavily detailed representation of the history of her family, portrayed in narrative form from left to right. Megan had meticulously painted all of the important events of the Steins' lives in gouache paint with gold-leaf accents: from their arrival at Ellis Island from the Old Country, to Megan's first period, to her stepbrother's promotion at Goldman Sachs.

Next to Megan's floor-to-ceiling mural stood a life-size sculpture. Erin O'Donaghue was putting the finishing touches of bronze patina on the surface of what looked like a takeoff of Michelangelo's *Pieta*. But in Erin's sculpture, where the Virgin Mary would be was a seated female who looked a lot like Erin herself—and instead of holding a freshly crucified Christ, she was cradling the naked body of Robert Pattinson.

Indigo felt dumb sitting and staring at a blank sheet of paper, waiting for an idea, two days before the show. Finally, she just started drawing, like she did back at her bunk, letting her hand lead her, and tried hard not to judge what it made.

After amassing page after page of scribbles, she finally plugged herself into her earbuds and hit play on a Ting Tings playlist on her iPod. She was determined to shut out the outside voices and her inside demons, the ones telling her she couldn't do it—screaming that she had no time, no ideas, no talent, no vision, and no ability. Remembering an exercise that Nick had given her to do when she was just eleven and he was lecturing his class on the subject of artist's block, Indy gave herself the task of drawing one of the empty chairs in the studio, just to prove that she could still draw from life. "Because once you tap into the fact that you still have a skill," she remembered him saying, "you can free up the muscle memory that goes into actual creativity." Indigo began to draw the chair.

Back then, he'd taught her that art was mostly about the cardio of just showing up and doing the work anyway. If the determination to create something great was there, it took a little patience. Very rarely did magic just flow out of the pencil or brush instantly—you had to clock the hours to see real results, like anything else that was worth doing.

Indigo began to clock the hours.

And after what seemed like ages of darting her eyes to the chair and back to the lines she made on the page, making sure the two looked like each other, and that the piece looked not just true to life but also good in its own right, Indigo realized that she was alone. It seemed the studio had cleared out for lunch as soon as she stopped consciously thinking about whether or not the other girls were staring at her. And it was a relief. Because even though the drawing of the chair turned out to be just okay—not great—it was enough to keep Indigo working.

She worked through the next period and the next. She worked through dinner, churning out drawing after drawing of that same stupid chair—each one slightly better than the last. And she realized in the process that she was able, at some point, to somehow focus on something besides the clamor of others in the space—in their space—in Nick's space. On Nick.

Indigo took tiny comfort acknowledging what she had accomplished, and paused her iPod, which was now blasting a Ted Leo and the Pharmacists song, having gone through all her other artists alphabetically, and landing straight back to *T*. She went to wash her hands, trying not to panic from the realization that she only had a stupid—however well drafted—series of colored-pencil drawings of a folding chair ready for the big show. And as she looked out the studio window above the sink, she saw hordes of girls on the hill in the dusk, wearing sweaters and sweatshirts and jackets over their summer clothes, walking toward the direction of Theater Row.

Crap.

The clock on the wall said that is was 7:45, which meant Puja's play, starring Lucy, was starting in fifteen minutes. Part of her wanted to stay in the quiet, safe, Nick-less studio for a while longer, but she also knew that she had hit a wall. She had no interest in going through the same process as before, crumpling up page after page of mediocre ideas. And if she drew another chair, she might go insane.

Instead, Indigo cleaned up her station, pressing her final chair drawing gently in between the last page and the cardboard backing of her Bristol pad before putting it away in her locker.

She buttoned up her jean jacket and raced out the studio toward the theater, running through the coolness of the approaching night down the path lined with evergreens. Soon, she saw that the front of the intimate Playwrights' Theater was busy with campers filtering in and taking seats according to their housing assignments.

The girls from the Neo-Expressionist cabin (who were going into seventh grade) sat up in the bleachers next to the campers in the Weimar Classicism bunks (who were going into eighth). On either side sat the thirteen- and fourteen year-olds from the Deconstructionist cabin—but, Indigo noticed, no girls in the Rococo, Marxist, or Pre-Raphaelite bunks. In fact, the entire audience was full of "upper-hill," or older, campers.

"Indy! Over here!"

Indy landed her eyes on Yvonne, who sat in an aisle seat all the way up on one of the back rows to the left. The Playwrights Theater was a "theater in the round" space with seats on all four sides of the stage, but not for too many butts. It was Indigo's favorite of the performance spaces at camp.

Yvonne Bremis waved her fleshy arm in the air at Indy, tapping the empty seat beside her as she did. She was wearing a tangerine sundress with small pit stains under the sleeves.

As soon as Indigo made her way next to Yvonne and plopped down in the seat next to her, it was like a load was taken off her chest. Indigo didn't have to worry about anyone asking her questions about where she'd been or what she was up to or what she was working on or why she wasn't at dinner. Yvonne was holding Indy hostage now, and she talked at her like she was on some kind of game show to determine who could say the most stuff without taking a breath.

"Oh my God, Indigo! Are you excited for Puja? Are you nervous for Lucy? This is crazy!" She produced a taco from nowhere and took a voracious bite. "Let me tell you," she continued, with her mouth full. "First of all, I want to apologize for hogging the armrest. I can't help myself, A," Yvonne said, finishing what was left of her snack. "And B, I also want to apologize if I smell a little bit—it was a hot day. I know it's cooler now, it's evening, obviously, what are you going to do, but I'm still sweating like some kind of beast, and I want you to know I'm aware of it, and I'm sorry if it offends you in any way."

"It's fine," Indigo said. "I can't…it's not a problem."

The lights began to lower, and Indigo was saved from any more talk about Yvonne's B.O.

"Silver Springs women!" Lillian practically shouted from the stage. "I am honored to welcome you all to the first event of Industry Showcase Weekend!" She paused for applause, but there was none. "When I say 'Industry,' you say 'Showcase!' 'INDUSTRY!'"

Nothing.

Lillian switched gears like a seasoned pro, or at least a camp director used to being ignored.

"So! We are truly blessed to be treated to tonight's very special evening activity—a production of Puja Nair's brand new play, *Torment*, starring our own C.I.T. with the M.O.S.T., Lucy SERRANO!"

Applause nearly drowned out the second half of Lucy's name without Lillian having to demand it. Lucy was clearly a fan favorite: the crowd was absolutely on board for whatever they were about to see, as long as it involved her.

"Now, remember—while I usually don't like to restrict access to any art because of the age group, Puja's play contains some adult themes and language that could be confusing or disturbing to lower hill campers. So, tonight's performance is strictly for us old-timers, right, ladies?"

There was a long silence, and the sound of someone clearing her throat. Then somebody in the audience shouted "Show us your tits!" and the crowd exploded. Yvonne laughed so hard, Indigo was worried she was hyperventilating. Once the audience finally settled down, Lillian's face was red—possibly from shame, but also because she, too, was laughing along with the crowd, for fear of otherwise seeming like a poor sport.

"Fair enough!" Lillian said. "Fair enough. So now, without further ado, Silver Springs is proud to present *Torment* by Puja Nair."

More applause scored the dimming of the house and theater lights, and a single spotlight landed on the center of the stage. A hush fell over the crowd. Lucy, wearing an insane amount of makeup and dressed in leggings and a skimpy tank top over a visible black bra, took her place in the light and began to address the audience. It was clear from the moment she landed onstage, before she'd delivered a single line, that she was playing a prostitute.

"Let me tell ya a few things about what it's like to work Thursday nights in Ko-reatown," Lucy said to the audience, in an exaggerated Chicago accent that hit the back wall with its volume alone. "First of all, you've gotta be packin'. I don't care if your john is a five-foot-four, chino-wearing motherfucker with tortoiseshell glasses and a fanny pack."

Lucy's accent began to shift into some bizarre amalgamation of Boston, New Jersey, and "ghetto."

"He *can* cut you, and he *can* hurt you," Lucy continued, in character. "It's part of the game. And bitches got to protect they'selves if they're gonna reckon any sort of street survival. You wanna know how I know? *Shit.* I learned it the hard way."

Blackout.

The song "I Know You Want Me" by Pitbull blasted through the state-of-the-art speakers that were mounted on all sides of the theater, as tech majors, dressed head to toe in black, moved in an impressive-looking set—including a bed, a dresser, and a nightstand—onto the stage.

As the lights transitioned from pitch black to a dim red, Tiffany Melissa Portman, the actress from Indy's bunk who helped her with her makeup for the social—took the stage and sat on the bed that was already positioned on the right-hand side of the stage. Tiffany was wearing a fake mustache, and her long hair was pulled up under a dark, scruffy wig that ended right below her ears. She had a pillow stuffed beneath a blue button-down shirt, which was tucked into a pair of skinny jeans. After the eight summers that Indigo spent at Silver Springs, watching girls play grown men onstage would never cease to be awkward.

Lucy came back out, this time in a slip and pink stiletto heels. She took her place at the lip of the stage as the lights came back up, flickering in a pretty great facsimile of low-rent, motel lighting. Those theater-tech girls were pretty talented.

Once the scene was set, Lucy began applying red lipstick out toward the audience, pretending she was looking into a mirror over the chest of drawers that was set to the left of the bed. Tiffany delivered her first line in a very deep voice.

"So, how much is it gonna be?"

"Five hundred for everything—a grand if you want me to spend the night," Lucy said, coldly, into the invisible mirror. She twisted her lipstick back down into its case, then tucked it between her breasts, into her bra.

"And your ad said that you..." Tiffany said. "...*partied.*" Tiffany cleared her throat and opened her legs wide, straddling the air in front of her. Is that how Tiffany thought men naturally sat?

Lucy spun her thick, shiny blond hair around as she reacted upstage to Tiffany's offer. Her hair was way too classy-looking for a hooker's.

"Yeah," Lucy said, sidling up to man-Tiffany. "I party. Are you holding?"

Holding, packing. What did Puja know from this world, and where did she learn this slang? She was from Great Neck, Long Island.

"You bet I am," Tiffany said, reaching into the back pocket of her skinny jeans to take out a prescription bottle of pills. "Catch." She threw the bottle to Lucy, who caught it in one hand, then looked at the label.

"Sweet," Lucy said as she placed the pills on the dresser.

"Do you mind if I turn on some music?" Tiffany mimed hitting a button on a bedside radio to cue an Al Green track on the stereo, at a low volume. While Al Green's musty, lascivious vocals filled the theater, Tiffany scooted down on the bed, closer toward the center of the stage, and to Lucy.

"Come over here, sugar," Tiffany said. "Give some of that sweetness to Poppa."

Lucy smiled and made her way over to Tiffany, then sat on the girl's lap and kissed her quickly. Indigo cringed watching Lucy slide off her slip to reveal her magazine-perfect body in a bra and panties. Lucy had no body fat, only lean muscles and a soft, flat belly. The last time Indy saw her friend that way it was…*Oh, God.*

Oh, God, no.

No.

Indigo wouldn't let her mind realize what her eyes had already put together, even though she knew exactly what came next.

Lucy, still in character, took her finger in her own mouth and traced the midline of her body down to the top of her underpants, then back up to Tiffany's mouth, which elicited an audible "Yeechhh!" from one of the front rows. Then Lucy began gyrating…in the same exact way she had done in the nanny-cam footage Indy had watched with Eleanor days earlier.

This couldn't be happening.

Indigo's heart sank as Lucy finished her lap dance, and then, right on cue, made her way over to the dresser. She poured out some prescription pills, crushing them up with the bottom of the bottle. She then took a credit card out of the wallet on the dresser and divided the powder into lines. And just as she did on the surveillance video for an audience of two, Lucy's head of bodacious curls went down as she snorted—or pretended to snort—line after line of "prescription pill dust."

Eleanor and Indigo's only smoking gun against Lucy turned out to be a toy pistol that shot bubbles. She was so mad at Eleanor for convincing her they had caught Lucy in a fireable offense, when all they had was rehearsal footage. Where *was* Eleanor, anyway? Indy scanned the audience, but it was too dark to see any faces.

Onstage, Lucy shook her curls like she was auditioning for Pantween all over again, and sniffed so loud the back row could hear. She rubbed the remainder of "pill dust" on her gums, cheating stage right to face Tiffany, who straddled something invisible off the side of the bed again. The lights lowered while the Al Green music faded out, to raucous applause.

"What an edgy play!" Yvonne yelped to Indigo, during the scene change. "Have you ever seen anything like it?" she marveled. Indy nodded, clapping along with the rest of the camp.

Unfortunately, she had.

20

The plot of the rest of Puja's play was all a blur. There was a drug deal gone bad, and somebody put a hit on Lucy's character. By the end, Lucy had laid slain in the center of the stage, her limp body anointed with stage blood placed just so, while a dramatic score drew the events to a close. When she sprung up to take her bow, the standing ovation that followed lasted five full minutes. The camp was under Lucy's spell.

As the houselights came up, Indigo tried her best to maintain a calm exterior around the staff and campers leaving the theater. But all she wanted to do was scream at Eleanor for mistaking a dumb rehearsal video of Lucy and Tiffany for actual footage of her and Nick fooling around and doing drugs. Indy prayed that she hadn't actually submitted it to Lillian yet. If so, they were going to look insanely stupid.

Another thing Indy hadn't even considered until that moment was the possibility that they had violated a camp rule by installing a nanny cam inside a staff dorm. They'd have to go in front of a committee and would probably be sent home once they were found responsible. Or, worse yet—Indigo would be sent home after Eleanor inevitably threw her under the bus.

Indy weaved in and out of the human traffic of audience members clearing out of the tiny space. She hopped over seats, drifting toward the exit, cutting in line and trying to be as inconspicuous as possible. Once outside, the cool night air made her jean jacket feel thin on her shoulders and arms, and the breeze blew through her long hair. The moon was high, and the pines were silhouetted against the voluptuous summer sky. Indy looked into the distance, but soon the exiting mass of upper-hill campers and staffers blocked her view. Yvonne was there, and Erin, Megan, Lena, Puja, Desi…pretty much everyone except Eleanor.

Then Indy noticed Nick exiting the theater. He was talking to Jen Rant.

Her body reacted the way it always had when she saw him—with intense waves of prickly warmth, like how it felt when you first realized you were drunk, combined with the chilly coldness of her fingers and toes losing circulation. She couldn't help but stare. He wore a dark blazer over an olive-green T-shirt and was freshly shaven. But he looked so good to her—it was like she hadn't seen him in forever, and only in that moment did she truly feel how much she missed him. How she was still attracted to him. How it wasn't up to her to decide who she was not supposed to want. The realization was almost a comfort.

Nick looked up and made eye contact with her. It was as if Indy's thoughts had been broadcast, and he was the only one tuned in to her frequency. He blushed and nervously ran his fingers through his hair, tucking the strands that fell on the left side of his face behind his ear. And then, seconds after meeting eyes with the student he once called Supergirl, Nick darted his eyes to the floor in what seemed like shame.

It broke Indy's heart. The fact that he'd also just seen Lucy's sexual tour de force on stage only made her feel worse. Lucy would always be the one looking incredible in front of the entire camp in her underwear, and Indigo would always be the one whose stare would be deflected, never returned. Lucy would be the one who gets looked at; Indy the one who did the looking. The Actress and the Artist—like it was some kind of sad Silver Springs fable. Why had she even tried to compete?

Her face felt hot and the shame of having destroyed his piece came flooding back. What if he knew? He probably did—and soon everybody else would, too. But Nick's opinion of her was all that mattered. If she could take back anything she'd ever done, Indy thought, it would have been that stupid night with the blowtorch.

"Hey, Indy—are you okay?" Megan appeared, putting her hand on her shoulder. "You know that Lucy didn't actually die, right?"

Indy nodded without missing a beat. "It just really made me sad how her character couldn't pull herself out of her horrible life." She looked down at the rocky ground, face flushed red with embarrassment. "You know what I mean?" Tears welled up behind her eyes and in her throat. She had to get out of there.

"Yeah, I guess so."

Indy turned on her heels and started back toward her bunk. Behind her, she heard Suzie McLandish ask Megan what her problem was.

"She's sad about that dead hooker," Megan answered knowingly.

Indy moved quickly toward the path that led to Ferlinghetti, assuming she'd already experienced the worst run-in of the night. In a few minutes she'd be back in her bunk, safe from the endless drama of the evening.

But Lillian Meehan had other plans.

"Hello, Indigo," said the camp director, stepping onto the path. She moved her eyebrows into "concern" position and kept a strained neutral expression in her mouth—she was neither smiling nor grimacing. It was terrifying. "Do you have a minute?"

Indy's mood, which had already plunged like a bungee drop, somehow plummeted a little lower.

"Of course," Indy said. She followed Lillian, pulling up her long black dress. It had been dragging through the dirt all evening and now had ugly brown dirt marks all over its hem.

They sat down on a bench between the back of the theater and the path. The picnic area in front of them was illuminated by one of several solar-powered "green lanterns" strung from cables that ran from one theater to the next during Industry Showcase Weekend. It was supposed to look festive, but the lights usually just attracted a shitload of bugs. And though they were somewhat out of the way of the exiting campers, Indigo still felt everyone's eyes on her. She was very conspicuously getting in trouble.

This had to be about the telltale Lucy tape. She considered feigning ignorance, blaming Eleanor, telling Lillian everything from the time she first crushed on Nick as a little girl—all of it. But then Lillian began talking, and Indy realized that her excuses were useless.

"Indy," Lillian began, making sure to speak in a non-patronizing manner and maintain eye contact, as she always did when addressing campers one-on-one. "I wanted to talk to you because I'm concerned. Of all the art majors at Silver Springs, I least expected to hear complaints about you."

"Complaints?" Indy asked cautiously. That could mean anything.

"Your work has been all over the place this summer. And then,

I heard you disappeared and were working out of your bunk? Is that true?"

"Sort of true. I was under the weather and didn't want to infect any of the other art majors with something contagious."

"Okay," Lillian said. "Fair enough. But your disappearance also coincided with a rather disturbing incident around the art studio. It seems some artwork that may have belonged to a staff member—I'm not going to divulge who—was destroyed in a small fire."

Indigo gulped.

"Do you know anything about that incident?" Lillian's eyebrows arched with generous anxiety on Indy's behalf, and her warm eyes beckoned with the benefit of the doubt.

The question hung heavy in the air. *What the hell*, she thought. She might as well get it over with.

"I did it," Indy replied, stone-faced. "It was me."

Lillian bowed her head and closed her eyes, like the confession was all too much for her to bear. As though it would have been easier for everyone if she had just lied.

"Oh, dear," Lillian breathed, "I was afraid you were going to say that."

"Am I in trouble?" Indy asked.

"I believe so."

Indigo looked at her feet.

"I'm sorry, Indigo. But vandalism isn't something we take lightly at Silver Springs."

"I'm so sorry," Indigo said, interrupting what seemed to be a meticulously planned speech. "It was a mistake, I promise…."

"That's not what you should be telling *me*. That's what you need to tell the Fairness Committee tomorrow morning." Lillian stood up as she spoke, smoothing out one of many wrinkles in her Eileen Fisher linen sheath dress. "You know the drill. A jury comprised of myself, your adviser, and two random teachers from your field of study will convene before breakfast tomorrow in the Harpsichord Room. We'll hear your case, listen to your explanation, and then vote on what we think would be a fair punishment."

"What sort of punishment?" Indy felt exhausted.

"You may be facing expulsion from the art show. And from camp entirely." Lillian let the revelation linger in the air for a beat between them. "And at the very least, I know your parents won't be happy to come up this weekend and find out your work isn't being shown."

"Right."

"Good night, Indigo," Lillian said as she walked back into the mass of campers and staff outside of the theater. Indy watched her walk toward the lanterns and the fireflies near the path, and finally, once Lillian was out of sight, spoke to herself, bluntly and at full speaking volume.

"Fuck. Me."

The walk back to the Beat cabin was interminable. Her dad and Yoshiko were going to be furious if they were to drive all the way to camp to learn that she was getting kicked out and had made absolutely nothing all summer. At least Lillian hadn't mentioned the Lucy tape. That was a boondoggle, but at least it still seemed to be under the radar.

But instead of thinking about what it would be like to endure the first Industry Showcase Day without any of her work displayed and how best to tell her parents about her humiliating blowtorch spree, Indigo mentally practiced exactly how she'd tell Eleanor off. First, she'd come in and slam the door behind her.

Then she'd ask her sarcastically whether Eleanor had any other rehearsal footage they could use to get Lucy fired. Maybe an old VHS tape from seven years ago, when Lucy got the lead in *The Pajama Game*?

Indy arrived at the bunk to the sounds of miscellaneous pre-bedtime chatter and gossiping from the rooms on either side of the hallway as she walked toward her and Eleanor's bedroom. "I heard she rehearsed for that role by charging all the Kinnetonka guys seven dollars an H.J." "I heard Tiffany walked around with a sock down her jeans for all of last week." "I'm so proud of Puja. I wish her parents had been here to see her play." "I don't know what my parents would say if I wrote a play about hooking." "They'd probably say, 'Write what you know'—or they wouldn't have had to, since you already had." "Has anybody seen my Chanel lip gloss?"

Indy burst into her room, expecting to unleash her temper on Eleanor right away. But the room was empty.

She studied her reflection in the full-length mirror across the room, the one behind the two trash bags full of her discarded artwork. She looked like a ghost of her former self—the time spent inside had kept her skin pale, and she'd definitely lost some weight in her face, eating only the dancer portions of the meals that Eleanor brought her. But her eyes looked blank; her eyebrows were tense. She had that little line between her brows that her stepmom routinely got Botoxed, and her mouth was dry, her nostrils flaring. Indy was pretty sure she looked like she was high on something. But she wasn't on drugs—she was just furious and hopeless. And now that Eleanor wasn't here, she didn't have anybody else to take her anger out on....

Besides herself.

Indigo rummaged through her drawers for something sharp

she could use to cut herself with, but there was nothing. All of the wire she'd used for her sculptures was back in the studio, and a quick rifle through Eleanor's dresser proved futile as well. All she found besides the cigarettes and pills her roommate had on tap were fuzzy size-zero Capezio wraparound sweaters, some expensive skirts and blouses, and pastel-colored, size 30AA La Perla lingerie.

Indigo made a beeline toward the bathroom. She'd swipe one of Yvonne's nail clippers or Eleanor's "complexion tool"—a glorified stainless-steel blackhead extractor, basically. She began to sort through the accumulation of nail, hair, skin, and tooth-related hygienic products in Yvonne's cubby before she found what she was looking for—a sharp, half-jaw, Revlon cuticle nipper. Indy slid off the plastic cover on the tip, listening intently for the sound of anybody coming. The chatter from the bedrooms seemed to recede as she tucked the tool safely inside her left hand, checking the mirror constantly for any signs of company. She crept, in relative quiet, toward the bathroom exit. All was clear. Until a crazy scream pierced the silence.

"WOOOOOOO-HOOOOOOOOO!"

Puja, screaming dementedly at the top of her lungs, burst through the hallway and past the bathroom entrance with her eyes lit up like some kind of psychedelic campfire. Indigo dropped the manicure tool on the tile floor in surprise. It collided with the tile and bounced into one of the stalls.

"Indy! Hi! It's so good to see you! Did you get out of bed? Have you combed your hair since I saw you last? Do you know I wrote AN IMPORTANT PIECE OF THEATER?" Puja was still shouting from the hallway, but the sight of Indigo near the sink had caused her to stop in front of the open bathroom entrance. Gradually, girls from the other suites, curious about whatever exactly was going on, drifted toward the shared bathroom.

"HEY, GUYS!!!" Puja, her eyes still manic, greeted the rest of Ferlinghetti—including Eleanor, who entered with Yvonne, in matching pajama sets in two very different sizes. So, Eleanor was busy recruiting and indoctrinating a new peon, thought Indy. Poor Yvonne.

"I SAID HEEEYYYYYY, GUYYSSSS!" Puja repeated.

"Are you feeling okay?" Indigo asked, because somebody had to.

"I AM FEELING GREAT, INDIGO!" Puja exclaimed at the top of her lungs. "Do you know *WHYYYY*?"

She swept all of the soaps, toiletries, and towels above the row of sinks onto the floor with a giant swoop of her right arm. They clattered satisfyingly to the floor.

"Do you know why!?" She repeated to the shocked group of girls who stared.

"Why?" Indy asked calmly.

"BECAUSE I wrote a HIT PLAY! And I am the BEST!!!" Puja began to dance like an old-timey cartoon of a giraffe, moving her neck to the left and to the right in silly, exaggerated motions. Then she Suzie-Q'ed her way over toward the showers and back.

Yvonne looked concerned and slipped out of the bathroom while Puja continued to dance and lecture at her gradually increasing audience of bemused bunk mates.

"DON'T YOU GUYS UNDERSTAND THE POWER AND MAGIC OF THIS PLACE?" Puja continued with grand, sweeping arm gestures.

"The bathroom?" Tiffany Melissa Portman asked, looking around.

"NO! *Camp!*" She finally stood still, and her eyes seemed to bulge out of her head with the realization that all of the girls in Ferlinghetti were present. "For TWO MONTHS out of the

YEAR we are able to MAKE OUR ART and NEVER HAVE TO WORRY ABOUT THE COMMERCE ELEMENT OF IT! I don't have to sell out a room! I just have to FOCUS ON BEING GREAT! Which I AM! I AM THE GREATEST AT WRITING PLAYS! I'm Vishnu and Kali and Jesus and Bathsheba and Katniss FRICKIN' Everdeen all up in one hot little package!!!"

Puja began to open all the stall doors in the bathroom. When she was done, she began running back to close them, naming each toilet as she did. "SCORPIO! Cancer! GEMINI! Sagittarius!!! READY OR NOT, here I COME!!"

The Beat cabin campers exchanged WTF looks. Finally, Yvonne returned to the bathroom, waving a manila envelope that had been ripped open. She shook her head in disappointment.

"Puja? Did you happen to eat this entire nutmeg that your parents sent you?"

"SO WHAT IF I DID?" Puja yelped. "I AM THE GREATEST AT WRITING PLAYS!" Puja's eyes became a little more narrow as she lowered her volume and made eye contact with the girls closest to her as though she was about to reveal a great secret.

"You know," she whispered, conspiratorially, "being a writer is basically like being God. You can control all the people you create, and they live in your world, which you also *created*." She got loud again. "ISN'T THAT BANAY-NAY???"

"Jesus Christ," Yvonne said, sticking her nose into the empty envelope. "She's as high as a kite."

"Nutmeg makes you *high*?" Tiffany crinkled her nose. She clearly knew a lot less about "holding" than the character she'd played earlier.

"If you eat enough of it," said Indy as they all watched Puja help herself to one of the bathrobes that hung outside the shower stalls. She put it on, then topped off her guru look with a string of gauze she wrapped across her forehead and tied in the back like a hippie headband.

"Let. Us. Go. SWIMMING!" Puja shouted.

"Sure!" exclaimed Eleanor, who Indy realized hadn't even tried to make eye contact with her since she came into the bathroom wearing matching pajamas with Yvonne. Leave it to Eleanor to freeze you out before you even got a chance to put her in her place.

Soon, with the encouragement of a lucid Eleanor and a hysterical Puja, all the other girls agreed that night swimming seemed like a great idea.

"Follow me, my disciples!" Puja shouted, and led the way out of Ferlinghetti toward the heated pool for an impromptu group baptism at the hand of a spice-fueled prophet. Indigo followed, in part to save face among her peers as a follower, and in part because she had nothing left to lose.

21

By the time the girls left the bunk, they were trailed by the rest of the Beat cabin residents. Word had gotten out that Ferlinghetti had weed they were going to smoke down by the pool, and that Puja, that dorky Indian playwright, was tripping on copious amounts of 'shrooms *and* acid that her dealer parents had sent her in a care package. By the time Indy, Eleanor, Yvonne, and Puja got to the pool and scaled the fencing that kept it confined during non-lifeguarded hours, the girls from Ginsberg, Burroughs, and Kerouac were right behind them, wearing swimsuits, pajamas, sweats, UGGs, or some sort of combination of all four.

"FIRST ONE IN IS A PLAYWRIGHT WITH GODLIKE POWERS!" Puja screamed before belly-flopping, bathrobe and all, into the deep end of the Olympic-size heated pool. Water splashed onto several of the girls, causing them to shriek in excitement. Campers from different bunks added to the ridiculousness of it all by jumping into the pool behind her, one by one.

There was shouting, splashing, and the requisite amount of awkward doggy-paddling, even by varsity-level swimmers, in the shallow end of the moonlit lanes. Some of the girls from the Modern Expressionist cabin removed the lap dividers and others fetched foam noodles from the shed to throw down into the onyx and ochre shimmer of moon on night undulating in the water's reflection. Puja, still raving like a loon, tried to grab whatever pool toys landed in her vicinity. "OFFERINGS! OFFERINGS! From my disciples! FRANKINCENSE! MYRRH! BRIDE OF FRANKINCENSE! MURRAY'S CHEESE SHOP! I kiss you! I thank you! I bless you! GESUNDHEIT!!!"

Indigo marveled at the chaos. She couldn't help but smile. Whatever anger or sadness or jealousy or alienation she felt back at Ferlinghetti began to drain away. It felt nice to stand back and watch these silly maniacs frolic, knowing it was likely her second-to-last night ever at Silver Springs.

"Marco!"

"Polo!"

"Polo Ralph Lauren!"

Campers from the Ensor and Munch bunks shouted to one another across the water, and whoever was left on the sidelines dove in. Suzie McLandish floated by, her breast implants pointing up toward Orion's belt in the sky as she backstroked toward Megan Stein, who doggy-paddled past the deep/shallow end marker, making sure to keep her color-treated hair dry. Desi the dancer, who did laps like she was getting a workout in, was wearing baggy clothes even in the pool.

And then Indy saw Lucy approach the pool from the other side of the fence with Tiffany Melissa Portman. They both wore hoodies over bikini tops and PINK sweats with flip-flops. Tiffany must have left Ferlinghetti to go collect Lucy and change clothes for the night swim. They were laughing and squealing, clearly still sharing a high from tonight's performance.

"Indy!" Lucy waved and shouted across the pool. "This is so nuts, right?!"

Indigo couldn't bear looking Lucy in the eyes, so she pretended she hadn't heard her. It was loud, after all.

But Lucy seemed to take this as a cue to walk over. Indy crossed her arms across her torso protectively as she approached, and suddenly they were face-to-face with each other—all that was between them now was a few inches of soaked concrete. Well, that and the events of the past few weeks.

"Why don't you jump in?" Lucy shouted, a slight, irritated edge to her voice.

"Because I don't want to." Some water splashed them from the pool, and they both jumped back.

"Will you go in if I go in?" Lucy was trying to use her calm "C.I.T.-dealing-with-a-difficult-child" voice.

"Look, I don't have to jump just because you want me to jump!" Indigo shot back, surprised at the anger that came out of her. Usually, she only turned against herself with that kind of ease.

"What the fuck is going on with you?" Lucy's face screwed up into a frown. She unzipped her hoodie and threw it on the ground, like she was making a point.

"What do you mean?" Indy sputtered back.

"You're acting like a total bitch!" Lucy tossed her hair dramatically. "I saw you in the audience tonight; I knew you were at the play, and you didn't even come backstage after to say hi."

"It's always about *you*, isn't it?"

Lucy just stared.

"It's *your* play, it's *your* summer job, it's *your* perfect blond hair and stupid gorgeous body and *your* acting career and all of it!" Tears welled up in the corners of Indy's eyes as she removed her denim jacket and threw it onto the ground.

"I've tried to reach out to you this summer, Indy, but sometimes you get so emotional." Lucy hung her head and spoke more calmly. "And then last week you totally disappeared."

Indy brought her arm up to wipe her face, now wet with both tears and wayward drops of pool water. As she did, Lucy reached out and grabbed her friend's forearm.

"Is this why you've been wearing long sleeves these past few weeks? Indy, are you cutting?" Lucy gestured to Indy's arm wound. All of a sudden, she got very intense and very quiet.

"Why do you care?" Indy shouted in response. Now she really started crying as Lucy moved closer.

"Stay away from me!" Indigo sobbed.

"Why are you so mad at me?" Lucy asked, practically shouting by now. "What did I ever do to you?"

Indy turned slowly and took a deep breath.

"You," she began, slowly and deliberately before clearing her throat.

"You. Fucked. Nick."

"WHAT?" Lucy gasped.

"You fucked Nick!"

"I did not! I thought we cleared this up! I told you! There was NEVER anything between us. Never!"

The small, moonlit heads of the wet revelers gradually turned to the edge of the pool as the girls became aware of the epic fight taking place between one of Silver Springs's most notorious duos.

"Knock it off with the Oscar-winning performance already, Lucy. I saw you two making out in the woods."

Lucy shut up for a second and looked Indigo right in the eyes.

"Are you kidding?"

"No." Indigo replied. "No, I'm not."

"What you *saw*," Lucy's eyes were huge with intensity, "is not what it looked like."

"What were you doing, then? Rehearsing for a love scene with my old painting teacher?" Indy said, averting her eyes quickly down to the ground. She had to be careful what she said.

"No," Lucy said, like it pained her. She took a deep breath.

"What happened that day," she continued, "was that Nick asked me to go to the woods with him to smoke a joint."

"Lame."

"You and I smoked pot in the same place, before you got all weird this summer!" Lucy snapped. "Anyway, I met him there, and the first thing he said was that he didn't have any pot. He said he was there because he'd gotten a text saying to meet me there, too. It was totally weird. Anyway. Then…" Lucy trailed off, and her eyes welled up. "Then he tried to make out with me."

"He what?"

"He tried to kiss me, okay? And he put his hand under my shirt. Or he tried to."

Indigo suddenly felt sick to her stomach.

"So, what happened?" she reluctantly asked, stepping back from the edge of the pool so Yvonne, who was totally oblivious to the drama, could do a cannonball.

"I pushed him away! I told him no, and he stopped. He said he got a flirty text from me earlier that led him to think something else, and I told him I didn't know what he was talking about, and then he went in to kiss me again."

What was Lucy saying? Could Eleanor have possibly set them up? And texted Indy to come to the lake so she would find them? There's no way she was *that* good.

"Anyway"—Lucy wiped her eyes—"after that, I ran back to camp and swore I'd never tell you about it because I didn't want you to think he was a creep. I know how crazy about him you are and how much he motivates you to get to the studio and work on your stuff. I didn't want to take that away from you."

"So you didn't kiss him back?" Indy asked, her faith in her friend slowly edging back.

"No!" Lucy said, tears running down her face by now. "You've been in love with him since I've known you! Friends don't do that to each other."

"Even if I'd never have found out about it?"

"I thought you knew me better than that, Ind." Lucy's eyes met Indigo's with a sincerity Indy recognized from summers past.

And just like that, her mood brightened. She even felt herself smile, involuntarily. Lucy, who was so relieved to see her best friend look happy for the first time in what seemed like ages, grinned back.

That's all it took for Indigo to suddenly connect to the world around her. Soon, she noticed what *else* was going on around them this entire time.

The pool party was in full swing, and nobody was looking at them anymore, since it became clear Indy and Lucy were making up.

They looked at each other.

"I'll go in if you go in," said Lucy.

They both kicked off their shoes, and Lucy slipped off her sweatpants. Indigo slid her black dress over her head and stood in her bra and underwear. And then, with a smile and a wink, Lucy dared her to take it all off. Indy unhooked her bra and held her boobs in her hands, while Lucy did the same with her bikini top.

By now, for obvious reasons, all eyes were back on them. But Indy was at peace with it. She wasn't worried about being compared to Lucy. She had nothing to lose, and she was giving herself completely to the experience, to the night, to her peers, and then to the coldness of the chlorinated water that embraced her goose bump–adorned, freckled, imperfect, beautiful nakedness once she splashed into the pool. By the time the two of them were in the water, giggling hysterically, Puja had scrambled up the steps, put her arms out like Jesus, and decreed, "SKINNY DIPPING!!!"

All bets were off.

Bras, pajama bottoms, panties, and bikini tops went flying onto the side of the pool as the distinguished young women of Silver Springs followed Indy and Lucy's leads and stripped bare. It was a free-for-all—splashing, screaming, and a chorus of giggly gasps scored the chaotic display of boobs and bellies and tushes of all shapes and sizes, as well as the bobbing wet heads of what seemed like the entire Silver Springs Academy for Fine and Performing Arts for Girls.

As the girls around her went wild, Indy dunked her head underwater and observed as the din of the pool vanished at once. She opened her eyes and enjoyed the sting of the chlorine and the disorientation. She couldn't see a thing in the dark pool water, besides the vague suggestion of bodies in motion. It was a pleasant kind of abyss. Like nothingness and freedom, cold and warmth—all at once.

Indy held her breath underwater, naked, and closed her eyes. She felt like a fetus in the womb—she even put her fingers in her ears to drown out the sounds that crept in from her fellow swimmers. But even then she heard screams and bobbed up to find out what the hell was going on.

As she treaded water and blinked the chlorine from her eyes, she saw Lillian come into the pool area, blowing her whistle energetically and futilely. She shone her flashlight beam across the water and shouted, "Ladies! Calm yourselves! Who started this? Ladies!"

All kinds of bacchanalian revelry continued under the glare of the searchlight. Puja, naked except for a bindi and a pair of rose-colored goggles, was doing the backstroke and chanting something about being Jesus Christ with a cuter rack. Tiffany had three or four foam noodles under each of her armpits that kept her afloat. "Look, guys, I made a raft!" she chirped happily. And Eleanor, who wouldn't take off her Danskin leotard, was sitting on the edge of the pool wearing a sour look on her face, probably seething that Lucy and Indigo seemed to be friends again.

"Shall we get the hell out of this pool?" Lucy yelled, from only a foot away.

"Yes, please. After you."

Lucy reached forward on the bars near the stepladder and climbed her way out of the deep end, followed by Indigo, who did the same. As they scampered naked toward their clothes, which lay strewn in clumps by the fence, Indy realized they were laughing together. It had been a really long time since they'd done that.

They grabbed their stuff and held their clothes in front of their bodies to cover themselves and dry off a little.

"It's so good to have you back, Indy." Lucy caught Indy's eyes.

"I know. I'm sorry I..." Indy trailed off, then corrected herself. Should she say what she was feeling? That it was *killing her* that she was dumb and weak enough to listen to Eleanor? That there was a DVD of Lucy somewhere on campus? That she had completely betrayed the person who'd always been there for her? She looked back at Lucy, who smiled. It was okay. Things could go unsaid between friends who'd known each other for that long.

And now she would set things right.

"I missed you so much," Indy said.

Lucy beamed brighter than the flashlight that shone onto the pool. Dripping wet, she and Indy re-dressed and then ran together, laughing, over the fence and down the hill, into the night.

22

The next morning, Indigo woke up feeling like she had risen from a coma. She got out of bed energized and fully rested from the chaos and misunderstandings that had muddied her experience at camp until this moment.

It was only when she remembered she had a meeting with the Fairness Committee that her heart sank.

Indy glanced over at Eleanor, who was still asleep, wearing her still-damp leotard from last night's pool party. The two of them still hadn't talked about their serious gaffe involving the video footage. It hardly mattered now that Indy was in serious trouble for something else.

All she wanted to do was go back to the studio and get to work. To use what would probably be her last day of camp to create something beautiful. Something worthwhile. Maybe she could use the same exercise she'd used to draw that chair to work on a new piece—one for the Industry Showcase Day exhibit.

That is, if they were even going to let her show her work. If only she had more time. It figured that Indigo had finally decided she *did* want to be at camp now that it was about to end. To make things even worse, she was about to face major public shaming in the artistic community for ruining someone else's work in a fit of temporary madness. Why couldn't she have just burned her *own* stuff that night?

Indy rifled through Eleanor's drawers for something to wear to the trial. All of her own clothes were dark or black and seemed to telegraph guilt. And with the weight she lost from her self-imposed quarantine in the bunk, Indy realized some of Eleanor's looser, elasticized tops would actually fit her as long as she let them open at the bust and wore a tank underneath.

She slipped on Eleanor's white diaphanous silky blouse over a stretchy cream camisole from Theory she found in another drawer. She paired it with a wraparound skirt—those were one-size-fits-all—and topped it off with a pair of pearl stud earrings her roommate had left on the top of her dresser.

Indy looked in the full-length mirror and, for the first time in a while, loved what she saw. Even though she didn't have anything display-ready for the art show she would likely be banned from anyway, she still had a little bit of time. She wanted to rise to the occasion and to make up for the damage she had caused. Not just for the scouts or her parents—she wanted to prove to herself that she was a true artist, not just some one-hit wonder who'd one time been mislabeled as a prodigy.

Indigo walked up the hill toward the main house with her head up high. The morning sun felt perfect on her skin, and the delicious breeze swept underneath Eleanor's skirt. It was all made that much better by the fact that she was friends with Lucy again.

As if on cue, she felt her phone vibrate from the inside of her army-navy bag. It was a text from Lucy.

Hey! So good 2 talk last night. See u at breakfast?

Indy texted back.

Good 2 talk, for real. But I actually have a Fairness Committee trial b4 bfast, so I don't know if I'll make it. I might be packing my stuff by then. : (

Seconds after Indy hit "send," Lucy's name popped up on her caller ID. "Hey, where are you?" Indy answered.

"I'm in my room! Are you going up to the main house now for Fairness Committee? Are you seriously on trial? For what?!" Lucy asked.

"I…it's complicated." If only she'd been more honest with her this whole time, she would've been able to fill her in on the vandalism drama. Or, had she trusted that Lucy would never have had anything going on with Nick, there wouldn't have *been* any vandalism drama in the first place. "Basically, I'm…being accused of destroying somebody's artwork. And setting the studio on fire. Well, parts of the studio on fire."

"Well, did you?" Lucy asked.

Indigo was quiet.

"Are you there?" Lucy asked again.

"Yeah, I'm here."

"Look, Indy—whatever happened, there's no way they can do anything to you. You're the hardest-working artist at this whole stupid place."

"Not lately."

"Is this about Nick?"

"Nick didn't force me to burn his painting," Indy said.

"Holy crap, Indy. You didn't!" Lucy laughed incredulously, then added, "I hate him."

"So do I," Indy said quietly. "Look, I have to run. I'll find you after the committee and tell you what happened, okay? And listen, Lucy—"

"Don't say it," Lucy said, cutting her best friend off. "I'm sorry, too."

Indigo ended the call and looked at the time—her trial would start in two minutes exactly. She climbed the steps up to the main house and caught her own reflection in the bay windows on the back entrance side of the mansion and smoothed down a flyaway strand of hair that obscured part of her pretty face. She was ready.

As she put her hand on the knob of the door that led to the Harpsichord Room, she couldn't help but notice how quiet and still the house seemed. Only her sandals creaking on the wooden floorboards made any noise at all, and part of her wished that she had the wrong day or the trial was called off or that the whole affair had been a vivid dream. But as she twisted the brass handle and pushed the heavy door in with all of her weight, she realized her judgment day was all too real. Behind the door, sitting in a semicircle of Ray Eames chairs, was her personal jury. Lillian, Jen, Jim Dybbs, and, for just an extra little dose of "fuck you," Nick, all sat patiently in front of the harpsichord, waiting to hear what Indigo had to say for herself.

"Come in, Indigo," Lillian said. "Have a seat."

The camp director gestured to the piano bench that sat opposite their makeshift coven. Indy, taking a moment to pull herself together and being sure not to rest her eyes on Nick, who was wearing an all-black ensemble of a black Talking Heads T-shirt over black jeans. Indy pulled her head up high and walked over to the bench. She kept her facial expression as neutral as she could and looked to Lillian without saying a word.

"Well," Lillian said, "none of us want to be here. But we've convened today to discuss the serious allegation of vandalism against Indigo, which is something that, if proven to be true, is punishable by suspension from the rest of camp, including all Industry Showcase events, as well as future ineligibility from the Silver Springs C.I.T. programs. Jen, why don't you begin?"

Jen Rant, who sat between Nick and Jim, cleared her throat. Everybody looked uncomfortable besides Indigo, who looked oddly calm and at peace with what had already begun. There was no stopping it now.

Jen finally began. "Well, a couple of weeks ago, I met with Indy regarding this summer's final project. And it did seem like she was not only distracted with personal matters, but that she was too busy making excuses and lying about her progress to actually produce any art."

"But there's no rule that says how you have to pace your work, is there?" Nick interrupted Jen.

"No," she responded, her face souring. "I was just saying, I'm concerned about Indigo for reasons beyond the vandalism."

"Well, she's on trial for vandalism, right?" Nick said. "Then let's just talk about that. There's no need to make things more complicated than they have to be, Jen."

Indy noticed as her adviser's face flashed from anger to sadness. She looked at Nick now, knowing his eyes were on Jen so he couldn't stare back, and she saw a bizarro version of the guy she'd loved forever. This Nick was selfish, disloyal, shallow, lecherous—somebody who'd seduce a girl who was barely sixteen into the woods so that he could have his way with her. Indigo quieted whatever instinct caused her to still be turned on by that abstract idea, and pushed down her rising feeling of jealousy as well. She'd trusted Nick with her feelings, and instead he lied to her and hit on poor Lucy. Indigo hated him in that moment. But it was indifference, not hatred, that was the true opposite of the adoration she'd felt for him just weeks before. It was going to take some time to get to that point.

"Fine," Jen said curtly. "Let's discuss the vandalism."

Jen reached into her purple messenger bag, which was, a bit immaturely, adorned with punk-rock stickers, pins, and badges. She removed a folder filled with glossy images of the studio fire, like it was a crime scene on *Dexter*. She removed one of the pictures—a close-up of Nick's burnt canvas from the garbage can. The skulls and paint were melted into the remains of soda cans from Indigo's pop ornaments, and the whole thing was covered in white foam. Jen held it up for the room to see and then passed it to Indy.

"Indy, does this look at all familiar to you?"

"Yes," Indigo said, holding the photo on her lap.

"Can you do me a favor and tell us how it got to this point?" Jen asked.

"I'd rather not."

The committee got quiet.

"Excuse me?" Jen said.

"I said I don't want to go over it." Indigo looked down. "I'm really sorry." She handed the photo back to Jen.

"It's okay if you go slowly, Indy," Jim Dybbs piped in. "You know, when I was a boy, I had a debilitating stutter and it was always humiliating whenever a teacher would call on me in class. All the other kids would laugh at me. I'd like them to see me now, married to a beautiful woman like Rebecca!"

There was a long pause.

"Indigo, why don't you want to tell us what happened?" Lillian broke the silence. "If it was some sort of accident...we could try to go easier. Starting a fire on camp property is a very serious offense in itself."

"I told you I did it," Indy replied calmly. "Just, please—tell me what my punishment is." She wasn't sure where all this brutal honesty was coming from, but it felt good.

"So, you purposely set out to destroy Nick's painting?" Jen continued, pursing her lips together.

"I mean, not exactly. But it was my responsibility that it was ruined, so I guess I'm guilty of vandalism." Indy looked down at her feet. What did Nick think of her now? She ruined his piece! If anybody had torched *her* artwork, she'd never forgive them.

Lillian spoke up. "Indigo, please explain to us what you mean. What happened?"

Indy paused. She could very well throw Nick under the bus—tell them that he was the one who was the root of all of her problems this summer. She could tell them about how he'd gotten her drunk, kissed her, then left her out to dry. How he'd made a move on Lucy, too, who was still underage, even if she was technically a staff member. But none of it really seemed worth it. She had had her fill of drama. Now she just wanted to make art.

"I made a mistake. I'm sorry." Indy reached up into the bun she had on the top of her head and loosened the bobby pin that kept it together. Her long hair came tumbling down her shoulders, and she shook it out with her other hand. She felt less vulnerable, she decided, with her hair everywhere. "I regret how I spent my time this summer. I regret this whole fire fiasco. I didn't mean to ruin anyone else's work. I screwed up. It's not like me. It's not like me at all. I'm so sorry."

There was another silence as the Fairness Committee took a moment to realize she was done speaking.

"Well, I think we've heard enough, Indigo," Lillian announced. "Please step out into the hallway while we discuss among oursel—"

"Wait!" Lucy burst into the room mid-sentence. The door slammed shut behind her.

"Lucy? Why are you here?" Lillian asked. "Shouldn't you be

setting tables with the other junior staff?"

"I had to say something," Lucy said, walking over to Indigo with a look of intention in her vivid blue eyes. She was out of breath and visibly shaken. Indigo noticed as Nick's expression changed. He shifted around uncomfortably in his chair, trying to seem casual. No one seemed to notice.

"I'm sorry to interrupt you all, but I can't do nothing while my best friend is being accused of something she would never do."

"But she did do it," Nick said, stony-faced. "She just admitted it…."

"Lucy." Indy looked to her friend. "Don't take the blame for me. I did it, not you."

"I didn't ruin anything in the studio," Lucy responded, "and neither did Indigo Hamlisch." She gave Nick a cold look. "I know she says she did, but the person who vandalized wasn't really her."

Where was she going with this?

"Look." Lucy struck a pose in the center of the room like Mariska Hargitay on a *Law & Order* poster. "Being an artist means that you have to be tapped into your emotional state, which changes wildly from day to day, from mood to mood. All of us in this room are artists in one way or another, right?"

"I used to…play the trumpet." Lillian said quietly.

Indigo watched Jim Dybbs nod from the corner of her eye.

"Well, we artists are majorly psychotic people." Lucy looked at each committee member. "Like, one day we could be on the top of the world. We're starring in a play or we're halfway through an awesome painting we're feeling really jacked up about. And the next thing you know we have a fight with our parents or we run out of money or the person we're crushing on ends up being a total a-hole."

Jen shot Nick a dirty look.

"Or maybe nothing happens at all!" Lucy continued. "But we feel like shit, and all of a sudden we can't make art anymore. Whether or not we show up at the easel or the studio or whatever." Indy looked at Jen, who suddenly looked embarrassed. "And that's when we can go nuts! And we can become people we don't even recognize. But you can't blame us for acting the way we're only acting when we're not ourselves. Because that's not who we really are all the time. It's just who we are sometimes."

"Are you finished?" Jen asked Lucy impatiently.

"No. I have one more thing to say."

Indy felt herself smile without trying to.

"Indigo Hamlisch is the hardest-working, most talented person I've ever met." Lucy looked at her friend. "For as long as I can remember, I wanted to grow up to be exactly like her."

Indy felt overwhelmed by the pins-and-needles quality of Lucy's sentiment.

"And whatever happened in the studio was an honest mistake she made. Everyone makes mistakes. And if I know Indy—and I *do* know Indy, longer than any of you in this room and better than anybody in the world ever could—she'll not only make up for this mistake. She'll do a better job on her project for the show than anybody else at this camp. Just please let her participate. And don't do anything dumb, like sending her home, or banning her from Silver Springs next year. I don't want to spend next summer—or any summer, really—without her. I mean, we just made up after fighting this long over a stupid misunderstanding about a boy."

Jen's face pinched up into a scowl. Nick turned red. Lucy smiled at Indigo.

"Besides," she added quickly, "it's not like the piece in question was all that amazing, anyway. It was just a dumb practice canvas.

The artist told me that himself. When we were walking in the woods."

Nick clenched his jaw nervously.

"Are you done, Lucy?" Lillian asked. "It's almost eight thirty, and breakfast is starting."

"I'm done." Lucy nodded.

"Then please go to the dining hall. And Indy, you can go to breakfast. We'll let you know our decision by noon."

"Thanks." Just as it looked like Jen's face was about to explode, Indy and Lucy walked out of the Harpsichord Room together.

Suddenly, things didn't seem so bad.

23

"Oh my GOD, did you see Nick's stupid face?"

"Nick's face! What about Jen's?" Lucy exclaimed, outside the dining hall. "She looked like Violet Beauregard from *Willy Wonka and the Chocolate Factory*, all puffed up like that! Only she was bright red instead of blue."

"I still can't believe she and Nick ever had a thing." Indy winced.

"I know. Gross."

"Gross!" Indy echoed.

They walked into the dining hall together as the younger campers from the French New Wave Cinema cabins filed in and took their seats at their assigned tables. "Lucy!" a cute seven-year-old drama major with cornrows squealed as she ran over and hugged her counselor's legs. "I practiced that Neil LaBute monologue again just the way you taught me to. Can I do it for you later?"

"Of course, Anjelica." Lucy smiled at the girl, who did an excited twirl and ran off to brag to her friends. Indy laughed. It was hard to believe she had doubted her loyalty all summer.

"Are you staying for breakfast? It looks like they're serving Balthazar scones...." Lucy looked at one of the platters going around the table to her right.

"Actually, I think I'm going to head to the studio."

"Yeah?" Lucy's eyes brightened.

"Yeah," Indy said. "I have an idea for something." Her eyes trailed off to the back of the dining hall, where she watched Eleanor arrive, looking haggard. "But first I have to do a little bit of materials-gathering."

It wasn't hard for her to find a hammer. Indigo remembered seeing a tool box in the recycling area next to the staff break room. She crept in and snatched it, making a mental note to return it later in case Lillian needed to hang another framed *Variety*, *ARTnews*, or *New York Times* rave review of a Silver Springs alumna's project.

Indy tucked the hammer into her purse and snuck out the pool entrance of the main house, successfully avoiding any potential encounters with older campers who had by now likely heard all about her Fairness Committee trial. There was no way she would willingly wear a scarlet letter in this situation. She was too absorbed in what she was about to do.

Indigo practically soared down the hill toward the cluster of mod, ski-lodge-looking chateaus that made up the staff housing. She arrived on the "Men's" side of the villa, which was easily identified as such from the stink of socks and Barbasol shaving cream from the first cabin, and the size fifteen jazz shoes outside of the next one, which must have housed Rashid.

She was still a little curious about which château was Nick's, but she no longer burned with the hatred of him that consumed her before. After she rejected the idea of snooping around to find his cabin, Indigo felt a quick pang of hurt that soon dissipated.

A stately weeping willow divided the cluster of men's housing from the women's, and soon she was tasked with finding which of the mini–ski lodges belonged to Lucy.

She peeked into the circular window on the front door of the first suite and saw a bottle of absinthe liquor, various pointe shoes, and a series of ancient black-and-white head shots of what looked like a very young ballet teacher named Renée Cornillion. The cabin next door looked like a mess from the front window that Indy could easily see into—the staffer hadn't bothered to draw her blinds. Indigo peeked in to see her Dead Kennedys T-shirt on the armchair in the front room. She didn't even need to confirm that the château next door to Jen Rant's was Lucy's. Even from the outside, the cabin smelled like her hair. That Pantween stuff was not messing around with its signature blend of herbs and spices or whatever.

Indy opened the front door to find a large studio with a made bed, a dresser like the ones in her own room, and a wall adorned with photographs. Pantween products and dog-eared copies of plays were everywhere.

Before she got down to the task at hand, she took a minute to look at all the pictures Lucy had on her wall and was touched to see how many were of the two of them from years ago. There they were in their awkward headgear-and-braces-with-rubber-bands phase. There they were on the camp lawn, dressed up as sexy cats at age eleven for the "Halloween in July" event five summers ago. The same weeping willow Indy had just passed drooped in the distance behind them, snugly positioned between their cat-ear headbands.

Remembering the time and what she was there to do, Indigo shook off her sandals and climbed onto Lucy's bed. She used the claw-end of the hammer to pry open one of the wooden ceiling panels and, standing on her tiptoes, looked inside.

Bingo.

Indy reached in and retrieved the nanny cam that Eleanor had mounted right where Indigo had suspected, judging from the angle of the tape they saw of Lucy by her dresser. She quickly stashed it in her bag, replaced the panel, and stepped off the bed. As she slipped her gold sandals back on, she smoothed down Lucy's bedding then left the same way she came in.

By now the sun was getting hot, and Indigo took off the white blouse she'd borrowed from Eleanor and wrapped it around her waist, freeing her arms and exposing the tank she wore underneath. By the time she arrived at her second destination—the area near the lake where she had seen Lucy and Nick—she felt comfortable in her skin. The mark on her arm was starting to fade a little now. It was a reminder of what she'd been through—not who she was. Even if the Fairness Committee verdict came back guilty, she could survive anything.

Indy found nanny cam number two dangling off one of the branches of a lusty Japanese maple, like a futuristic birdhouse right under the rock where she and Lucy had smoked that joint. She leaned the branch down to her height and untangled the copper wire that kept the camera fastened.

Finally, she walked over to Theater Row, past the fountain and the swing set and the benches and the pines, and found Lucy's rehearsal studio. It was in the Tudor housing that held about five or six mirrored cubicles in each space. Somebody was tap-dancing in one of the cubes and someone else was singing scales along with a piano. Last-minute preparation for Industry Showcase Day was obviously in full swing in all corners of the camp. Indy kept her eyes on the tops of the cubicle dividers, which ended far before the ceiling did. When she landed on what looked like a teddy bear perched on top of one of the dividers, she walked through the maze of sounds directly toward it.

The stuffed bear was wearing a *Phantom of the Opera* mask and cape, and held a little rose. It rested atop the cork-and-linen divider of a cube labeled "Rashid Beatts/Lucy Serrano." Indy opened the mercifully unlocked aluminum door and pushed one of the two folding chairs in the carpeted space up to the corner where the stuffed animal sat. She stood on the chair for support and grabbed the suspiciously heavy bear, then stashed it in her bag, which now bulged with the weight of her and Eleanor's entire failed scheme.

By the time she had snuck out of the rehearsal studios unseen, more and more campers were walking along the paths. Her timing must have been perfect—breakfast was over by now, and the girls were just now racing to their home bases—studios, rehearsal spaces, and music halls—for a last-minute round of line-cramming, scale-practicing, and crash-dieting that proceeded the upcoming festivities.

As Indigo headed back toward the art studio, she noticed Jen Rant in the distance. Jen looked up from her purple messenger bag, which she held like a nursing infant, saw Indy, and shook her head before looking away. Before she resumed her journey, Indigo waited for Jen to disappear.

It was a good thing she'd gotten an early start on the day. Right after Indy arrived back at the painting studio, it became overrun with other art majors. Suzie McLandish was hunched over a drafting table, furiously inking a twenty-five-page graphic novel about a super-heroine she'd created called Breast Implant Girl. The lead character looked sort of like a super-pretty version of

Suzie, and it was clearly meant to be some kind of postfeminist commentary on the plastic surgery her parents bought her. Megan was putting the finishing touches on her colorful mural—she had only to add detail to the part of her Stein family history that depicted her aunt's adoption of a Chinese baby girl after her fertility treatments didn't take.

Indigo tried not to think about what everybody in the room looked like naked now that she had T.M.I. from last night's swim, and also tried not to psych herself out by looking too intently at the beautiful work everybody in the studio was making. Instead, she set herself up in the only corner of the studio that was empty—the part that had been taped off since the infamous blowtorch incident. She'd be like a phoenix rising from her own ashes.

Indy ripped the masking tape off the paint-splattered, slightly charred wooden floorboards. She cleared off the surface of the worktable next to the blowtorch station and dumped out all the contents of her purse—nanny cams, teddy bear, and hammer, along with a tube of ChapStick, a tiny sketchbook, tampons, tissues, wallet, and everything else. She unwrapped Eleanor's blouse from around her waist and dumped that on the table as well.

Inspired and focused, she reached into the cabinet where Nick kept the goggles and removed the tarp from the blowtorch, which hung on the wall in the corner. But this time she would be creating, not destroying.

Indy put on Nick's goggles and fired up the torch. Soon the smell of melting plastic and metal replaced Nick's distinctive sweat-and-soap scent on his goggles. The nanny cams morphed into something shiny and globby and otherworldly and beautiful once the fire got to them. Their plastic exteriors disappeared under the heat to reveal multicolored wires that looked like futuristic rainbows. As the lens and the microchip insides warped and shifted shape under the glare of her thumb-sized torch flame, Indy thought about how great it would be if all of her deeds against Lucy were destroyed alongside the video she torched.

Soon she had three cow patty–sized piles of warped plastic, glass, and metal in front of her. The remnants of the three nanny cams sat there in their twisted beauty, the lenses still positioned to the center of each like the jam dots in homemade thumbprint cookies. Indigo marveled at the effect. They were like pretty robot eyes, or precious stones she couldn't wait to make some kind of jewelry out of. Her mind abounded with inspiration and possibilities. For the first time in what seemed like forever, what *not* to make was a bigger dilemma than what she *would* do in the studio. Then, finally, she had a thrilling idea.

She was going to build a three-eyed monster.

Possessed by her creative direction, Indigo rooted through the studio trash to look for newsprint, scraps, or any other kind of paper debris she could use as the base for a plaster-of-paris mold. But it was recycling day, which meant the bins full of paper waste were already on their way to the compost heap in town.

Then Indigo remembered the garbage bags full of discarded sketches, scribbles, and journal pages full of ramblings from when she'd been sequestered in her room. The bags were still in there—she hadn't hauled them to the Dumpster yet. Indigo rushed out of the studio to make it to the Beat cabin before somebody else got rid of them. She didn't even think to take off Nick's welding goggles—all she could think about was creating this sculpture.

As soon as she exited the studio, Indy saw Lillian waiting for her on the lawn.

"Hi."

"Hello, Indy." Lillian nodded. I was just at Ferlinghetti, looking for you—I figured you might be here."

"Am I banned from the show? From Silver Springs?" Indigo no longer cared about the events of this morning or even of the last month. She cared only about her project now, and the sooner Lillian told her the verdict of this morning's Fairness Committee, the sooner Indy would know whether she was going to make her papier-mâché "triclops" beastie here at camp, or at her parents' place back home.

"Well, I want you to know that this was not an easy decision. It came down to a vote, the results of which were—"

"Am I getting. Kicked. Out," Indy asked again.

"No," Lillian said, evenly. "We'd like you to stay."

"Thank you!" Indigo exclaimed. The relief she felt made her realize how much she *did* care about this place. She got to stay! Indy was even tempted to give Lillian a hug but then thought better of it.

"…Provided!" Lillian added. "You finish your Industry Showcase submission and stay out of trouble until the application period for C.I.T.s begins in the fall." A smile formed on Lillian's lips. "We all actually think you would make a wonderful staff member next year."

"All of you?" Indy said, genuinely surprised to hear the staff's opinion of her. Was what she did really not *that* bad? Should she not have felt all that guilt? There's no way this was a fair outcome, but she felt grateful enough for the second chance to know she wouldn't take it for granted.

"Well, to be honest, one committee member thought you…lacked certain qualities. But we'll just leave it at that." Lillian crossed her arms around her chest. "And Indigo?

Please be careful using that blowtorch."

Indy looked Lillian in the eyes, and then, remembering she was wearing welding goggles, broke out into a huge grin.

"I always am."

Lillian smiled back. And Indigo, relieved that the whole ordeal was finally over, ran all the way back to her bunk.

She burst into her bedroom. But instead of finding the two trash bags of scrap paper she was looking for, she found Eleanor and Yvonne sitting on the floor instead, playing cards. Between the two girls lay a stunning assortment of prescription-pill bottles and loose tablets.

"Hello?"

"Oh, Indy!" Yvonne threw down her cards abruptly like she'd been caught doing something terrible. "How are you? You look nice. Is everything okay? We sort of heard about you maybe being in trouble? I mean, not like the blond chick from *Dirty Dancing* 'I'm in trouble, Baby! Get your dad to help me out!' kind of 'in trouble,' but that maybe you were going to get…'"

"I'm not getting expelled." Indigo felt herself smile in great relief. "They just told me—or Lillian did. I can come back next summer. And I'm still in the show." She couldn't believe her luck.

"Terrific," Eleanor responded, as dry as a wind tunnel. "Yvonne, go! It's your turn."

"Oh!" Yvonne picked up her hand of cards from the floor—half of them were turned up already. "I guess, I'll…raise you four Ativan?" Eleanor showed her hand—all aces—then swept the stash of pills to her side of the room.

"Aw, darn it!" Yvonne said, smiling. Either she was a phenomenally good sport or she was relieved to have a friend who paid this much attention to her. Indigo had been replaced. And not a moment too soon.

"Have you guys seen the two garbage bags that were in here earlier?" she asked.

"Oh, yeah!" Yvonne nodded as Eleanor dealt another hand of cards. "I put those in my and Puja's room. I hope that's okay."

"You'll find that all your other stuff is in Puja's room, too," Eleanor added, not bothering to look up. "I just figured you might be more comfortable hanging in there from now on." Eleanor looked up from her hand of cards and stared at Indigo with a reptilian coldness that chilled her from across the room.

"I hope that's okay!" Yvonne repeated. "I knew it was gonna be awkward, so just tell me if it's awkward. I mean, not like, 'Ooh, let's experiment with our bodies and listen to folk music—college roommate–style awkward,' but—"

"It's fine," Indy interrupted. "It's great."

"Oh, and Indigo," Eleanor continued, "that DVD you lent me is on your bed. The one labeled 'rehearsal'?"

"Oh, right. Thanks."

She turned around to fetch her bags, and as she left, heard Eleanor ask Yvonne, "Wait. Was she wearing my skirt?"

24

Everything about Indy's sculpture turned out even better than she'd intended. As she formed the monster's body, soldered the nanny-cam-lens eyes onto its papier-mâché head, and wove shreds of Eleanor's white blouse into its scalp for hair, she found that her hands were taking her piece to a higher level than she dreamed. She'd also decoupaged the chair drawings she'd churned out before Lucy's play onto an actual chair that the robot sat upon for a meta, surrealist statement that would have blown René Magritte's mind.

So when her piece took center stage at the Industry Showcase Art Show and was even awarded best in show, however grudgingly, by Jen Rant, who headed the judging committee—Indigo tried her hardest to look surprised.

"Excuse me! Can I have everyone's attention, please?"

Lillian, wearing a smart navy pantsuit and a golden brooch in the shape of the Silver Springs coat of arms, stood in the center of the Stein Gallery—one of several glisteningly clean and modern-looking exhibition spaces located on the northwest corner of the Silver Springs campus. The Stein Gallery was named after Megan's family, who had donated enough money to make sure it was the biggest one at camp after Megan encountered some spatial challenges displaying her work the summer she was going through a Claes Oldenburg phase. In fact, Megan's mural, which was mounted on the wall opposite the gallery's main entrance, even depicted her father writing a check for its donation, her own sculpture of a huge, vinyl Subway foot-long floating in the background.

"I want to say, first and foremost, what a sublime blessing it is to have Silver Springs campers, their parents, and all of you talented professionals together on such a creatively fulfilling occasion." Lillian beamed into a sea of young and old faces.

"What is she talking about?" Leo Hamlisch, wearing a Hawaiian shirt, whispered to Indigo. Yoshiko, who stood next to them in a black satin shift dress and fedora, smiled appreciatively.

"Welcome to the fortieth annual Silver Springs Industry Showcase Day art show!" Lillian announced.

The adults gathered in the Stein Gallery all applauded on cue. Yoshiko took an Instagram pic of Indigo's piece on her iPhone and then one of her standing next to it. Indy didn't mind—she had even put on some black eyeliner and lip gloss, for a look that was way more becoming than the one she rocked at the Kinnetonka Social.

"We are so proud of you," Yoshiko said sincerely and a little too loudly.

The Steins shot them a look. In response, Leo mimed zipping his lips and throwing away the key.

"Now, as you all know," Lillian started up again as the crowd's attention began to wane, "we like to foster a noncompetitive creative environment here at Silver Springs."

Everyone stopped slurping the gallery wine and chewing on

their Carr's water crackers for enough time to participate in the biggest group eye roll ever seen in a non-flash-mob setting.

"That said, some works truly are exceptional and deserve special recognition," Lillian continued. "And today we'd like to announce that the work of art that best represents a clear vision, a bold statement, a visually compelling aesthetic, and a promising talent…is *Blinky at the Races* by Indigo Hamlisch!"

Indigo's dad hugged her tight, and Yoshiko began to cry.

"Indy, would you mind coming up and saying a few words about your sculpture?" Lillian beckoned.

Indy, through her joy, thought about how, only days earlier, she was dirty and isolated in her bunk, throwing drawing after drawing into the trash. She smoothed down her hair and walked over to Lillian, then reluctantly took the mic from her hands.

"I guess," she began slowly and with gradually more confidence, "I wanted to make a statement about revenge, technology, and surveillance." She cleared her throat. "Blinky is a monster who can see what you do day or night. He's like a nondenominational cyborg Santa Claus. With a conscience."

"What are the monster's eyes made out of?" somebody in the crowd shouted at her. Indy recognized the voice immediately.

"Those are nanny cams," she responded, blushing an even deeper shade of red. Even though she'd decided she hated him the day before, Nick looked incredible in the blazer he wore to the Dylan concert, over a button-down shirt and black jeans. "And the lashes are made out of a DVD I sliced up into little strips. The DVD had special meaning to me." He nodded in response to her answer.

Lillian stepped in.

"Congratulations, Indigo. And thanks to all of you—campers and parents alike—for making Silver Springs a mecca for such artistic vibrancy. And to all of our very important industry guests—I invite you to explore the works of our young artists. These are your future stars! After this, please join us in the dining hall for a quick brunch. Then there will be a one PM fully clothed performance of *Oh, Calcutta!* in the Herzog-Streisand Theater. Following that, please join us for a concert of Ani DiFranco songs arranged as chamber music in the Miranda July wing of the main house. Thank you, and enjoy!"

Indy rejoined her dad and Yoshiko, who was still choked up with pride.

"Congratulations, kiddo." Leo Hamlisch hugged his daughter again.

"Thanks." Indy grinned. "Do you guys wanna take a walk after this? I don't really want to see either of those performances, but I should probably say hi to Lucy."

"Oh!" Leo looked around. "Are Mr. and Mrs. Serrano here this year?"

"No. She's a C.I.T., remember?"

"Of course. Well, let's find her and say hello. I haven't seen Lucy since…well, since I passed her on that billboard on Madison and Ninetieth." Leo popped a Tic Tac into his mouth, then put the case back into his shirt pocket. "How much dough do you think she rakes in for that kind of a gig?"

"Leo, stop it. Don't talk numbers in front of people, it's déclassé," Yoshiko scolded her husband.

"Oh, please. This camp is all about cash, and you can't even talk about it? That's like going to the Kentucky Derby and not talking about horses. Or how much you won from the horses." Leo laughed.

"Mr. and Mrs. Hamlisch!" Lillian cut through the crowd to say hello. "You must be so proud of Indy."

"We are." Leo beamed.

"She's very talented. And she really did a complete turnaround over the last twenty-four hours, with this piece. It's incredible." Lillian clapped her hands together.

"Indy works fast when she's excited about something." Leo put his hand on Indy's back.

"By the way"—Lillian lowered her voice—"I want you to know how much it meant to receive your recent donation."

"Well"—Leo winked—"those new printmaking facilities weren't going to build themselves."

Lillian smiled back, and Indy felt weird. In no way did her dad's money talk negate the sense of accomplishment she felt around her piece. But, she figured, his donation was probably relevant to her Fairness Committee verdict. For the first time, she felt she had a better insight into the machine that kept this place running. This odd, terrible, wonderful place.

"Indy!" Lucy burst into their group with her big, bright Lucyness.

"Hey, look who it is!" Leo gave her a bear hug as soon as he saw her.

"Hi, Mr. Hamlisch! Hi, Yoshiko!" Lucy smiled sincerely and then turned to Indigo. "So, what's this I heard about you winning best in show?"

Indy cocked her head to the side, brushing off the compliment like dust off her shoulder. "It's all very political who wins these things."

"BullSHIT!" Lucy exclaimed, causing the heads of the dads—and moms—who weren't already checking out the pretty blond to turn in her direction. "This is the best piece you've ever produced. You made this art show your *bitch*. And I'm really proud of you."

"Aw. Thanks, Luce."

"It's good to see you two haven't changed," Leo said. "You know, I remember when the two of you were as flat as two rowing paddles."

"Leo, SHUT. UP." Yoshiko looked mortified.

"Come on, let's sneak some wine," Lucy whispered to Indigo.

"Be right back, Dad." Indy turned to leave with her.

"Okay, Peanut. Yoshiko and I will meet you at the dining hall." Leo trailed off as he took his wife's arm. "I wonder if they'll have those gruyere frittatas this year.…"

Indy and Lucy made their way toward the snack table, dodging Mr. and Mrs. O'Donaghue, who wore matching ascots printed with alternating shamrocks and anchors. Also nearby were Yvonne's conservative parents, the Bremises, who were taking notes on the most offensive pieces in the show so they could cite them in a sternly worded letter to Lillian at a later date. Puja's dad, food critic Reginald Nair, was chewing a piece of gouda for what seemed like forever, next to his stunningly beautiful actress wife, whose huge saucer eyes peeked out underneath her dark bangs, which were as thick as a slice of chocolate pound cake.

Lucy snuck some wine into her aluminum earth-friendly water bottle and gave it to Indigo, who took a swig. They drifted over to the side of the room and leaned against the wall together, checking out the scene.

"You know, I never said thanks," Indy said, handing her back the bottle.

"Thanks for what?"

"Thanks for showing up at Fairness Committee and defending me."

"Of course! You're the most original artist I know. And so is your process." She shrugged. "So what if you burned some stuff."

"I just really appreciate you barging in like that and sticking up for me. I mean, without you, I wouldn't have been able to create this piece. And I love this piece." Indigo knew Lucy would never know in full what she meant.

"Look." Lucy took another swig of wine. "I will always be there to throw myself in front of whatever dumbness gets in the way of you making art. Whether it's a Fairness Committee, a case of writer's block, or an obsession with some stupid guy." She smiled at Indy. "I'm your biggest fan."

Indy felt a sense of gratitude wash over her.

"Likewise." She gestured to Lucy's water bottle for another swig of wine. "I know I've said it before. But I really, really regret making such a thing out of my crush on Nick. I mean, imagine all the work I could have made if I hadn't wasted my summer thinking about him."

Indigo handed Lucy the bottle and caught her reflection in the glass doors that led to the hallway. She felt chic, trim, and sophisticated in her white, crisp button-down and black skinny jeans.

"What if the energy you spend thinking about a boy is the same energy you put into your work," Lucy wondered. "Like how calories are calories?"

"Totally," Indy agreed. "I need that energy if I'm going to live, let alone make stuff that I don't want to burn with a torch."

"I still can't believe you burned Nick's painting. You're such a badass." Lucy shook her head and giggled.

"But you know what I mean. Jealousy, boys, sex, money…" Indy said and sighed, watching a couple of the hotter dads check out Lucy's boobs in her staff T-shirt. "Those are all distractions from making art."

"I dunno." Lucy squinted her eyes to think about it. "I mean, without that stuff, what would you ever have to make art *about?*" She sounded very confident, Indy realized. Maybe Lucy was smarter than she'd honestly ever given her credit for. "Without those feelings, without *life*, your art just sucks. It means nothing."

"I guess I just need to figure out how to balance thinking about guys with thinking about art," Indy finally concluded.

"Eh," Lucy said, shrugging her shoulders. "One thing feeds into the other." She took a final swig, emptying the bottle. "Good art just needs passion."

Indy looked across the gallery at Nick, who was shaking hands with each of the O'Donaghues like he was a campaigning politician. His eyes were lit up with the same spark—the same desire—she recognized from their late night in the studio together, before they moved in to kiss. It seemed like he wanted something from that wealthy couple as badly as he wanted her then. It was strange to see.

Indy saw Jen Rant trying as hard as she could to schmooze with the Steins. But as Jen tried to seem congenial and feminine, her hunger just read as urgent. Marty and Ellen Stein looked like they couldn't escape. Indy observed how Lillian worked the room and made sure all of the pictures on the wall were hung evenly. She saw Jim Dybbs and his hot wife making out in the corner of the gallery. And as disgusting as it was to see Jim rub his hippie-dippie beard all over his wife's flawless made-up face and groping her shapely butt with his hairy hands—it was sort of sweet. They were in love.

"You know what I think?" Indigo began, out loud to herself as much as to her best friend. "More than anything, these, these...*people* around us—whether they're distractions or obstacles or mentors or crushes." Indy paused for a second to think, then said, "They're all just here to be our muses."

"Yeah," Lucy said back, nodding.

"I mean, isn't that what a muse is supposed to be? Somebody who inspires you? Or gets in your way to the point where you want to prove them wrong? Or basically helps you to express yourself even if they're not trying to?"

"Totes."

"Who says that a muse has to be some Greek babe?"

"Well, that's what a muse is for dudes, I guess." Lucy began twirling her hair on her index finger.

"Fuck dudes," Indy shot back.

Lucy laughed and took her hand.

"Oh, Indy. Don't worry. You'll find somebody new to crush on as hard as Nick." Indy looked Lucy in the eye just as she realized how sad she was. Letting go of liking Nick was the hardest thing she had to do this summer, including the all-nighter she'd pulled to finish her final project, the days she spent in her room, and the depression and guilt that went into, then followed, the act of actually cutting herself. Her eyes welled up as she realized she was lonely now that she didn't have Nick to think about. He kept good company in her mind.

Lucy reached out for a hug. "Nick was a good muse," she whispered as Indy squeezed back.

The gallery was nearly empty by now. Only a few random stragglers surveyed the art, taking notes on their iPads and in their Moleskine notebooks.

"Ms. Hamlisch?" An older man with sharp features under tortoiseshell glasses approached Indigo and held out his hand. He wore brown slacks and a tweed blazer, and Indy couldn't help but think she'd seen him somewhere before.

"Yes?" Indy replied, politely. She didn't recognize him as anyone's dad.

"I'm Peter Franks. From the Franks-Curren Gallery in New

York?" He gave her a warm smile. "Could I possibly have a moment of your time?"

"Oh, yes, of course." Indy looked to Lucy for guidance while she silently freaked out.

"I'll be waiting for you outside." Lucy grinned.

A little bit later, Indigo walked through the glass doors of the Stein Gallery and down the hallway toward the ladies room. As she glided down the corridor with her shoulders back, she let herself process what had happened in the last fifteen minutes. A real gallery owner, Peter Franks, wanted to put a bid in for the exclusive rights to her next sculpture series for his space in TriBeCa. He'd given her his business card and arranged to have her come tour the gallery upon her return to New York. Maybe it was luck. And maybe she actually had done this on her own. It felt amazing.

"Well, hello."

No.

It had to be comic timing, seriously. Nick was exiting the men's room as Indigo approached and the two of them were suddenly alone in front of the water fountain. Indigo could hear Lillian say her good-byes from the next room, then close the front door. Now it was really just the two of them in the gallery, or it seemed that way.

"Hi." Indy suddenly felt dizzy. She paused, and, not knowing what to say, announced, "I'm going to pee."

"Congratulations," Nick joked. He smiled and showed off his perfect teeth as Indigo felt the familiar rush of sexual feelings charge into her body. "Hey." He reached out to touch Indy's bare arm, which formed goose bumps on contact. "I just wanted to say how incredible your piece is. I mean, I know that you know. You're smart enough to know how talented you are, and not many people are both." He paused. "You know…bright and good."

Indy smiled, taking in the compliments like a plant responding to sunshine.

"I guess what I wanted to say," Nick continued, "is that I'm proud of you. You've grown up a lot in the short amount of time I've known you, Indigo. And I'm glad you didn't get in trouble. I did all I could."

"You stuck up for me?" Indy completely forgot that she had to pee and felt only the magnetic force of the spot in front of Nick where she stood.

"Of course I did," Nick responded, running his fingers through his hair with one hand and bringing the clear plastic Dixie cup of red wine to his lips with the other. His lips were stained from the inside with burgundy.

"Hey." He gulped down the rest of the cup. "About that night when you and I…"

"Yes?" The memory of it rushed Indy's senses. "What about it?"

Nick's eyelids looked heavy. "That was really nice." He put the cup down on the water fountain and moved a step closer. Indy's heart leapt. But she did not budge.

"Yes," she replied, a familiar mixture of pain and desire quickly growing inside her.

"And I just wanted to tell you," he continued, moving even closer so that she could smell his hair and skin next to hers the same way she did in the studio that night.

"Yes?" she asked. She could feel her heart pounding against her chest.

"I…" Nick's eyes glanced down at her body, and back up into her eyes. "I think you're the real deal."

"I'll bet you say that to all the girls," Indy whispered back.

He smiled. "Maybe," he said. "But you're my favorite girl."

His hands wrapped around Indy's waist and he brought her in, close to him, like she'd always dreamed about. He leaned in close enough for her to feel his warm breath on her lips. "You did it, Supergirl."

Indigo felt pleasure and terror wash over her as she realized Nick was about to kiss her again. But before he did, she gathered all of the resolve and strength she still had inside of her and pulled away.

It was time to let him go.

"Sorry, Nick," she said.

Nick looked confused and hurt, but Indy felt no sympathy for him. She just felt the small spark of confidence that her life was about to change with this very decision, for the better.

"Well." He frowned at his shoes. "Congrats again on your piece. It's…it's remarkable."

"I couldn't have done it without you." Indigo smiled, and then she walked away.

The best part was that she truly meant it.

Acknowledgments

Thank you first and foremost to my literary agent, Scott Mendel, and my editors Cindy Eagan and Elizabeth Bewley, as well Pam Gruber. Thank you, second but also somehow foremost, to Holly Schlesinger, who revised the drafts of the proposal and the structure of this before it was actually a thing, and Gillian Berrow, who helped me shape that aforementioned thing into a Great Thing.

Thanks also to Jack Fagan, Ellen, Joe and Phil Klausner, Amy Poehler for the blurb and for being a flawless rock star in general, Cecily Von Zeigesar for being an inspiration, Eryn Oberlander, Kara Baker, Melissa Myers, Sarah Self, Erin Junkin, Greg Hodes, Justin Ongert, Erica Gray, and everyone at Poppy and Little, Brown.

Finally, thank you for reading this. People who appreciate my work make my life extraordinary. I am so lucky to have fans as wonderful as you.

CPSIA information can be obtained at www.ICGtesting.com
Printed in the USA
LVOW131443220513

335061LV00002B/148/P